Faith on the Frontier

VIVIAN BELLE

STERLING RIDGE PRESS LLC

Published by: Sterling Ridge Press, LLC www.sterlingridgepress.com

ISBN: 978-1-966093-17-6
Printed in the United States of America

First Edition: March 2025

For permissions, contact: support@vivianbelle.com or visit www.vivianbelle.com

Dedication

To my cherished readers,

These pages hold more than just words—they contain my heart's deepest belief in the power of courage when facing life's untamed frontiers. Like Emma, many of us stand at the crossroads between safety and the wild unknown, between what others expect and what our souls quietly long for.

I wrote this story for anyone who has ever felt the pull to venture beyond comfortable boundaries, for those who understand that true treasure isn't always found in gold, but in the courage to trust your own path—even when others doubt you can navigate it.

In your hands, may this tale be more than entertainment. May it be a companion when you face your own mountains, a reminder that faith isn't just about believing in something greater, but also about believing in yourself and in the possibility of love even in unlikely places.

You've honored me by stepping into this journey through Montana's rugged landscape. My hope is that when you close this book, you carry with you the same courage that Emma discovered—to stand firm for what matters, to open your heart when it's easier to keep it guarded, and to find purpose in creating something meaningful from life's untamed possibilities.

With profound gratitude for allowing my words into your world,

Vivian

About The Author

Vivian Belle is a talented author known for her sweeping **Historical Christian Romance** novels set against the untamed beauty of the American frontier. With a deep love for history and storytelling, she brings to life **resilient heroines, steadfast heroes, and faith-filled journeys** in the vast, rugged landscapes of the past.

Nestled in the **majestic mountains of northern West Virginia,** Vivian finds endless inspiration in the rolling hills, winding rivers, and boundless sky that mirror the spirit of her stories. When she's not writing, she enjoys **kayaking on tranquil waters, hiking through breathtaking mountain trails, and, of course, getting lost in a good book.**

Vivian's novels capture the heart of **faith, love, and perseverance**—where strong women and honorable men overcome life's trials to find hope, home, and happily-ever-after. Whether she's exploring the great outdoors or crafting her next frontier romance, Vivian's passion for adventure and storytelling shines through in every word she writes.

You can find out more about Vivian and her latest releases at www.vivianbelle.com or follow her on social media for updates and behind-the-scenes glimpses of her writing process. Stay connected—you won't want to miss the heartfelt stories of love and family she has in store!

Also by Vivian Belle

Where the Heart Finds Home

Faith on the Frontier

Love in Hopewell Creek

Contents

Chapter 1

The stagecoach rattled violently as the wheels hit yet another rut on the rugged Montana road. Emma Abbott gripped the worn leather strap hanging from the ceiling, her gloved fingers white with tension as her body lurched forward. Across from her, a weathered cattle broker dozed despite the jarring ride, his chin bouncing against his chest with each bump.

"Not much farther now," the driver called down, his voice barely audible over the thundering hooves and creaking wood. "Blue Ridge is just beyond that next rise."

Emma straightened her spine and adjusted her navy traveling dress, now wrinkled and dust-covered after days of travel. The journey from Boston had been grueling—train to St. Louis, then another to Helena, followed by this bone-rattling stagecoach for the final leg. Each mile had taken her further from the refined society she'd known all her twenty-four years and closer to an uncertain future.

"Thank you," she called back, her voice carrying a cultured Eastern accent that seemed as out of place as she felt. She reached into her reticule and touched the folded deed to the Abbott Ranch, the paper now soft from countless readings. Her uncle Thomas's final gift to her and her ticket to freedom.

The cattle broker stirred, his rheumy eyes opening as he cleared his throat. "First time in Montana Territory, miss?"

"Yes," Emma replied with a polite smile. "I'm relocating here permanently."

The man's bushy eyebrows rose. "Permanently? You don't say. Meeting a husband out here?"

"No," Emma said firmly. "I've inherited my uncle's ranch. I intend to run it myself."

The broker's surprised chuckle held no malice, but his patronizing tone was unmistakable. "Well, good luck to you, miss. Ranching ain't no tea party. This country breaks men twice your size."

Emma met his gaze steadily. "Then I suppose I'll have to be twice as determined."

Before he could respond, the stagecoach crested the rise, and Emma's attention was drawn to the window. Below them stretched a valley, green with spring's tentative arrival. Nestled within it was Blue Ridge—smaller than she'd imagined from her uncle's letters, but undeniably real. A main street lined with wooden buildings, a white steepled church, scattered homesteads, and beyond them all, the majestic mountains that gave the town its name.

A flutter of nerves mingled with excitement in her chest. Somewhere beyond those buildings lay the Abbott Ranch—her ranch now. The thought still felt foreign.

The stagecoach thundered down the slope, and Emma caught her first glimpse of the people of Blue Ridge—men in work clothes and wide-brimmed hats, women in practical dresses, children darting between buildings. So different from Boston's crowded, fashionable streets.

As they approached the town, the driver called out, "Whoa!" The horses slowed to a trot, then halted before a weathered building with "BLUE RIDGE STATION" painted across its front.

"Here we are, folks. Blue Ridge, Montana Territory," the driver announced. "McGinty's Mercantile is just up the street if you're needing supplies. The Blue Ridge Inn is for those staying over."

Emma gathered her small handbag while the cattle broker descended first. The driver jumped down and offered her his hand. Taking a deep breath, she accepted his assistance and stepped down into the dusty street, her practical boots—purchased specially for this journey—meeting Montana soil for the first time.

The air was different here—crisp, tinged with pine and something wild she couldn't name. Distant mountains loomed like sentinels against the vast blue sky. For a moment, Emma stood transfixed, drinking in the scene.

"Miss? Your trunks," the driver prompted, already unloading her luggage from the roof.

"Oh, yes. Thank you." Emma turned her attention back to practical matters. "Is there someone who might help transport these to Abbott Ranch? It's about a mile outside of town, I believe."

The driver paused, trunk in hand. "Abbott Ranch? Thomas Abbott's place?"

"Yes," Emma nodded. "He was my uncle."

The man's weathered face softened. "Thomas was a good man. Sorry for your loss, miss."

"Thank you. Did you know him well?"

"Well, enough to share a drink now and then. Quiet sort, but fair." He set her trunk down beside her. "As for getting out there today—that might be tricky. Stage came in late, and most folks with wagons will have headed home already."

Emma surveyed the street, trying to hide her dismay. She hadn't anticipated this obstacle so early in her venture.

"McGinty might know someone," the driver suggested, gesturing toward a large building with a wooden sign proclaiming 'McGINTY'S MERCANTILE' in bold letters. "He knows everybody's business in Blue Ridge."

"I appreciate your help," Emma said, reaching into her reticule for a coin to tip him.

With her smaller bag in hand, Emma made her way toward the mercantile, leaving her trunks under the stagecoach awning. The boardwalk creaked beneath her feet, and she felt the curious stares of passersby, their gazes lingering on her fine clothes and eastern bearing.

A bell jangled as she pushed open the door to McGinty's. The scent of coffee, leather, and spices greeted her, along with the sight of shelves packed with goods ranging from tools to fabrics to canned foods. A few customers browsed the aisles, while a red-haired man with a generous mustache arranged items behind a wooden counter.

"Good afternoon," Emma said, approaching the counter. "Are you Mr. McGinty?"

The man looked up, surprise flickering across his friendly face. "That I am, miss. Patrick McGinty, at your service." His Irish lilt was unmistakable. "Just arrived on the stage, have you?"

"Yes," Emma nodded. "I'm Emma Abbott. My uncle Thomas owned a ranch outside of town."

McGinty's expression shifted to one of recognition and sympathy. "Thomas Abbott's niece! We heard he'd left the place to family back East, but didn't expect—" He paused, seeming to catch himself. "Well, didn't expect you'd come all this way. Thomas spoke of you fondly."

"You knew him well?" Emma asked, a pang of grief surprising her. Though she'd corresponded with her uncle, they hadn't seen each other for years.

"As well as anyone knew Thomas," McGinty said with a chuckle. "Private man, your uncle, but respected. Always paid his bills on time and helped neighbors when needed." He studied her curiously. "Will you be selling the ranch, then?"

"No," Emma replied firmly. "I intend to live there and run it myself."

McGinty's eyebrows rose, and nearby conversations quieted as other customers turned to look at her.

"Is that so?" came a smooth voice from behind.

Emma turned to find a tall man watching her with amused interest. His clothes were finer than those of the other men she'd seen in town—a black vest over a crisp white shirt, polished boots, and a hat that he now removed to reveal dark hair and keen eyes. Handsome in a predatory way, like a sleek panther.

"Jedediah Walker," he introduced himself with a tip of his hat. "Folks call me Jed. I own the Silver Spur Saloon." His eyes assessed her with an intensity that made Emma instinctively straighten her posture. "Welcome to Blue Ridge."

"Thank you," Emma replied, maintaining her composure under his scrutiny.

Jed smiled, revealing perfect teeth. "I've had my eye on the Abbott property for some time. Approached your uncle several times with generous offers, but he was... attached to the place. Perhaps you'd consider selling to a local who knows the land's value."

"As I just told Mr. McGinty, I have no intention of selling," Emma stated. "The ranch is my home now."

Jed's smile didn't falter, but something flickered in his eyes. "A lady like yourself, running a ranch? That's ambitious. Ranching is difficult work—dangerous, even. Not suited to a woman's delicate constitution."

Emma met his gaze steadily. "My constitution is stronger than it appears, Mr. Walker. And I'm quite capable of learning what I don't already know."

"I'm sure you are," Jed said, though his tone suggested otherwise. "Still, should you reconsider, my offer remains open. Very generous, I assure you."

"I'll bear that in mind," Emma replied coolly, "though I don't anticipate changing my decision."

Jed inclined his head, then glanced at McGinty. "Put Miss Abbott's purchases on my account, Patrick. Consider it a welcome to Blue Ridge." He turned back to Emma. "Our little community looks after its own. You'll find us quite hospitable."

There was something in his tone—a veiled warning beneath the charm—that set Emma on edge. Before she could respond, the bell above the door jangled again, and a tall figure with a deputy's badge entered.

"Afternoon, Patrick," the newcomer said, nodding to McGinty before his eyes landed on Emma. He straightened, removing his hat to reveal sandy hair and honest brown eyes. "Ma'am."

"Deputy Lewis," McGinty greeted him. "This here's Miss Emma Abbott, Thomas's niece from back East. Miss Abbott, Deputy Samuel Lewis."

The deputy's expression brightened with recognition. "Miss Abbott! We've been expecting you. Sheriff Davies mentioned you'd written about your arrival."

Emma nodded, recalling the brief letter she'd sent to the local authorities, announcing her intention to claim her inheritance. "Yes, though I find myself in need of assistance. My trunks are at the stagecoach station, and I need transportation to the ranch."

"I'd be happy to offer my services," Jed interjected smoothly. "My carriage is quite comfortable."

"That won't be necessary," Deputy Lewis said quickly, his tone professional but firm.

Jed's smile tightened almost imperceptibly. "Of course. Another time, perhaps." He turned to Emma with a slight bow. "Miss Abbott, until we meet again. Welcome to Blue Ridge."

As he exited, Emma felt tension release from her shoulders.

"Don't mind Jed," McGinty said quietly. "He's just sore about Thomas refusing to sell to him all these years."

"Why is he so interested in my uncle's land?" Emma asked.

McGinty and Deputy Lewis exchanged glances.

"Your uncle's property is well-situated," Lewis explained diplomatically. "Good water, decent grazing. Valuable to anyone looking to expand their holdings."

Emma sensed there was more to the story, but the deputy had already moved on.

"If you'll give me a list of what you need, Miss Abbott, I can help you gather supplies while Patrick prepares the rest," Lewis offered. "I've got the sheriff's wagon outside. We can load your trunks and be at the ranch before sundown."

Relief washed over Emma. "Thank you, Deputy. I appreciate your kindness."

"Samuel, please," he said with a warm smile. "Or Deputy Sam, if you prefer. We're not overly formal in Blue Ridge."

As Emma began selecting essentials—coffee, flour, sugar, lamp oil—other customers drifted closer, curiosity evident in their expressions.

"So you're really planning to run old Thomas's place by yourself?" asked an older woman examining fabric nearby.

"I am," Emma confirmed, selecting a sturdy work apron from a display.

The woman exchanged glances with her companion. "Where's your husband, dear?"

"I'm not married," Emma replied, growing weary of the question but maintaining her politeness.

"A young woman alone? In these parts?" The woman's companion looked scandalized. "It isn't proper. Or safe."

Deputy Lewis cleared his throat. "Miss Abbott is Thomas Abbott's legal heir, Mrs. Hendricks. She has every right to claim her property."

"Of course she does," McGinty added, placing Emma's selections in a crate. "And she'll have neighbors to help when needed, just like anyone else."

Emma gave both men a grateful look, touched by their defense.

As they finished gathering supplies, the bell jangled again, and a woman about Emma's age entered, a young boy in tow. Her simple dress and sun-kissed complexion spoke of outdoor work, but her smile was warm as she approached the counter.

"Patrick, Tommy and I need—" She stopped, noticing Emma. "Oh, I'm sorry, I didn't mean to interrupt."

"Not at all," McGinty said cheerfully. "Clara, meet Miss Emma Abbott, Thomas's niece from Boston. Miss Abbott, this is Clara Jacobs, one of your neighbors. Her homestead borders Abbott Ranch on the east."

"It's a pleasure," Emma said sincerely, extending her hand.

Clara's grip was firm, her eyes curious but kind. "Likewise. This is my son, Tommy." The boy, about seven years old, offered a shy nod. "We were sorry to hear about your uncle. He was a good neighbor."

"Thank you. I'm looking forward to seeing his—my—ranch," Emma replied.

Clara's expression held surprise. "You'll be staying, then? Running the ranch yourself?"

McGinty chuckled. "That's the question of the hour, Clara. And yes, she is."

"Good for you," Clara said. "It won't be easy, but—" She glanced at her son with pride. "We women can manage more than most folks give us credit for."

A widow, Emma realized, feeling an immediate kinship with this woman who clearly understood what it meant to defy expectations.

"You're close by?" Emma asked. "Perhaps we could call on each other sometime."

Clara's face lit up. "I'd like that. It gets lonely sometimes, just Tommy and me." She hesitated, then added, "I could show you around, help you get acquainted with the area."

"I'd appreciate that very much," Emma said sincerely.

As Deputy Lewis helped Emma complete her purchases, more townsfolk filtered in, each introducing themselves with varying degrees of curiosity and skepticism. By the time they loaded the last of her supplies into the sheriff's wagon, Emma had met the blacksmith, the schoolteacher, and half a dozen others whose names blurred together.

"Quite a welcome committee," Lewis commented as he helped Emma onto the wagon seat. Her trunks and supplies were secured in the back, along with a crate of chickens McGinty had included—"Thomas's flock died off after he passed," he'd explained.

"Everyone's been very... interested," Emma replied diplomatically as Lewis took the reins.

He chuckled. "Blue Ridge doesn't see many new folks, especially not educated Eastern ladies planning to run ranches alone. You've given them something to talk about."

The wagon pulled away from the boardwalk, and Emma felt dozens of eyes following their departure. The main street soon gave way to open country, the dirt road winding through rolling hills covered in spring grass.

"Beautiful, isn't it?" Lewis asked, noting Emma's wide-eyed gaze at the landscape.

"It is," she agreed, drinking in the vastness of it all. "My uncle's letters described it, but I didn't fully comprehend until now."

Lewis nodded. "Most don't. Takes seeing it with your own eyes." He hesitated, then added, "Miss Abbott, I should warn you—the ranch hasn't been properly maintained since your uncle's passing. The buildings are sound, but it's been seven months..."

"I understand," Emma said, though her heart sank a little. "I'm prepared for work."

"I know there is a ranch hand living in a cabin near your uncle's home. His name's Mark McKay. Quiet fellow, he keeps to himself. He might be willing to help, at least until you get settled."

Emma made a mental note of the name. "Thank you. I'll need all the help I can get."

As they rode in comfortable silence, Emma reflected on her journey—not just the physical miles traveled, but the distance between the life she'd left and the one stretching before her. In Boston, her parents had been horrified by her decision to leave.

"Have you lost your mind, Emma?" her mother had demanded. *"Abandoning a perfectly suitable match with Edward Sinclair to chase some... frontier fantasy?"*

"It's not a fantasy, Mother," she'd replied. *"It's an opportunity to live on my terms."*

Her father's disappointment had been even harder to bear. "You're throwing away everything we've built for you. Security. Position in society. For what? A plot of dirt in the wilderness?"

But they didn't understand. Couldn't understand how the thought of marrying Edward, becoming an ornament in his collection, existing solely to host his parties and bear his children, had made her feel as though she were slowly suffocating.

Uncle Thomas's letters had been her escape, his stories of Montana painting pictures of a life where people were valued for their character and capabilities, not their pedigree or connections. When a letter had arrived providing her with details of his illness and death along with the deed to his ranch, Emma had seen it for what it was—not just an inheritance, but a chance at freedom.

"Miss Abbott?" Lewis's voice pulled her from her thoughts. "We're here."

Emma looked up to see a wooden arch spanning the road ahead, the words 'ABBOTT RANCH' carved into the crossbeam. Her heart quickened as they passed beneath it. The property opened before them—rolling pastureland dotted with a few grazing cattle, a stream winding through the valley, and ahead, nestled against a backdrop of pine trees, a timber-framed house with a front porch.

As they drew closer, Emma could see the house and yard needed a good cleaning, but it was solid and welcoming. A weathered barn stood nearby, along with several smaller outbuildings.

Lewis brought the wagon to a stop before the house. "Home sweet home, Miss Abbott."

Emma sat motionless for a moment, taking it all in. This was hers. This house, this land, this opportunity—all hers to shape as she wished.

"Thank you, Deputy," she said finally, her voice thick with emotion she hadn't expected.

He helped her down from the wagon, understanding in his eyes. "Take your time. I'll start unloading your things."

Emma nodded gratefully and approached the house. The porch steps creaked under her weight, the weathered boards solid despite their age. She ran her hand along the porch railing, feeling the roughness beneath her gloved fingers. The front door was locked, but the key had been sent with the deed. She retrieved it from her reticule and inserted it into the lock with trembling fingers.

The door swung open on protesting hinges, revealing a dim interior. Emma stepped inside, the floorboards groaning beneath her feet. Dust motes danced in the shafts of evening sunlight filtering through the windows. The air was stale but not unpleasant—it smelled of wood smoke, old books, and something indefinably masculine that must have been her uncle's scent.

The main room was sparsely furnished. A stone fireplace dominated one wall, a wooden rocking chair positioned before it. Bookshelves lined another wall, filled with volumes whose titles Emma couldn't wait to explore. A sturdy table with four chairs stood in what served as the dining area, and a doorway led to what she assumed was the kitchen.

"It's perfect," she whispered to herself, tears pricking at her eyes. The enormity of what she'd done—leaving everything familiar behind—suddenly hit her, bringing equal measures of fear and exhilaration.

She moved through the house, exploring each room. The kitchen was simple but functional, with a cast-iron stove, a dry sink, and cupboards that, upon inspection, contained basic dishware. A bedroom revealed a wooden bed frame with a straw mattress that would need fresh ticking, a chest of drawers, and a small mirror. The study was clearly where Thomas had spent most of his time—a desk piled with papers, more books, and a comfortable chair.

"Miss Abbott?" Lewis called from the doorway. "Where would you like your trunks?"

"The bedroom, please," she replied, composing herself and returning to the main room. "It's through that door."

While Lewis carried in her luggage, Emma continued exploring. A ladder in the corner of the main room led to a loft, which she discovered contained another bed frame, neatly made up but dusty. Storage, perhaps, or accommodation for a guest, she thought to herself.

Back downstairs, she found Lewis setting her crate of supplies on the table.

"There's a pump out back for water," he explained, "and the outhouse is beyond that. Thomas dug a proper well, so you'll have clean water year-round. I imagine the stove needs a good cleaning, but the chimney appears sound as well as the other structures on the property. I checked them the last time I rode by."

"You've been keeping an eye on the place?" Emma asked, touched by the gesture.

Lewis nodded. "Sheriff Davies asked me to. We all respected Thomas. Wanted to make sure his property was waiting for whoever came to claim it." He hesitated. "There's something else you should know, Miss Abbott. There's been some... interest in this land lately."

"Mr. Walker's offers, you mean?"

"Not just offers," Lewis said grimly. "There've been strangers riding the boundaries, looking for I don't know what. And one of the out-buildings had a broken lock last month—nothing taken that I could see, but someone was poking around."

Emma frowned. "Why would anyone trespass?"

"I'm not sure. Could be some drifter thinking the property has been abandoned," Lewis admitted. "But be careful, Miss Abbott. Not everyone in these parts is as welcoming as they should be to newcomers." He glanced out the window, where the sun was beginning its descent toward the mountains. "I should head back before dark. Will you be all right here alone tonight?"

Emma squared her shoulders. "I'll be fine, Deputy. I came prepared." She indicated her reticule, where the handle of a small pistol was just visible.

Lewis's eyebrows rose. "You know how to use that?"

"My uncle insisted in his letters, just in case if I ever decided to come this way. Thinking on it now, it's almost as if he were preparing me," Emma said. "I had lessons back in Boston."

"Good," Lewis nodded approvingly. "I'll stop by tomorrow to check on you. And Clara Jacobs's place is just over that rise to the east if you need anything urgent."

After Lewis departed, Emma stood on the porch, watching the wagon disappear down the road. The silence that followed was profound—no city noises, no bustling households, just the whisper of wind through grass and the distant lowing of cattle.

For the first time since leaving Boston, she was truly alone.

Rather than frightening her, the realization was liberating. No one to judge her choices or dictate her actions. No social obligations or suffocating expectations. Just Emma Abbott and the land that was now hers.

With newfound energy, she returned inside to begin making the house habitable. She tied an apron over her travel dress, rolled up her sleeves, and set to work sweeping, dusting, and unpacking essentials. She found clean linens in a trunk at the foot of the bed and made up the mattress with fresh bedding.

By the time darkness fell, Emma had cleaned the kitchen sufficiently to prepare a simple meal of beans and salt pork from her supplies. She lit the lamps she'd found and cleaned, casting a warm light throughout the main room.

As she sat at the table with her modest dinner, Emma noticed a leather-bound book on the bookshelf that looked newer than the others. Setting aside her plate, she retrieved it and opened the cover to find her uncle's handwriting. It was a journal, dated the previous year.

April 15, 1884

Spring has finally arrived in full force. The creek is running high with snowmelt, and the pastures are greening up nicely. Spotted the first calves of the season today—three healthy ones. Mark says we should expect at least ten more in the coming weeks.

Emma flipped through the pages, finding detailed accounts of ranch life—cattle counts, weather observations, notes on repairs and improvements. Her uncle had been meticulous in his record-keeping. This would be invaluable, as she learned to manage the ranch.

Towards the end of the journal, the entries grew shorter and more sporadic.

August 30, 1884

The cough is worse. Dr. Hargrove says it's consumption. Not much to be done at my age. Mark knows what to do if I don't make it through winter.

September 18, 1884
Made arrangements with Muldoon at the bank. Everything goes to Emma if I pass. The girl deserves a chance at something real, not that puppet show they call society back East. She's got spirit, just like her mother had before she married my stuffed shirted brother. Maybe here she'll find what matters.

October 2, 1884
Told Mark to stay on as long as he wants after I'm gone. Paid him six months' wages in advance. Good man, Mark. Quiet, but solid. Hope Emma keeps him on when she comes. She'll need someone who knows the land.

Emma brushed away tears as she closed the journal. Her uncle had known her better than she'd realized, despite the distance between them. He'd known of her unhappiness in Boston and offered this lifeline—not as an afterthought, but as a deliberate choice.

"Thank you, Uncle Thomas," she whispered to the empty room.

Chapter 2

Rising from the table, Emma moved to the window. Night had fully descended, and the vast Montana sky was ablaze with stars—more than she'd ever seen in Boston, where city lights dimmed the heavens. The silhouettes of mountains were just visible against the starlit backdrop, ancient and enduring.

A movement caught her eye—a flickering light in the distance, too steady to be a star. A lantern, perhaps, in a window or carried by someone on foot. It appeared to be coming from the direction of the woods that bordered the western edge of the property.

Mark McKay perhaps? Lewis had mentioned he lived in a cabin nearby. Emma wondered about this man her uncle had trusted enough to leave in charge of his beloved ranch.

The sound of hoofbeats approached from the direction of the road. Emma tensed, remembering Lewis's warning about trespassers. She moved away from the window, dousing the lamp in the main room to avoid being silhouetted against the light.

Through the darkness, she watched a rider approach—a solitary figure on horseback, moving with purpose toward the house. The rider dismounted smoothly, securing the horse to the hitching post, then paused, apparently noticing the smoke rising from the chimney.

Emma's hand moved over her reticule, where her small pistol rested. The figure mounted the porch steps, boots heavy on the wooden boards. Then came a knock—firm but not threatening.

"Hello?" a deep voice called. "Anyone there?"

Emma hesitated, her heart pounding.

"I'm armed," she called out clearly. "State your business."

There was a pause, then: "Mark McKay. I work—worked—for Thomas Abbott. Saw the smoke and light coming from the windows and came to investigate."

Emma relaxed slightly, recalling her uncle's words in the journal. Good man, Mark. Quiet, but solid. She relit the lamp and approached the door, pistol still in hand but no longer aimed.

When she opened the door, she found herself facing a tall man with broad shoulders outlined in the dim light. His hat shadowed his features, but she could make out strong lines in his face and the wariness in his stance.

"Mr. McKay," she said, lowering the pistol. "I'm Emma Abbott, Thomas Abbott's niece from Boston."

The man stiffened almost imperceptibly. "Miss Abbott." He removed his hat, revealing dark hair and piercing eyes that assessed her with undisguised skepticism. "Thomas said you'd come."

"I arrived today," Emma explained, suddenly aware of her disheveled appearance after hours of cleaning. "Deputy Lewis helped me settle in."

McKay nodded but said nothing, his expression unreadable in the dim light.

"Would you like to come in?" Emma offered, stepping back from the doorway. "I've just been reading my uncle's journal. He spoke highly of you."

McKay hesitated, then inclined his head and entered, ducking slightly through the doorway. In the lamplight, Emma could see him more clearly—a man of perhaps thirty, weathered by sun and wind, with an intensity about him. He moved with the fluid grace of someone accustomed to physical labor, though there was a coiled tension in his bearing that suggested he was rarely at ease.

"You've been caring for the ranch since my uncle's passing?" Emma asked, gesturing for him to take a seat at the table.

McKay remained standing, his hat in his hands. "Someone had to. Cattle need tending. Horses too."

"I appreciate that," Emma said sincerely. "Uncle Thomas mentioned in his journal that he paid you six months' wages in advance."

"He did," McKay confirmed. "That time's up, but I've continued to watch over everything. Didn't seem right to leave it all to ruin."

A man of integrity, then, continuing work even without compensation. Emma's estimation of him rose.

"I'd like to hire you to continue," she said directly. "I know little about ranching, but I'm a quick learner. Having someone with experience would be invaluable."

McKay's expression shifted slightly—surprise, perhaps, though his features quickly returned to their stoic set. "You're planning to stay, then? Run the ranch yourself?"

"I am," Emma replied, growing weary of the question but keeping her tone even.

"It's hard work," he said, studying her fine hands and citified clothes. "Not what you're used to, I'd imagine."

"No," Emma admitted, "but I didn't come all this way to fail, Mr. McKay. I intend to learn whatever is necessary."

Something that might have been respect flickered in his eyes. "You'll need help. More than just me. A ranch this size usually has at least three hands during calving and branding season."

"Then we'll hire more when required," Emma said practically. "For now, I'd be grateful for your assistance and knowledge."

McKay was quiet for a long moment, seeming to weigh his options. Finally, he gave a single nod. "I'll stay on. Same wages Thomas paid."

Relief washed over Emma. Having an experienced ranch hand—especially one her uncle had trusted—would make all the difference.

"Thank you," she said. "Perhaps tomorrow you could show me around the property? I'd like to understand what I'm working with."

"Dawn," McKay replied. "We start at dawn in ranching country."

Emma straightened her spine. "Dawn it is."

For the first time, McKay's expression softened almost imperceptibly. "Thomas said you had spirit. Guess he was right."

The simple statement touched Emma deeply. "I hope to prove him right about many things, Mr. McKay."

McKay put his hat back on, apparently considering their business concluded. "I'll be by at first light. Get some rest, Miss Abbott. Tomorrow will come earlier than you think."

With that, he turned and left as quietly as he'd arrived, his tall figure disappearing into the darkness.

Emma closed the door behind him, leaning against it as her mind processed the encounter. Mark McKay was not what she'd expected—more imposing, less communicative, yet somehow reassuring in his solid presence. He clearly doubted her abilities, but he hadn't dismissed her outright, which was more than could be said for the many she'd met today.

Returning to the table, Emma picked up her uncle's journal again, finding comfort in his words. Tomorrow would bring challenges, but also the first real steps toward the life she'd chosen. A life of freedom, purpose, and possibility.

Outside, the Montana night stretched vast and star-filled above her new home, while somewhere in the darkness, cattle lowed softly and a distant coyote called to the moon. Emma Abbott, Boston socialite turned rancher, smiled at the unfamiliar sounds of her new horizon.

Chapter 3

The first light of dawn had barely begun to streak the sky when Emma jerked awake, momentarily disoriented by the unfamiliar creaks and shadows of her new bedroom. She blinked at the rough-hewn ceiling, her mind racing to place herself until memory flooded back—Montana, the ranch, her inheritance, her new beginning.

A rooster crowed in the distance, and Emma swung her legs over the side of the bed, wincing at the soreness that permeated her muscles after yesterday's cleaning frenzy. The floorboards felt cool beneath her bare feet as she crossed to the window and pulled back the faded curtain. The eastern horizon glowed with the promise of sunrise, painting the vast Montana landscape in shades of indigo and charcoal.

"Dawn," she murmured, remembering Mark McKay's terse instruction from the night before.

Emma hurried to dress, selecting her plainest skirt and a sturdy shirt waist—still far too fine for ranch work, but the best she could manage until she acquired more suitable clothing. She twisted her auburn hair into a practical knot at the nape of her neck, foregoing the elaborate style she'd worn in Boston.

The fireplace in the main room held only gray ashes. Emma knelt to restart it, grateful for the box of matches she'd purchased at McGinty's. The kindling caught quickly, and soon a small fire chased away the morning chill. She pumped water into a kettle for coffee, thankful once again the kitchen pump worked smoothly despite months of disuse.

While the water heated, Emma stepped onto the back porch, eager for a look at the ranch as the sun rose above the mountains. The sight took her breath away. Rolling hills stretched toward distant mountains, their peaks tinged pink with the first touch of sunlight. Dew sparkled on the late spring grass, and birds called from the trees bordering the property. The beauty of it struck her with unexpected force—this was hers now, all of it.

A sense of purpose straightened her spine. She would make this work, whatever it took. She quickly rushed inside, poured a cup of coffee, and returned outside.

Emma descended the porch steps, determined to familiarize herself with the immediate surroundings before Mark arrived. The barn stood sturdy and weathered about fifty yards from the house, with smaller outbuildings clustered nearby—a chicken coop, a smokehouse, and what appeared to be a tool shed. Beyond these, a large corral.

Except—Emma stopped short, frowning. The corral gate stood wide open, and the enclosure was empty.

"No, no, no," she muttered, dropping her cup of coffee as she hurried toward the open gate. Hoof prints in the mud showed where the horses had wandered out, heading toward the open pasture.

Emma scanned the horizon and spotted them—five horses grazing peacefully about a quarter mile away. Relief flooded her, but it was short-lived. The animals needed to be returned to the corral before Mark arrived, or he'd think her completely incompetent.

This was her first test as a rancher, and she refused to fail.

In Boston, she'd taken riding lessons and occasionally visited her friend's farm, where she'd watched the stable hands work with horses. Treats often helped lure them back, didn't they?

Emma hurried to the house and returned with a sliced apple. Holding it before her like an offering, she approached the nearest horse—a sturdy brown gelding who watched her with wary eyes.

"Come now," she called, her voice gentle. "I have something for you."

The horse lifted its head, nostrils flaring at the scent of apple. It took a tentative step toward her, then another.

"That's it," Emma encouraged, stretching out her hand with an apple slice flat on her palm as she'd been taught.

The gelding came close enough to snatch the treat, then immediately backed away, chewing contentedly but showing no interest in following her.

Emma suppressed a flare of frustration. This wasn't working. She needed a lead rope, or perhaps grain, to entice them. Returning to the barn, she searched until she found a halter and lead rope hanging on a peg.

Back outside, she approached the horses again. The brown gelding had wandered a few yards farther away, joining his companions.

"Come here," Emma called firmly, trying to project confidence she didn't feel. "Time to go home."

The horses flicked their ears but continued grazing. Emma moved closer, halter ready, but as she approached, the animals simply shifted away, maintaining their distance with infuriating ease.

After fifteen minutes of increasingly desperate attempts, Emma was flushed with exertion and no closer to corralling the horses. Her skirt hem was sodden with dew, her boots caked with mud, and her carefully arranged hair was coming loose, wisps falling around her face.

"This can't be so difficult," she muttered, setting her jaw in determination. If she couldn't bring them in, she would at least drive them toward the corral. She began waving her arms and calling out, hoping to startle them in the right direction.

The horses regarded her with what seemed like equine amusement before trotting farther away, their tails swishing in the morning air.

Emma was about to make another attempt when the sound of approaching hoofbeats made her freeze. Turning, she saw Mark McKay riding toward her, his expression unreadable under the brim of his hat. He sat tall in the saddle, his movements fluid and confident as he guided his horse directly to her.

Mortification washed over Emma. She straightened, attempting to salvage her dignity despite her disheveled appearance and obvious failure.

"Good morning, Mr. McKay," she managed, keeping her voice level.

Mark dismounted in one smooth motion, his boots hitting the ground with barely a sound. He surveyed the scene—the open corral gate, the horses, Emma's muddied clothes—and his mouth tightened slightly.

"Morning. Looks like you've got some strays," he said simply, his deep voice betraying no mockery, though Emma was certain he must find the situation laughable.

"The gate was open when I came out this morning," she explained, determined not to sound defensive. "I was attempting to bring them back."

Mark nodded, his piercing blue eyes assessing her briefly before he turned his attention to the horses. Without another word, he swung back onto his mount and rode toward the scattered animals. Emma watched, unable to mask her fascination as he worked.

His movements were purposeful yet relaxed, guiding his horse with subtle shifts of weight and pressure from his knees rather than yanking on the reins. He approached the group from the side, not head-on as she had done, and began a gentle arc that seemed to invisibly gather the horses.

The animals responded to his presence differently than they had to hers. They lifted their heads, alert but not fearful, and when he maneuvered behind them, they began moving in the direction he indicated—toward the corral. Within minutes, he had them trotting obediently through the open gate.

Emma approached as Mark dismounted again. Up close, she noticed details she'd missed in their brief encounter the previous night—the faint scar along his left cheek, the quiet intensity in his gaze, the confident economy of his movements.

"Thank you," she said sincerely. "I fear I was making rather a mess of things."

Mark secured the gate latch before answering. "Horses need proper handling. Takes practice." His tone wasn't unkind, just matter-of-fact.

Emma nodded. "I have much to learn."

Something shifted in Mark's expression—perhaps surprise at her ready admission. "Most do, coming from the city." He ran his hand along the gate's frame, his brow furrowing. "This latch was forced open."

"Forced?" Emma moved closer to see where he was pointing. "You mean it didn't just come open on its own?"

"No." Mark's fingers traced splintered wood near the latch. "Someone opened it deliberately."

A chill ran through Emma, despite the strengthening morning sun. "Deputy Lewis mentioned there had been trespassers."

Mark's jaw tightened.

Someone had been on her property while she slept, intentionally causing mischief—or worse. "Who would do such a thing?"

Mark straightened, his expression guarded. "Hard to say. New property owner arrives, some folks get curious. Others don't like change."

"Or perhaps someone like Jed Walker wants to discourage me from staying," Emma said.

Mark's eyes met hers, sharp and assessing. "That's a serious accusation, Miss Abbott."

"It's merely an observation, Mr. McKay." Emma lifted her chin. "In my experience, men like Mr. Walker don't readily accept being denied what they want."

A muscle worked in Mark's jaw. "You've met Walker already?"

"Yesterday, at the mercantile. He wasted no time offering to purchase this ranch."

Mark nodded, as if this confirmed something he'd suspected. "Walker's been buying up property all through this valley. Your uncle refused to sell, no matter the price." He glanced toward the distant mountains. "Thomas had his reasons."

There was something in his tone—a hint of knowledge held back—that piqued Emma's curiosity, but before she could question him further, Mark turned and began walking towards the barn.

"I'll fix this gate properly," he said. "Then I'll show you the property lines. You'll need to know what you're defending."

Emma watched him stride toward the barn, tension evident in his broad shoulders. There was clearly more to the story of Jed Walker's interest in Abbott Ranch, and Mark McKay knew at least part of it, she sensed. She would get answers, but pushing now would only make him retreat further behind that hard facade.

In the meantime, she had a ranch to learn about.

Chapter 4

The morning sun had climbed higher by the time Emma emerged from the house, having changed into a different skirt and taken a few moments to tidy her hair. Mark was finishing repairs on the corral gate.

"Will this prevent further tampering?" Emma asked, approaching with two steaming cups of coffee.

Mark glanced up, seeming slightly surprised by the offered drink. After a moment's hesitation, he accepted the cup with a brief nod of thanks. "Should hold against anything short of an ax."

Emma sipped her coffee, studying the horses now contentedly milling about the corral. "Are these all that remain of my uncle's stock?"

"Five horses and about two dozen head of cattle," Mark confirmed. "Thomas was scaling back toward the end. Used to run twice that many cattle."

"I see." Emma absorbed this information. "And these are sufficient for our immediate needs?"

Something flickered in Mark's expression at her use of "our," but he simply nodded. "More than enough for now. That gelding there—" he indicated the brown horse Emma had attempted to lure with apple slices, "—is relatively gentle. Might suit you once you're more comfortable."

"I've ridden before," Emma said, perhaps too quickly. "In Boston."

The corner of Mark's mouth twitched almost imperceptibly. "City riding and ranch riding aren't quite the same, Miss Abbott."

"Please, call me Emma," she said, realizing the formality between them would quickly become tedious in the casual atmosphere of ranch life. "And I'm aware there will be differences. I don't presume to know everything simply because I've sat on a saddle a few times in a Boston riding park."

Mark studied her for a moment, seeming to reassess his impression. "Emma, then," he said finally, his deep voice wrapping around her name in a way that made her unexpectedly aware of his proximity. "Call me Mark. 'Mr. McKay' makes me sound like my father."

It was a small concession to friendliness, but Emma recognized it as significant coming from this reserved man. "How long have you worked here, Mark?"

"Two years this summer," he replied, draining the last of his coffee. "Time to see those property lines, if you're ready."

Emma set her empty cup on a fence post. "I am. Shall I attempt to saddle a horse?"

Mark's expression suggested he was calculating the time it would take to teach her versus doing it himself. "I'll handle it this time."

Emma watched as he entered the barn and then returned with a saddle. He entered the corral and placed the saddle on the brown gelding he mentioned. His hands moved with practiced ease, adjusting straps and checking the cinch with a thoroughness that spoke of years of experience.

"You need to check every connection," he explained, seeming to warm slightly to the role of teacher. "A loose cinch means a sliding saddle, and that means a rider on the ground."

Emma nodded, committing the steps to memory. "My uncle's journal mentioned you've helped with more than just the horses. He seemed to trust you with every aspect of the ranch."

Mark's hands stilled momentarily before continuing their work. "Thomas was a good man. Fair employer. Made it easy to be loyal."

"I hope to earn the same trust," Emma said.

Mark glanced at her. "Time will tell." He led the gelding toward her and held it steady as Emma mounted, her movements more practiced than he might have expected.

Once both were mounted, Mark led the way along a well-worn trail that skirted the edge of the property. Emma found herself relaxing into the rhythm of the horse's gait, appreciating the smooth stride of the animal beneath her. The morning air was crisp and sweet with the scent of pine and prairie grass, and despite her earlier frustrations, she felt a rush of joy at the sheer beauty surrounding them.

"The northern boundary follows that creek," Mark explained, pointing to a ribbon of water glinting in the sunlight. "Good water source year-round. To the east is the Jacobs place—Clara's homestead."

"She seems kind," Emma observed. "I met her briefly in town yesterday."

Mark nodded. "Decent neighbor. Tough woman. Been on her own since her husband died two years back."

"She mentioned she might show me around the area," Emma said. "I thought I might visit her today after we're finished here."

"Good idea," Mark said. "Clara knows how to survive out here. You could learn from her as well."

They rode in companionable silence for a while, the horses' hooves making soft thuds against the earth. Mark pointed out landmarks and boundaries, explaining water rights and grazing patterns with unexpected eloquence. For a man of few words, he became more talkative when discussing the land itself.

"Beyond this ridge marks the western edge," he said as they crested a gentle slope. "Beyond that is forest land, then more rugged mountains."

Emma reined in her horse beside his, gazing at the sweeping vista before them. The view was breathtaking—rolling pastures giving way to pine forest, with the majestic peaks of the Rockies rising in the distance, still capped with snow despite the spring warmth.

"It's beautiful," she breathed.

Mark glanced at her, something softening in his gaze. "Most beautiful place I've ever known," he agreed.

"I can see why my uncle loved it so much," Emma said. "His letters always spoke of the grandeur of Montana, but words hardly do it justice."

"Thomas appreciated what most take for granted," Mark said, his voice taking on a reverent quality that surprised her. "He didn't just see land to be used—he saw something worth preserving."

Emma studied him, intrigued by this glimpse of passion beneath his reserved exterior. "You sound as though you share that view."

Mark seemed almost embarrassed by his momentary openness. He adjusted his hat, gaze returning to the distant mountains. "Land speaks to those willing to listen," he said simply. "Thomas listened. I listen."

They continued their circuit of the property, Mark pointing out features Emma might have overlooked—a spring-fed pond perfect for watering cattle, a sheltered dell where calves were typically born, a particularly fertile stretch that would make excellent garden land closer to the home.

"The garden's overgrown now," he explained as they rode past a plot near the house where wild grasses had reclaimed once-tilled soil. "Thomas kept vegetables, some herbs. Nothing fancy, but enough to supplement supplies from town."

"I'd like to restart it," Emma said decisively. "Perhaps Clara could advise me on what grows well here."

Mark nodded. "She's got a good hand with plants. Between that and canning, she manages to feed herself and the boy year-round."

As they approached the barn again, Emma felt a new confidence building within her. The property was manageable—larger than she'd initially thought, but not overwhelmingly so. With Mark's help and her own determination, she could make this work.

"Thank you for showing me around," she said as they dismounted. "I have a much better understanding of what I'm working with now."

Mark took the reins of both horses, his expression thoughtful. "It's good land. Needs work, but good bones." He paused, seeming to choose his next words carefully. "Your uncle knew you'd come some-day. Said you had grit and belonged here."

The simple statement touched Emma deeply. "I'm beginning to think he knew me better than I realized."

Mark's mouth curved in what might almost have been a smile. "Thomas had a way of seeing into people." He led the horses into the barn, and Emma followed, watching as he efficiently removed the tack and began brushing down the animals.

"I plan to go into town for more supplies today," Emma said, leaning against a post as Mark worked. "Is there anything we need for the ranch that I should purchase?"

Mark considered this. "Feed store should have oats for the horses. McGinty has seeds if you're serious about that garden. And you'll need more practical clothes if you're planning to do actual ranch work."

Emma glanced down at her city-made skirt, now dusty from the ride. "Yes, I rather thought as much. Would you be able to hitch the wagon for me?"

Mark nodded. "After I finish with the horses. It needs checking over first—hasn't been used in months."

"I appreciate your help," Emma said sincerely. "I know this must be an adjustment for you as well, having someone new in charge."

Mark's hands stilled momentarily on the horse's flank. "Change is part of life out here," he said finally. "Seasons turn, people come and go. Land remains."

There was something almost philosophical in his words, a depth that contrasted with his practical exterior. Emma found herself wondering about this enigmatic man—what had shaped him, what had brought him to her uncle's ranch, what kept him tied to this land when he could clearly find work anywhere with his skills.

But those were questions for another time. For now, she had a ranch to learn more about and supplies to gather from town. One step at a time, she would build the life she'd chosen in this wild, beautiful place.

Chapter 5

The ride into Blue Ridge took less time than Emma expected, the wagon rolling steadily along the dirt road despite its months of disuse. Mark had checked it thoroughly, oiling wheels and testing harnesses before pronouncing it sound, and Emma was grateful for his thoroughness as she guided the team of draft horses into town.

Blue Ridge looked different coming in from this side of town—smaller than her first impression, but more vibrant. Children played in the dusty street, women hung laundry behind modest homes, and men moved purposefully between the various businesses.

Emma drew the wagon to a halt outside McGinty's Mercantile, remembering to secure the brake as Mark had shown her. She gathered her reticule and the list she'd prepared, feeling a small surge of accomplishment at having driven herself to town. Small victories, she reminded herself, would eventually add up to the life she envisioned.

The bell above the door jangled as she entered the mercantile. Patrick McGinty looked up from where he was stocking shelves, his face breaking into a welcoming smile.

"Miss Abbott! Good to see you again," he called cheerfully. "Settling in all right at the ranch?"

"As well as can be expected," Emma replied with a smile. "There's much to be done, but all in due time."

"That's the spirit," McGinty approved. "What can I help you with today?"

Emma produced her list. "Quite a few things, I'm afraid. Seeds for a garden, some tools, fabric for work clothes, and various household necessities."

McGinty nodded, already moving to gather items. "Thomas always planted in mid-May—should be safe from frost by then. I've got good bean and potato seeds, some corn, and squash too."

As McGinty assembled her order, other customers entered the store, each greeting Emma with varying degrees of curiosity and warmth. News traveled fast in small towns, and it was clear that everyone knew who she was and why she had come.

"So you've met the McKay fellow?" asked an older woman examining fabric nearby. "Keeps to himself, that one. Never says more than two words together in town."

"He's been very helpful," Emma replied diplomatically, unwilling to gossip about her employee. "I'm fortunate to have someone who knows the property so well."

The woman raised her eyebrows skeptically. "If you say so, dear. Just seems strange to me, a young woman alone with a man of his... mysterious background."

Emma bristled at the implication. "Mr. McKay was my uncle's trusted employee, and now he's mine. There's nothing improper about our professional relationship."

"Of course, dear," the woman replied, though her tone suggested otherwise. "We're just concerned for your well-being, being new to our ways and all."

The door opened again, and Clara Jacobs entered with Tommy in tow.

"Miss Abbott!" he exclaimed, breaking free of his mother's grasp to rush toward her. "Did you really come all the way from Boston? Is it true you own the ranch now?"

Emma couldn't help smiling at his enthusiasm. "Yes, to both questions, Tommy. Though I'm still learning how to be a proper rancher."

Clara approached more sedately, offering Emma a warm smile. "Good afternoon, Emma. I hope you don't mind Tommy's curiosity—he's been full of questions since we met yesterday."

"Not at all," Emma assured her. "It's refreshing to encounter such honest interest rather than veiled disapproval."

Clara's eyes flickered toward the older woman, who had suddenly become overly interested in examining a bolt of calico. "Yes, well, some folks have rather traditional views about what women can and cannot do." She lowered her voice. "But those of us actually doing the impossible know better, don't we?"

"Indeed we do."

"I was hoping to invite you to dinner this evening," Clara continued. "Nothing fancy, but it would give us a chance to get better acquainted."

"I'd be delighted," Emma replied sincerely. "What time should I arrive?"

"Around six? My place is just visible from your east pasture—the small house with a fence around it."

"I remember," Emma nodded. "Mark pointed it out during our ride this morning."

Clara's expression showed subtle surprise. "He's speaking to you already? McKay said more than three words together?"

Emma laughed. "He's not quite as taciturn as everyone suggests. At least, not when discussing the land."

"The land is probably the only thing he truly cares about," Clara observed. "That and Thomas's memory. He was devoted to your uncle—wouldn't leave even after he passed."

This confirmed Emma's impression of Mark's character—steadfast, loyal, and deeply connected to the ranch beyond mere employment. "I'm grateful for his dedication. I'd be quite lost without his guidance."

McGinty returned with the last of Emma's items. "That should do it, Miss Abbott. Want me to have the boy help load these into your wagon?"

"Yes, please," Emma agreed, paying for her purchases from the funds she'd brought from Boston.

As McGinty's young assistant began carrying packages out, Emma turned back to Clara. "Is there anything I can bring for dinner tonight?"

"Just yourself," Clara assured her. "And perhaps a willingness to hear some plain talk about surviving out here as a woman on your own. It's not easy, but it's worth every struggle."

Chapter 6

Clara's homestead was modest and welcoming, with a neatly swept yard and carefully tended flower beds adding cheerful color to the practical dwelling. As Emma approached, driving the wagon herself, she noticed chickens scratching in a small yard and smoke rising from the chimney.

Tommy burst out the door before she'd fully stopped the team. "Miss Abbott! You came! Mama's making rabbit stew, and I helped pick the carrots!"

Emma smiled, setting the brake and climbing down. "That sounds wonderful, Tommy. I haven't had rabbit stew in years."

"Really?" Tommy asked, his eyes wide. "We have it all the time. I caught the rabbit myself with my snare!"

"That's very impressive," Emma said sincerely. "Perhaps you could teach me how to set snares sometime. I have much to learn about country living."

Tommy's chest puffed with importance. "I know all about snares and fishing and which berries you can eat. Mama taught me."

Clara appeared at the door, wiping her hands on her apron. "Tommy, let Miss Abbott get inside before you offer to teach her everything you know," she said with fond exasperation. "Come in, Emma. Dinner's nearly ready."

The interior of Clara's home was as neat and welcoming as the outside—simple furnishings arranged for practicality, with thoughtful touches like wildflowers in a jar on the table and handmade quilts adding color to the modest space. Delicious aromas wafted from the iron pot hanging over the fire.

"It smells wonderful," Emma said appreciatively.

"It's just simple fare," Clara replied, "but filling. Please, sit. The bread's just about done."

Over dinner, Emma enjoyed Clara's practical wisdom and Tommy's innocent curiosity. The conversation flowed easily, touching on everything from gardening techniques to the best way to mend clothes to last through hard ranch work.

"Those city clothes won't hold up to ranch life," Clara observed, nodding at Emma's attire. "I noticed you bought fabric at McGinty's. Do you sew?"

"Decorative needlework was part of every Boston girl's education," Emma said wryly, "but practical sewing is another matter. I fear my skills aren't equal to creating an entire wardrobe, but I'm determined."

Clara smiled. "I can help with that. I make all our clothes—necessity taught me well."

"I'd be most grateful," Emma said sincerely. "There's so much to learn, and it's overwhelming at times."

"That's how I felt when William first brought me out here," Clara admitted, her expression softening at the memory of her late husband. "I was a shopkeeper's daughter from St. Louis—knew nothing about homesteading. But we learn what we must to survive."

Tommy, having finished his stew, looked up eagerly. "Can I be excused, Mama? I want to get my collection to show Miss Abbott."

Clara nodded indulgently. "Just for a few minutes, then it's time to wash up for bed."

As Tommy scampered off to retrieve his treasures, Clara refilled Emma's cup with fragrant herbal tea. "He's taken a shine to you," she observed. "It's good for him to have new people to talk to. Gets lonely out here sometimes, just the two of us."

"He's a wonderful boy," Emma said sincerely. "You've done an impressive job raising him on your own."

"We manage," Clara said simply. "It's not the life I imagined, but it's a good one. William left us this land, and working it connects Tommy to his father's memory."

Emma nodded, understanding the sentiment. "That's how I feel about Uncle Thomas's ranch. It's a connection to him, and to something authentic."

Clara studied her thoughtfully. "It's more than that for you, though, isn't it? You're running from something back East."

Emma started, surprised by Clara's perceptiveness. "Is it that obvious?"

"Only to someone who recognizes the look," Clara said gently. "I had it myself once—that mix of determination and relief at escaping something. You don't have to tell me what it was."

Emma traced the rim of her cup, considering how much to reveal. "I was expected to marry a man of my parents' choosing—a suitable match, they called it. A life planned out to the smallest detail, with no room for my own desires or dreams."

Clara nodded, understanding. "And now you're here, where no one's path is predetermined. It's terrifying and liberating all at once, isn't it?"

"Yes, it is," Emma agreed, relieved to be understood. "I don't regret my decision to come here at all."

"That's how you know you've made the right choice," Clara said firmly. "But Emma—" her expression grew more serious, "—you should know what you're facing here. It's not just the physical hardships or learning new skills. There are those who won't want you to succeed."

"You mean Jed Walker," Emma guessed.

Clara nodded, lowering her voice, though there was no one to overhear. "He's been buying up properties all through this valley. Pressuring folks to sell, especially those of us on our own. Your uncle flat-out refused him, no matter the price."

"But why? What makes this land so valuable to Walker?"

Clara shook her head. "I have my assumptions as to why. Jed owns the saloon, has interests in several businesses in town, but the past year, he's focused on acquiring land—specific parcels, including mine and yours. It's not like the land is particularly fertile compared to other areas."

"Deputy Lewis mentioned there had been trespassers on my property," Emma said. "And this morning, someone deliberately messed with the corral gate, letting the horses loose."

Clara's expression darkened. "That's how it starts. Subtle things—missing tools, damaged fences, livestock frightened. Nothing you can prove was deliberate, but enough to wear you down."

"Has this happened to you?" Emma asked, concerned for her new friend.

"A few times," Clara admitted. "Nothing I couldn't handle, and it stopped after a while. I think Walker decided I wasn't worth the trouble—my little homestead is just a side piece to what he really wants."

"Which is?"

"Your land, primarily. And the Carson place on the other side of town. Both back up to the mountains." Clara hesitated. "There are minerals in those mountains—gold, copper..."

Tommy returned proudly displaying a collection of interesting rocks, bird feathers, and a shed antler. "Look what I found, Miss Abbott! Mr. McKay taught me which rocks are special." He held up a quartz specimen. "This one has gold in it—see the little flecks? Mr. McKay says there are lots of these in the stream by your place."

Emma and Clara exchanged meaningful glances over Tommy's head.

"That's fascinating, Tommy," Emma said, examining the rock with new interest. "Mr. McKay seems to know a great deal about the land."

"He knows everything," Tommy affirmed with childish certainty. "He showed me how to track deer and where the best fishing spots are." His expression grew serious. "Mama says I should listen when he talks because he's smart."

"Your mama is very wise," Emma agreed, glancing at Clara.

After Tommy had been sent to bed and the women were alone again, Clara spoke in hushed tones. "Be careful how you approach McKay with questions. He's private, especially about anything to do with Thomas or the land. But if anyone knows why Walker wants your property so badly, it's him."

"Do you trust him?" Emma asked directly.

Clara considered the question. "I trust him to be loyal to Thomas's memory and to the land he loved. I trust him with my son. Beyond that?" She shrugged. "McKay's a mystery to most folks around here. Showed up two years ago, keeps to himself, works hard. Thomas trusted him completely, which counts for something."

Emma nodded, processing this information. "I should head back before it gets too dark. Thank you for dinner, and for your candor. It means a great deal to have someone I can speak openly with."

Clara walked her to the wagon, helping her check the horses' harnesses. "Any time you need advice or just a friendly ear, my door is open. We women must stick together out here."

As Emma drove back toward her home, her mind whirled with everything she'd learned. The ranch, it seemed, was more than just a fresh start for her—it was wrapped in mystery and coveted by powerful interests. And at the center of it all was Mark McKay, a man of few words who quite possibly knew more than he was saying.

Chapter 7

Emma woke with a start, her heart racing as something clattered against the bedroom window. She sat upright, momentarily disoriented, before recognizing the beams of her uncle's—her—bedroom. A tree branch scratched against the glass, driven by a morning breeze that rustled through the trees outside.

Letting out a relieved breath, Emma pushed aside the homespun quilt and swung her legs over the side of the bed. She padded to the window and peered out at her property—her home—spread before her in the early morning light.

The corral gate stood secure, the horses within grazing peacefully. No sign of trespassers or trouble. Just Montana awakening to a new day, the land stretching toward distant mountains with nothing but possibility between.

Emma dressed quickly in one of her plainer dresses and twisted her hair into a simple knot.

The house creaked comfortingly as she moved through it. She started a fire in the cast-iron stove in the kitchen and pumped fresh water for coffee. While the water heated, Emma stood on the back porch, breathing in the crisp morning air. Birdsong filled the silence, punctuated by the occasional lowing of cattle in the distance. No rumble of carriages, no calls of street vendors, no constant hum of city life. Just peace.

"I am so glad I came here. This is paradise," she murmured to herself, tucking away a stray strand of auburn hair that had escaped her pins.

After a simple breakfast of bread and jam—purchased from McGinty's the day before—Emma decided to explore her uncle's study more thoroughly. She'd glimpsed it briefly upon arrival, but had been too overwhelmed with cleaning and settling in to give it proper attention.

The study door creaked as she pushed it open. Dust motes danced in the shafts of morning light streaming through the single window. The room smelled of leather, paper, and pipe tobacco—her uncle's scent preserved like a memory. Emma ran her fingers lightly over the desk, feeling the worn grooves.

Bookshelves lined the walls, their contents a fascinating mix of practical manuals on ranching and farming alongside volumes of poetry, history, and philosophy. Uncle Thomas had been a learned man despite his frontier lifestyle—or perhaps because of it. Out here, one had time to think, to read, to contemplate.

Emma's attention was drawn to a row of leather-bound journals on the bottom shelf, some labeled with a year, others not.

Kneeling, she selected one from several years back and opened it carefully. Her uncle's strong, slanting script filled the pages.

May 18, 1880

Spring planting finished today. Expect a good yield from the north field if the weather holds. Spotted three new calves in the east pasture—all healthy. With God's blessing and a little luck, the herd will grow nicely this season.

Emma smiled, turning pages and watching the seasons pass through her uncle's eyes. His entries were practical but occasionally philosophical, especially when describing the land or changes in the weather. She could almost hear his voice in the words, steady and thoughtful.

As she reached for another volume, a note sticking out with a name written on it caught her eye—Mark McKay. Curious, she turned to the entry.

June 10, 1883

Hired a new hand today—Mark McKay. Young fellow doesn't say much about where he's from, but knows horses better than any man I've met. Has a way with them that can't be taught. Seems to be running from something, but don't we all have ghosts? His work speaks for itself.

Emma's curiosity deepened. She flipped forward several months.

September 22, 1883

McKay proved his worth today. Flash flood nearly took three calves down the creek. He rode into water that would have given most men pause, brought them all out without a scratch on them. When I thanked him, he just nodded like it was nothing extraordinary. But it was. Beginning to think Providence sent him my way.

She continued reading, piecing together the growing relationship between her uncle and his taciturn employee. Thomas's respect for

Mark was evident in every mention, evolving from approval to genuine affection.

December 25, 1883

Christmas dinner with just me and McKay. Not much for talk still, but he seems less guarded. Gave him a new knife—fine steel with a bone handle. He looked at it like nobody'd ever given him a gift before. Maybe they haven't. Later found a hand-carved chess set on my porch—his work, though he denied it when I thanked him. Quality craftsmanship. The man has depths not easily plumbed.

Emma searched the room until she found the chess set tucked away in a wooden box on a shelf. The pieces were beautifully carved, each one unique but balanced with its counterpart. She ran her finger over the knight, feeling the smoothness of wood worked by patient, skilled hands.

She returned to the journals, time slipping away as she became engrossed in her uncle's words. The entry that finally made her pause came from early the previous year:

March 8, 1884

Mark finished the cabin today—built it himself from trees we felled last autumn. Offered to pay him extra, but he refused. Said having his own place on the property was payment enough. I understood. A man needs his own hearth, his own four walls. I've come to think of Mark as the son I never had. Not that I'd tell him so—he'd likely saddle up and ride off, uncomfortable with such sentiment. Thank the Lord for sending him my way.

"The son I never had." Emma whispered the words, a lump forming in her throat. No wonder Mark had stayed on after Thomas's death, watching over the property without pay. His devotion went beyond employment—it was something akin to family.

She was so absorbed in the journals that she didn't immediately register the sound of hammering from outside. When it finally penetrated her awareness, she startled, nearly dropping the book in her hands. Setting it carefully aside, she rose and moved to the window, peering out toward the source of the noise.

Mark was on the barn roof, methodically replacing the damaged shingles. He moved with efficiency, each strike of his hammer sure and practiced. He'd shed his coat in the warmth of the morning sun, and Emma could see the play of muscles across his shoulders as he worked.

Gathering the journals, Emma decided to speak with him. If her uncle had thought so highly of Mark, perhaps she needed to make more effort to understand the reserved man who knew this land so intimately.

Outside, the day had warmed considerably, the late spring sunshine burning away the morning chill. Emma shielded her eyes as she looked up at the barn roof.

"Good morning, Mr.—Mark," she called, correcting herself.

He paused mid-swing, turning to look down at her. "Morning, Miss Abbott."

"Emma," she reminded him, setting the journals on a nearby barrel. "I didn't expect to see you so early today."

Mark tapped another nail into place before responding. "Roof needed fixing before the next rain. Been meaning to get to it."

"I appreciate your attention to detail," Emma said, genuinely impressed with his initiative. "I was just reading some of my uncle's journals. He documented everything about the ranch."

Mark's hands stilled momentarily before resuming their work. "Thomas was thorough. Liked to keep track of things."

Emma nodded, watching him work for a moment before continuing. "He wrote about you quite a bit."

This time, Mark's pause was more pronounced. He glanced down at her, his expression unreadable beneath the shadow of his hat.

"He thought very highly of you." Emma hesitated, uncertain if she should share the depth of her uncle's feelings. "He valued your knowledge and skill."

A flicker of something—perhaps discomfort, perhaps gratification—crossed Mark's face before he turned back to his task. "Thomas was a good man. Fair judge of character."

Emma sensed his reluctance to discuss the subject further, but pressed on gently. "How much longer do you think you'll be working on the roof? I thought perhaps we could share lunch afterward. I'd like to ask you about some of the ranching methods my uncle mentioned in his journals."

Mark seemed to consider this, hammering another nail with precision. "Another hour should do it. Don't go to any trouble."

"It's no trouble," Emma assured him, already planning what she could prepare. "I'll need your advice if I'm to make this ranch successful."

Mark gave a brief nod, which Emma took as agreement. She gathered the journals and headed back to the house, her mind already working through questions she wanted to ask.

Inside, Emma returned the journals to the study and began preparing lunch. Her cooking skills were limited—in Boston, servants had handled such tasks—but she was determined to expand her skills. From the supplies she'd purchased in town, she assembled cold sliced ham, bread, cheese, and pickles, arranging them as attractively as she could on one of her uncle's mismatched plates.

As she worked, her thoughts drifted to Mark. There was something compelling about his quiet strength and dedication. Clara had called him a mystery, and Emma found herself increasingly curious about the man who had earned her uncle's deep respect and trust.

She knew little about him beyond his obvious ranching skills. Where had he come from? What had brought him to Montana? What were the "ghosts" her uncle had alluded to in his journal? Emma reminded herself not to pry too deeply—Mark's privacy was clearly important to him. Yet, she couldn't help wondering about the man who now represented her strongest connection to both this land and her uncle's memory.

A knock at the door pulled her from her thoughts. Mark stood on the porch, hat in hand, his dark hair damp with perspiration from his work on the roof.

"Roof's finished," he said simply. "Should hold through spring storms now."

"Perfect timing," Emma replied, gesturing him inside. "I've just finished preparing lunch. It's simple fare, I'm afraid."

Mark stepped into the house, his tall frame making the room feel suddenly smaller. He looked slightly uncomfortable.

"Don't usually come in," he admitted, seeming to read her thoughts. "Thomas and I mostly talked outside. Or at his porch table."

"Would you prefer to eat on the porch?" Emma asked, sensing his discomfort.

Relief flickered across his face. "Might be nice. Good day for it."

Emma nodded, gathering the food and two cups of coffee. "Let me bring these out, then."

On the porch, they settled at the small wooden table. Mark waited until Emma was seated before taking his own chair, a small courtesy that spoke of good manners beneath his rugged exterior.

"Please, help yourself," Emma said, gesturing to the food.

Mark nodded his thanks and began assembling a sandwich, his movements economical and precise. They ate in silence for a few moments, the quiet broken only by the distant calls of birds and the occasional snort from the horses in the corral.

Emma finally broke the silence. "I must admit, I'm finding my uncle's journals invaluable. He documented everything from cattle counts to weather patterns. Did he always keep such detailed records?"

Mark nodded, swallowing a bite of sandwich. "Never saw a man take such care with his writing. Said it helped him make sense of things, seeing them on paper."

"He mentioned several techniques for gardening that seemed suited to this climate," Emma continued. "I hope to restart the garden plot you showed me yesterday."

"Good soil there," Mark agreed. "Thomas grew enough to see him through winter most years. Potatoes, beans, carrots. Some corn when the season was right."

Emma took a sip of her coffee. "He also wrote about the livestock—said he once had twice as many cattle as there are now?"

"Fifty heads at his peak," Mark confirmed. "Started scaling back when his health began failing. Sold most off gradually. Kept the best breeding stock."

"Could we build the herd back up?" Emma asked.

Mark studied her for a moment, as if reassessing her commitment to ranching. "Could. Takes time. Money for initial stock. Careful management."

"I have some funds set aside," Emma said thoughtfully. "Not an endless supply, but enough to make a start if we're judicious."

Mark's eyebrow raised slightly at her use of "we," but he didn't comment on it. "Best to go slow. Learn the rhythms first. Cattle need constant attention, especially come calving season."

Emma nodded, appreciating his candid advice. "That makes sense. I don't want to take on more than I can manage at the outset."

They continued eating, the silence between them growing more comfortable. Emma studied Mark when he wasn't looking—the weathered lines around his eyes that spoke of years squinting into the sun, the capable hands that moved with such certainty, the set of his shoulders that suggested both strength and the weight of unspoken burdens.

"May I ask you something?" she said finally.

He glanced up, wariness flitting across his features. "Depends on the question."

Emma smiled slightly at his honesty. "Fair enough. I was wondering what brought you to Montana originally? My uncle mentioned you arrived about two years ago."

Mark took a slow sip of his coffee, his expression closing like a shutter over a window. For a moment, Emma thought he wouldn't answer.

"Needed work," he said finally. "Heard Montana had opportunities. Found your uncle's place. He was hiring."

It was a simple explanation that revealed nothing of substance.

"Where were you before, Montana? The journals mentioned you're particularly skilled with horses."

Mark set down his cup, his jaw tightening almost imperceptibly. "Moved around. Colorado for a while. Wyoming. Worked ranches mostly."

Emma nodded, accepting the sparse details. "I imagine you've seen a great deal of the West, then."

"Enough," Mark agreed. His eyes met hers. "My turn for a question."

Emma raised her eyebrows, surprised by his initiative. "Of course."

"Why Montana?" he asked directly. "A woman like you could have sold this place without ever leaving Boston. Why come all this way? Take on all this work?"

It was a fair question, and one Emma had asked herself more than once during the grueling journey west. She considered how much to reveal, then decided on honesty.

"I needed to escape," she admitted. "In Boston, my life was... predetermined. My parents had arranged a marriage to a man they approved of—Edward Sinclair, from a prominent family with the right connections. He was handsome, wealthy, and utterly convinced of his own importance."

Mark listened silently, his eyes never leaving her face.

"The match made perfect sense to everyone except me," Emma continued. "Edward saw me as an ornament, a suitable hostess for his business dinners, eventually the mother of his heirs. My education, my thoughts, my desires—none of that mattered. I would simply be an extension of him."

"Sounds suffocating."

Emma looked up, surprised by his perceptiveness. "Yes, exactly that. I felt as though I couldn't breathe. When a letter arrived with the deed to my uncle's ranch, it was like someone had opened a window in a sealed room. I saw a chance for something else—a life of my own choosing."

"Your parents objected," Mark guessed.

"Vehemently," Emma confirmed with a small smile. "They couldn't fathom why I would reject such a 'perfect' arrangement to run off to the wilderness. Mother said I'd lost my mind. Father called me ungrateful and willful."

"Were they wrong?" Mark asked, a hint of something almost like humor in his eyes.

Emma laughed, the sound carrying across the quiet ranch yard. "Perhaps not about the willful part. But I haven't lost my mind—I've found it. For the first time, I'm making my own decisions, facing the consequences of my own choices. It's terrifying and exhilarating all at once."

Mark nodded, as if her answer satisfied something in him. "Freedom's worth fighting for. Thomas understood that."

"Did he?" Emma asked.

"He didn't come west by accident," Mark said. "Had his reasons for leaving civilization and the finer things in life behind. Never talked much about it, but I gathered he was running from something too. Or toward something he couldn't find back East."

Emma considered this new perspective on her uncle, whom she'd only known through letters and now his journals. Perhaps they were more alike than she'd realized.

"What about you?" she asked. "What were you running from? Or toward?"

Mark's expression shuttered again. He stood and said. "Should check those horses. Need new shoes before long."

Emma recognized the deflection but didn't challenge it. "Of course. Thank you for sharing lunch with me. And for fixing the roof."

Mark nodded, his eyes meeting hers briefly. "Food was good. Thank you."

It was a small thing that thanks, but Emma sensed it represented more than mere politeness. As he descended the porch steps and headed toward the corral, she realized that getting to know Mark McKay would be a slow process—like coaxing a wild animal to trust. But her uncle had obviously deemed it worthwhile, and Emma was inclined to agree.

She collected the dishes, her mind still turning over what little she'd learned. Mark remained a mystery, but at least now she understood a fraction more about the man who would be crucial to her success in this new life.

Chapter 8

The next morning dawned clear and warm, perfect for Emma's plans to survey the garden plot. After a breakfast of porridge and strong coffee, she gathered a notebook and pencil to sketch out her ideas, drawing inspiration from her uncle's journals.

The garden area lay fallow, overtaken by weeds after much neglect, but Emma could see its potential. Good southern exposure, protected from harsh winds by a stand of trees, with the creek nearby for irrigation. She paced the perimeter, making notes about dimensions and considering what to plant.

"Potatoes here," she murmured to herself, marking the spot in her notebook. "Beans along this side where I can set up poles."

So absorbed was she in her planning that she didn't hear the approach of a horse and rider until a shadow fell before her. Looking up, Emma found herself face to face with Jedediah Walker, sitting astride a gleaming black stallion that pawed impatiently at the ground.

"Miss Abbott," Walker greeted her, removing his hat with a flourish. "A pleasant surprise to find you engaged in such... rustic pursuits."

Emma straightened, instinctively smoothing her skirts as she faced him. "Mr. Walker. I wasn't expecting visitors."

"Please, call me Jed," he insisted with a charming smile that didn't quite reach his eyes. "I was riding past and thought I should pay my respects to our newest town member. How are you finding ranch life so far?"

"Educational," Emma replied diplomatically, not missing the way his gaze swept over the property with an assessing eye. "Though I doubt your route took you 'past' my ranch by accident, Mr. Walker."

Walker's smile widened, acknowledging her perception. "Direct, aren't you? I've always appreciated forthrightness in business matters." He swung down from his horse, looping the reins around a fence post. "Speaking of business, I've been giving our previous conversation some thought."

Emma felt a prickle of unease. "I believe I made my position clear. The ranch is not for sale."

"Even the most firmly held positions can evolve with new information," Walker said smoothly, removing a folded paper from his vest pocket. "I've taken the liberty of preparing an official offer for your consideration."

He extended the document, and Emma reluctantly accepted it, unfolding it to scan the contents. Her eyes widened involuntarily at the figure written there—a sum that far exceeded what she would have estimated the property's worth to be.

"This is... substantial," she admitted, looking up at him suspiciously. "Unexpectedly so."

"I value this land appropriately," Walker replied, his eyes sharp despite his pleasant tone. "Unlike some, I recognize its true potential."

"And what potential would that be, exactly?" Emma asked, folding the paper deliberately. "What makes Abbott Ranch worth such a generous offer?"

Walker's expression remained unchanged, but Emma sensed a calculation behind his easy manner. "Location, primarily. The property has excellent access to water, good grazing land. Strategically positioned."

"For what strategy, I wonder?" Emma pressed.

A flicker of irritation crossed Walker's face before his smooth mask returned. "For someone unaccustomed to our ways, you ask very pointed questions, Miss Abbott."

"I find direct questions yield the most honest answers," Emma replied evenly. "Though not always from those who prefer veiled intentions."

Walker's charm slipped momentarily, revealing something cold and calculating beneath. His jaw tightened, and his eyes hardened to flint. For an instant, Emma glimpsed the true man behind the genial facade—and felt a chill despite the warm spring day.

Just as quickly, the mask slid back into place. He chuckled, as if they were sharing a joke. "You're a formidable woman, Miss Abbott. I admire your spirit, though it might serve you better in more civilized surroundings."

"I find the air quite refreshing here," Emma said firmly. "And to address your offer directly—I must decline. This ranch is not merely property to me; it's my home and my future."

Walker studied her for a long moment, his assessment almost tangible. "The frontier can be unforgiving to those unprepared for its challenges. Accidents happen. Equipment fails. Livestock disappears." His tone remained conversational, but the implications hung in the air between them. "A woman alone faces particular... difficulties."

"Are you threatening me, Mr. Walker?" Emma asked, her spine straightening.

"Merely offering friendly advice," he replied, his smile returning. "It would be a shame to see you struggle when a simple business transaction could spare you such hardship."

"I appreciate your concern," Emma said with cool politeness, extending the folded offer back to him. "But I've never been one to shy away from challenges."

He made no move to take the paper. "Keep it. Consider it at your leisure. My door is always open, should you reconsider?" Looking down at Emma, he tipped his hat. "I do hope we can be friends rather than... otherwise."

"I prefer honest friends, Mr. Walker," Emma replied steadily. "Ones whose intentions are as clear as their words."

Something dangerous flickered in Walker's eyes, but his voice remained pleasant. "Clarity comes with time and understanding. I look forward to our next conversation."

With that, he wheeled his horse around and rode away, leaving Emma standing with the unwanted offer in her hand and an unsettled feeling in her stomach.

Once he was out of sight, Emma released a deep breath and shuttered. The encounter had left her shaken, not so much by the veiled threats as by the calculated intensity she'd glimpsed beneath Walker's charm. He was a man accustomed to getting what he wanted.

Emma tucked the offer into her pocket and returned to the house, her enthusiasm for garden planning temporarily dampened. She needed to understand what made her property so valuable to Walker—and what he might do when thwarted.

Chapter 9

The rhythmic sound of hoofbeats announced Mark's arrival later that afternoon. Emma looked up from the books she'd been reviewing at the kitchen table—her uncle's account ledgers, which she was struggling to decipher. Through the window, she watched Mark dismount and lead his horse to the water trough.

Emma rose, deciding to meet him outside rather than wait for him to knock. She needed to tell him about Walker's visit, to see if his reaction might confirm her growing suspicions about the saloon owner's interest in the ranch.

Mark looked up as she approached, touching the brim of his hat in greeting. "Afternoon."

"Afternoon. I'm glad you've come. There's something I need to discuss with you."

He must have caught something in her tone, for his expression sharpened. "Problem?"

"Jed Walker paid me a visit this morning," Emma said without preamble.

Mark's entire demeanor changed instantly. His posture stiffened, and his eyes narrowed, scanning the property as if expecting to find Walker still present. "What did he want?"

"Officially? To make another offer on the ranch." Emma withdrew the folded paper from her pocket. "An extremely generous one, at that."

Mark's jaw tightened visibly. "And unofficially?"

"To intimidate me, I believe," Emma said frankly. "He made several remarks about the 'dangers' a woman alone might face. The usual misfortunes that might befall an inexperienced rancher."

Mark's expression darkened further, anger evident in the hard set of his mouth. "Threatening you."

"Not explicitly," Emma clarified. "But the implication was clear enough."

Mark reached for the paper she held. Emma watched closely as he unfolded it and read the offer. His eyebrows rose slightly at the figure.

"High," he commented tersely.

"Suspiciously so," Emma agreed. "Which only confirms my feeling that there's more to his interest in this land than he's admitting. He mentioned something about the property being 'strategically positioned,' but wouldn't elaborate when I pressed him."

Mark refolded the paper with deliberate care, his hands betraying tension despite his controlled movements. "Walker's been buying land all around the valley. Pressuring folks to sell. Some have."

"So I've heard," Emma nodded. "Clara mentioned it when I had dinner at her place. She also said there are rumors about minerals in the hills—possibly gold or copper. Could that explain his interest?"

Mark's gaze shifted to the distant mountains that bordered the western edge of the property. "Yes."

"Why didn't my uncle sell, then?" Emma asked. "If the land might contain valuable minerals, surely that would make it worth more than as a cattle ranch."

"Thomas had his reasons. Wasn't just about money for him."

"Well, whatever my uncle's reasons, I share them. I have no intention of selling to Mr. Walker, regardless of his offers or his intimidation tactics."

Mark studied her, as if taking her measure. Whatever he saw seemed to satisfy him, for he gave a single, approving nod. "Good."

"But I am concerned," Emma admitted. "Walker doesn't strike me as a man who accepts defeat gracefully. Clara mentioned experiencing some troubles after refusing his offers—damaged fence, missing tools. And we've already had the corral gate incident."

"I'll keep a closer eye on things," Mark said firmly. "Ride the property lines daily. Check for signs of trespassers."

"I appreciate that," Emma said sincerely. "I also think it might be wise for you to start teaching me about ranching, as we discussed. Your presence around the property might discourage Walker or his men from causing mischief."

Mark nodded again. "Makes sense. We'll start soon—basic ranch skills. Riding, roping, maintenance. Things you'll need to know, anyway."

"Thank you," Emma said, relief evident in her voice. "I don't want to appear afraid, but I'm not foolish enough to ignore potential threats, either."

"Caution isn't fear," Mark said, his voice low and certain. "It's wisdom in wild country."

Emma smiled at his succinct philosophy. "Well then, we'll proceed with caution—and determination. I may be new to ranching, but I'm not easily discouraged."

Something that might have been approval flickered in Mark's blue eyes. "Thomas said you had grit. Seems he was right."

"I hope to prove worthy of his faith in me—and yours."

Mark looked somewhat uncomfortable at this personal turn in the conversation. He gestured toward the barn. "Should check that new tack I ordered from McGinty's. Tomorrow we'll start with proper horsemanship—city riding won't help much out here."

Emma recognized the change of subject for what it was, but didn't mind. They had established an understanding, and that was enough for now. "I look forward to it. And Mark—" She caught his eye as he turned to go. "Thank you. For staying on. For helping me."

Mark held her gaze for a moment longer than usual, something unreadable passing through his eyes. "Thomas would've wanted it that way," he said finally, touching his hat brim before heading toward the barn.

Emma watched him go, thinking that while Mark McKay might attribute his actions to loyalty to her uncle, there was something more there—a personal code of honor that went beyond obligation. It gave her confidence that whatever challenges Walker might present, she wouldn't face them alone.

Chapter 10

Sunday morning dawned bright and clear, perfect weather for Emma's first attendance at Blue Ridge's church. She dressed with care in her nicest dress that wasn't overly formal—a blue cotton with modest trim that she hoped would strike the right balance between respectful and not ostentatious.

As she pinned her hair into a neat arrangement, Emma reflected on her first week in Montana. So much had happened in such a short time—meeting the townsfolk, beginning to understand the ranch, encountering Walker's unsettling interest in her property, and starting to unravel the mystery that was Mark McKay. Through it all, she'd felt her uncle's presence guiding her, especially through his journals, which she continued to read each day.

Mark had declined her invitation to accompany her to church, merely shaking his head when she'd mentioned it the day before. "Not one for crowds," he'd said simply, and Emma hadn't pressed. She understood that Sundays were a day of rest for him, spent in his own way in the solitude of his cabin.

The drive into town was pleasant, the wagon rolling easily along the now-familiar road. Blue Ridge looked different on a Sunday morning—quieter, more serene. People in their Sunday best walked toward the white clapboard church, nodding greetings to each other as they gathered.

Emma parked the wagon where others had left their conveyances and smoothed her skirts before approaching the church steps. She was still very much the newcomer, and while some townspeople had been welcoming, others remained reserved in their judgment of the Eastern woman who presumed to run a ranch alone.

"Emma!" Clara called, waving from the churchyard where she stood with Tommy, who was fidgeting in his Sunday clothes.

Relief washed over Emma at the sight of a friendly face. "Good morning, Clara, Tommy. What a beautiful day for services."

Tommy grinned up at her, his hair slicked down in an obvious attempt at tidiness that was already failing. "Ma made me wear this collar. It itches something fierce."

"Thomas!" Clara admonished, though her eyes twinkled with amusement. "Miss Abbott doesn't need to hear your complaints."

"Actually, I sympathize completely," Emma told the boy with mock seriousness. "Formal clothes are instruments of torture designed to make us appreciate our everyday garments."

Tommy's eyes widened at this unexpected alliance, and he giggled. "See, Ma? Miss Abbott understands."

Clara shook her head, smiling. "Don't encourage him. Come, let's go in. Reverend Thompson will be starting soon, and the best seats fill quickly."

As they approached the church steps, Emma became aware of curious glances and whispered conversations. She held her head high, returning greetings with a warm smile, determined to make a good impression despite any preconceptions the townsfolk might harbor.

Inside, the church was simple but lovely—polished wooden pews, clear glass windows that let in the morning light, and wildflowers arranged at the pulpit. Emma followed Clara to a pew about halfway down the aisle, nodding to those she recognized from her visits to town.

"Don't mind the staring," Clara whispered as they sat. "They're just curious. Most of them don't mean any harm by it."

"Most of them?" Emma whispered back.

Clara's eyes flickered meaningfully toward a group of well-dressed women near the front. "The self-appointed moral committee. They've already decided you're either incredibly brave or completely foolish for taking on the ranch alone. Possibly both."

Emma suppressed a smile. "And what's your assessment?"

"That it's none of their business," Clara replied firmly. "And that anyone who manages to leave Jed Walker speechless, as I heard you did yesterday, deserves my respect."

A hush fell over the congregation as Reverend Thompson entered. He was tall and lean, with silver hair and kind eyes that crinkled at the corners as he smiled at his flock. His simple black suit and clerical collar lent him a dignified air without pretension.

"Good morning, friends," he began warmly. "What a blessing to gather on such a beautiful day the Lord has made. I see we have a new face among us—" his eyes found Emma with a welcoming smile, "—Miss Emma Abbott, Thomas Abbott's niece from Boston. Welcome to our humble congregation, Miss Abbott."

Emma nodded politely as heads turned her way, a warm blush rising to her cheeks at being singled out.

"Thomas was a valued member of our community," the reverend continued. "A man of principle and quiet faith. We miss his wisdom and steady presence. How fitting that his legacy continues through family."

The simple tribute to her uncle touched Emma deeply. She hadn't known the extent of his involvement in the community, having corresponded with him primarily about the ranch and his observations of the natural world. This glimpse of his social connections made her feel closer to him somehow.

The service proceeded with familiar hymns and prayers, bringing Emma a sense of continuity despite the vast differences between this frontier church and the grand cathedrals of Boston. Faith remained constant, a thread connecting her past to her present.

Reverend Thompson's sermon focused on the parable of the talents from Matthew's Gospel, his resonant voice filling the modest church as sunlight streamed through the windows.

"The Lord entrusts each of us with different gifts," he said, his gaze sweeping across the congregation. "Some receive land to steward, other skills to build, teach, or heal. The question isn't what we've been given, but what we choose to do with it."

Emma leaned forward slightly, struck by how the message seemed to speak directly to her situation.

"Fear," the reverend continued, "causes us to bury our talents—to hide what God has entrusted to us. But faith..." he paused, his eyes briefly meeting Emma's, "faith gives us courage to multiply those gifts, even when the path seems uncertain."

He spoke of the pioneers who had established Blue Ridge, who had faced hardship with determination and community spirit. "They didn't come west because the journey was easy, but because the promise was worth the struggle."

As the sermon concluded, Emma felt a renewed sense of purpose. Her decision to claim her inheritance wasn't just about escaping Boston's constraints—it was about honoring the gifts she'd been given and having faith in her ability to build something meaningful.

"We face trials not to break us, but to strengthen our faith," Reverend Thompson said as he brought his message to a close. "Just as gold is refined by fire, so too are we refined by challenges. Let us support one another through these trials, remembering that we are called to be neighbors in the truest sense of the word."

The congregation responded with murmurs of agreement and several amens. The service concluded with a final hymn, the blended voices filling the small church with harmonies that stirred Emma's heart. For the first time since arriving in Blue Ridge, she felt a true sense of belonging—a connection to something larger than herself.

As the congregation began to disperse, Reverend Thompson made his way to Emma, extending his hand in greeting.

"Miss Abbott, I'm delighted you could join us today," he said warmly. "Your uncle was a dear friend and a man of exceptional character."

"Thank you, Reverend," Emma replied, touched by the comparison. "I've been discovering more about him through his journals. He rarely mentioned his involvement with the church in his letters to me."

"Thomas wasn't one to boast of his good works," the reverend nodded. "But he was generous with both his time and resources. This church's roof was repaired last year, largely through his efforts."

"I had no idea," Emma said.

"He believed in building community," Reverend Thompson continued. "Something I suspect you value as well."

"I do," Emma confirmed. "Though I'm still finding my place here."

"These things take time," he assured her. "But know that you are welcome among us, regardless of what whispers you might hear." His eyes twinkled with understanding. "Small towns have long memories and active imaginations."

Emma smiled gratefully. "I appreciate your candor, Reverend. And your sermon today—it spoke to me quite profoundly."

"The Word has a way of finding those who need it most," he replied. "I hope we'll see you next Sunday."

"You will," Emma promised.

As the reverend moved on to greet other parishioners, Emma was approached by several townspeople, each seeming more curious than the last.

"Miss Abbott," said a plump woman in a flowered bonnet, "I'm Edith Wilson, Tucker's wife. We run the trading post. Such a pleasure to meet Thomas's niece at last."

"The pleasure is mine, Mrs. Wilson," Emma replied politely.

"We were all quite surprised to hear a young Boston lady would be taking on ranching," Edith continued, her eyes assessing Emma's neat appearance. "Such a... challenging endeavor for someone of your background."

"I find new challenges invigorating," Emma replied evenly.

"Of course, dear," Edith patted Emma's arm. "And you have that McKay fellow helping you, I understand. Quite the mysterious character, isn't he?"

Before Emma could respond to the obvious fishing for gossip, Clara appeared at her side.

"Emma, I'd like you to meet Dr. Emily Hargrove," Clara said, introducing a tall woman with intelligent eyes and a no-nonsense manner. "Emily, this is Emma Abbott."

"A pleasure," Dr. Hargrove said, shaking Emma's hand firmly. "I knew your uncle well—treated his rheumatism in his final years. A remarkable man."

"Thank you for caring for him," Emma said sincerely. "I wish I could have been here during his illness."

"He spoke of you often," the doctor replied. "He was quite proud of your education and independent spirit. Said you were the only one of his relatives who truly understood his choice to leave Boston for Montana."

This revelation warmed Emma's heart.

"Thomas wasn't one for flowery sentiments," Dr. Hargrove added with a small smile. "But those who knew him could see his pride in you. If you need anything—medical or otherwise—my door is always open."

"I appreciate that," Emma said.

As they spoke, Emma noticed Deputy Lewis standing somewhat awkwardly nearby, dressed in his Sunday best, hat in hand. When their eyes met, he approached with a respectful nod.

"Miss Abbott, good to see you again," he said. "Settling in all right at the ranch?"

"As well as can be expected, Deputy," Emma replied. "I've had some help from Mr. McKay in learning the basics."

"McKay," the deputy echoed, a slight furrow appearing between his brows. "He's kept clear of trouble since arriving. I'll give him that. Keeps to himself mostly."

Emma felt a strange impulse to defend Mark. "He's been invaluable in helping me understand the property. My uncle trusted him completely."

"Thomas was a good judge of character," Deputy Lewis conceded. "Still, a woman alone at that isolated ranch… I'd be happy to ride by occasionally, just to ensure everything's secure."

"That's very kind," Emma said, noting Clara's raised eyebrow beside her. "But I assure you, I'm managing well."

"Of course," the deputy nodded. "Just know the offer stands. This territory can be unpredictable."

A commotion near the church steps drew their attention. A man was leaning unsteadily against the railing, his clothes disheveled despite the Sunday morning hour. Emma recognized him as one of the men who had been loitering outside the saloon on her first day in town.

"Mason," Deputy Lewis said under his breath, excusing himself to approach the intoxicated man.

"Jed Walker's right-hand man," Clara explained quietly to Emma. "Showing up drunk at Sunday service—that's a deliberate provocation."

Emma watched as the deputy firmly but calmly escorted the man away from the church grounds. The incident cast a momentary shadow over the morning, reminding her of the tensions underlying the peaceful community facade.

"Speak of the devil," Dr. Hargrove murmured, nodding toward the street.

Jed Walker sat atop his black stallion across from the church, observing the congregation's departure with calculating eyes. When his gaze met Emma's, he tipped his hat with exaggerated courtesy, a smug smile playing at his lips.

"He doesn't even pretend to respect sacred ground," Clara said disapprovingly.

"I don't think Mr. Walker respects much of anything," Emma replied, holding the man's gaze steadily until he finally turned his horse and rode away.

"That man has brought nothing but trouble since he arrived three years ago," Dr. Hargrove said, her voice low. "He's bought up a few of the businesses in town, and people live in fear of crossing him."

"Not all people," Emma said.

"You've got spirit, Emma Abbott," Dr. Hargrove observed with approval. "This town could use more of that."

As the churchyard gradually emptied, Emma found herself the recipient of numerous invitations—to Mildred Harper's boarding house for dinner in the future, to Lydia Williams's sewing circle the following Wednesday, to the schoolhouse where Abigail Adams wanted to introduce her to the children.

The sense of community, despite its complications and undercurrents, warmed Emma deeply. This was so different from Boston's rigid social hierarchy, where acceptability depended on family name and bank accounts rather than character and contribution.

"Would you like to join Tommy and me for dinner?" Clara asked as they walked toward their wagons. "Nothing fancy, but there's plenty."

"Thank you, but I should get back to the ranch," Emma declined regretfully. "Mark mentioned checking the north pasture fences this afternoon, and I am eager to learn all I can."

Clara nodded understandingly. "Next Sunday, then. And remember, I'm expecting you on Wednesday at the sewing circle. We can begin those work clothes we discussed."

"I wouldn't miss it," Emma promised, climbing into her wagon.

As she drove back toward the ranch, Emma reflected on Reverend Thompson's sermon again. Faith to multiply what she'd been given, not bury it in fear. Courage to face trials, knowing they refined rather than destroyed.

The wagon crested the final hill, and Emma's breath caught as it always did at the sight of her ranch spread before her—the house, the barn, the corrals, all nestled against the backdrop of distant mountains. Her inheritance. Her responsibility. Her future.

Near the barn, she could make out Mark's tall figure working with one of the horses. He glanced up at the sound of the wagon, raising a hand in acknowledgment of her return.

Emma lifted her own hand in response, a sense of rightness settling over her.

$\mathcal{C}hapter\ 11$

Emma ducked as the cast-iron skillet erupted in flames. Frantically searching for something to smother the fire. The bacon she'd been frying had transformed from breakfast to inferno in the blink of an eye.

Emma grabbed the lid from a nearby pot and slammed it over the skillet. The fire hissed angrily beneath the metal before reluctantly subsiding, leaving behind only wisps of acrid smoke that stung her eyes.

Coughing, Emma flung open the kitchen window and back door, waving her apron to disperse the smoke. Outside, the Montana morning continued undisturbed—birds singing, horses nickering in the corral, the world blissfully unaware of her culinary disaster.

"So much for proving my competence," she muttered, lifting the lid cautiously to reveal charred remains that bore no resemblance to food.

After yesterday's inspiring church service, Emma had awakened, determined to take on more responsibility around the ranch. Cooking a proper breakfast, instead of grabbing a hunk of bread and jam, had seemed like a reasonable meal to start her day.

Her mother would be horrified to learn that her daughter, raised with servants to handle such matters, was attempting to fry bacon.

She scraped the blackened mess into a pail, wincing at the smell. "At least no one witnessed this disaster."

"Something burning?"

Emma nearly dropped the skillet at the sound of Mark's voice. He stood in the doorway, hat in hand, expression unreadable as he surveyed the smoke-filled kitchen.

"Just experimenting with cooking techniques," Emma said, attempting dignity despite her flushed face and disheveled appearance. "I've discovered that extreme heat doesn't improve bacon."

A slight twitch at the corner of Mark's mouth might have been the ghost of a smile. "Happens to everyone," he offered, stepping into the kitchen. "First time I tried cooking, nearly burned down my cabin."

"I fear my education left some practical gaps."

Mark nodded toward the stove. "Fire needs watching. Bacon needs turning." He hesitated, then added, "I could show you. Later."

Emma looked at him in surprise, recognizing the offer for what it was—an unexpected kindness. "I'd appreciate that."

"Meantime," Mark continued, "thought we'd start your riding lessons today. Weather's good. Horses are ready."

"Yes, of course." Emma gestured ruefully at her soot-streaked apron. "Let me change first. I doubt this is appropriate riding attire."

"Meet you at the corral in fifteen minutes," Mark said, already turning to leave. He paused at the door. "Bring a hat. Sun gets strong."

After he departed, Emma hurried to her room, removing her soiled apron and splashing water on her face from the basin. She changed into her sturdiest skirt and a plain shirtwaist, then searched through her trunk until she found a broad-brimmed hat she'd purchased for garden work back in Boston.

As she pinned her hair securely, Emma caught her reflection in the small mirror hanging on the wall. The woman looking back at her appeared different already—her skin slightly tanned from days in the Montana sun, her expression more determined.

"You can do this," she told her reflection firmly. "If you can face down Jed Walker, you can certainly learn to ride properly on the frontier."

Mark was waiting at the corral when she arrived, two horses already saddled. Emma recognized the gentle brown gelding from her previous experience and the more spirited bay that Mark typically rode.

"Good hat," Mark observed, nodding approvingly at her choice.

"Thank you," Emma replied, absurdly pleased by the simple compliment. "Now, where shall we begin?"

"Basics. Some things you already know, others probably not," Mark said, leading the brown gelding forward. "You've ridden before, but English-style. Western's different."

"Different how?"

"Longer stirrups. Different balance. One hand on the reins, not two." Mark adjusted the stirrups on her saddle as he spoke. "Western saddle's designed for long days working cattle. Comfort over form."

Emma approached the horse and stroked its velvety nose. "Does he have a name?"

"Rusty," Mark said, patting the gelding's neck. "Thomas named him for his color."

"Hello, Rusty," Emma said softly. "We're going to become good friends, I hope."

"Left foot in stirrup. Spring up, swing right leg over. Settle in gently, don't plop down. Just as you did the other day."

Emma mimicked his instruction. Her skirt bunched awkwardly despite her best efforts, and she made a mental note to ask Clara about riding clothes at their next meeting.

"Good," Mark said once she was seated. "Back straight. Relax your shoulders. Reins in left hand, not too tight."

Emma made the adjustments. The western saddle did feel more secure than what she was accustomed to in Boston, with its high cantle and horn providing stability.

"Now what?" she asked.

"Now we ride," Mark said simply, mounting his horse in one smooth motion. "Follow me. Nice and easy."

He led them at a walk out of the corral and toward the open pasture, where they would have room to practice without obstacles. Emma focused on maintaining the posture he'd shown her, conscious of his occasional glances to check her form.

"How long have you been riding?" she asked as they fell into a comfortable rhythm side by side.

Mark considered the question. "Since I was six. My father taught me."

It was the first personal detail he'd volunteered, and Emma didn't want to discourage him with excessive curiosity. Instead, she said lightly, "You must have been a natural."

"Fell off plenty," Mark admitted. "Learning's not about avoiding falls. It's about getting back on."

"A philosophy that applies to more than horsemanship, I suspect," Emma observed.

Mark glanced at her, a new assessment in his eyes. "Your uncle said something similar once."

"You were very close to him, weren't you?"

"Closer than I've been to anyone in a long while."

The admission hung between them as they rode, the rhythmic sound of hoofbeats filling the silence.

"Thomas found me trying to decipher one of his books," Mark continued unexpectedly. "I could read some—basics. But nothing complex. He offered to help. I refused at first."

"Why?" Emma asked, genuinely curious.

"Pride," Mark said simply. "Didn't want charity."

"But you changed your mind."

Mark nodded. "Thomas said it wasn't charity to share knowledge. Said it was an investment. In me." The memory seemed to soften something in his expression. "We'd sit on the porch after supper. Read for an hour most nights."

Emma could picture it clearly—her uncle and this reticent young man sharing quiet evenings, surrounded by the vast Montana landscape. "What did you read?"

"Started with newspapers. Moved to novels. History." Mark's mouth quirked slightly. "Your uncle preferred poetry. Said it spoke truths plain words couldn't reach."

"That sounds like him," Emma said warmly. "His letters were often sprinkled with poetry."

They had reached a wide, flat area perfect for riding practice. Mark demonstrated how to guide the horse, using subtle pressure from the reins and legs, rather than yanking on the bit.

"A horse is your partner, not your servant," he explained. "Needs to trust you. You need to trust it."

Emma practiced the techniques he showed her, finding that Rusty responded well to gentle guidance. When she successfully completed a figure-eight pattern, she couldn't suppress a triumphant smile.

"Well done," Mark said, and though his expression remained largely impassive, Emma detected approval in his voice.

"Thank you," she replied. "It feels different from riding in Boston."

"City riding's about looking proper. Ranch riding's about working together."

They continued practicing for another hour, with Mark patiently correcting Emma's form when needed and demonstrating new techniques. By the time they returned to the corral, Emma felt both exhausted and exhilarated.

"Same time tomorrow?" she asked as they dismounted.

"If the weather holds," Mark agreed. He hesitated, then added, "You're a quick study. Thomas would be pleased."

The simple praise warmed Emma more than she cared to admit. "I had a good teacher," she replied.

Mark busied himself with unsaddling the horses, seemingly uncomfortable with the compliment.

"Mark, there's something I've been meaning to ask you."

He glanced up, a wariness entering his expression.

"It's about protection," Emma clarified quickly. "I've been thinking about what happened with the corral gate and Walker's veiled threats. I took some shooting lessons in Boston, but I'm afraid my experience is limited. I can shoot, but I wonder if I should know more."

"Smart thinking. Firearms are necessary out here."

"Would you be willing to give me some instruction?" Emma asked. "I understand if you'd rather not—"

"We'll start today," Mark interrupted. "Your uncle kept a rifle above the fireplace. Know how to use it?"

"Only in theory," Emma admitted. "But I'm willing to learn."

Mark nodded decisively. "Let me finish with the horses. Meet you at the house in an hour."

Chapter 12

When Mark arrived, he stood somewhat awkwardly on the porch, as if uncertain about entering the main house. Emma ushered him in with a warm smile.

Mark carefully lifted the Winchester from its place above the mantel, checking it with practiced hands. "Good condition. Thomas kept it clean."

"He wrote about hunting in his journals," Emma said. "Though I gathered it was more necessity than sport."

"Meat for winter," Mark agreed. He held the rifle with comfortable familiarity. "Basic rules first. Always treat a gun as loaded. Never point at anything you don't intend to shoot. Finger off trigger until ready to fire."

Emma nodded, absorbing the instructions seriously. "I recall those principles from my lessons in Boston, though we focused on smaller firearms."

"Speaking of which," Mark said, "there's something else you should know about." He gestured toward the study. "Mind if we go in there?"

Curious, Emma led the way to her uncle's study. Mark moved to the heavy oak desk and knelt, running his hand along the floorboards underneath it.

"Thomas showed me this," he explained, pressing against what appeared to be an ordinary plank. A section of flooring shifted slightly. "Just in case."

Emma watched in amazement as Mark lifted the board, revealing a hidden compartment beneath. Inside lay two pistols, boxes of ammunition, and a small leather pouch.

"A hidden cache," Emma breathed. "I had no idea."

"Your uncle believed in being prepared," Mark said, lifting one of the pistols and checking its mechanism. "These are loaded and ready. Colt Navy revolvers. Reliable."

Emma knelt beside him, peering into the secret space. "What's in the pouch?"

Mark handed it to her. "See for yourself."

The leather bag contained several gold coins and a folded piece of paper. Emma carefully unfolded it to find a hand-drawn map of the ranch property, with numerous areas marked with X's and annotations in her uncle's handwriting.

"What does this mean?" she asked, showing the map to Mark.

"Survey marks. Thomas was... interested in the land's features."

Something in his tone suggested there was more to the story, but Emma decided not to press for now. Instead, she refolded the map and returned it to the pouch.

"Let's focus on the firearms first," she said. "I am eager to learn how to use them properly."

Mark nodded, seemingly relieved by the change of subject. "We'll start with this pistol. Simpler to handle for beginners."

He replaced the floorboard, leaving one pistol and a box of ammunition out. "We'll practice behind the barn. Less likely to attract attention."

They walked together to a secluded area where Mark had set up several bottles on a fallen log about twenty paces away. He explained the mechanics of the revolver, showing Emma how to load, cock, and fire safely.

"Remember," he cautioned, "breathe steady. Squeeze the trigger, don't pull. Both eyes open."

Emma took the pistol, surprised by its weight. She aligned the sights as Mark had instructed, drew a steady breath, and squeezed the trigger. The report was louder than she expected, but she managed not to flinch too badly. Her shot went wide, missing the bottles entirely.

"Not bad," Mark said. "Adjust your grip. Like this."

He moved closer, positioning her hands correctly. Emma was acutely aware of his proximity, the warmth of his chest near her back as he guided her arms.

"Elbows locked," he said, his voice low near her ear. "That's it."

Emma tried again, focusing on the corrections he'd made. This time, the bottle on the far left shattered satisfyingly.

"I hit it!" she exclaimed, unable to contain her excitement.

A rare smile broke across Mark's face, transforming his typically solemn features. "Good shot."

Encouraged, Emma continued practicing under Mark's guidance. She successfully hit enough targets to feel reasonably confident in her ability.

"You've got a steady hand," Mark observed. "Good eye, too."

"My father would be scandalized," Emma said with a small laugh. "He always said firearms were unladylike."

"Out here, practical trumps proper," Mark replied. "Being able to protect yourself isn't unladylike. It's necessary. Next, I want you to load and shoot the rifle."

"I've never handled a rifle before."

"Heavier than the pistol. More powerful," Mark explained, handing her the Winchester. "Let me show you how to load it first."

Emma watched attentively as his deft fingers demonstrated, loading the rifle, his movements precise and practiced. The weapon seemed to be a natural extension of his hands.

"Your turn," he said, passing her a cartridge.

Emma's fingers felt clumsy by comparison, but she managed to load the rifle without fumbling too badly. "Like this?"

"That's right," Mark nodded. "Now, holding it properly is different from the pistol."

Mark stepped behind her, reaching around to position the rifle against her shoulder. "Butt tight against your shoulder," he instructed, his breath warm against her ear. "Left hand supporting the barrel, right on the trigger guard."

Emma was intensely conscious of his chest pressed lightly against her back, his arms encircling her as he adjusted her grip. She found her focus wavering.

"Eyes on the target," Mark reminded her, his voice low. His hands rested briefly over hers, showing her how to sight along the barrel. "Breathe in, then halfway out. Hold it there when you squeeze the trigger."

Emma nodded, unable to trust her voice. Mark stepped back, and she immediately felt the chill of the air where his warmth had been.

"Ready?" he asked.

"I think so," Emma said, settling the rifle firmly against her shoulder. She sighted on a bottle at the far end of the log, drew a breath, and squeezed the trigger.

The rifle exploded with a force Emma hadn't anticipated. The recoil slammed into her shoulder and threw her off balance. She stumbled backward, losing her footing completely, and landed unceremoniously on the ground.

"Oh!" she gasped, more from surprise than pain.

Mark was at her side instantly, concern etched on his features. "You all right?"

Emma felt heat rush to her face. "Only my pride is injured," she assured him, accepting his offered hand. His grip was strong and steady as he pulled her effortlessly to her feet.

"Should've warned you better about the kick," Mark said, a hint of contrition in his voice. "Rifle's got more power than the pistol."

"I gathered that," Emma replied, brushing dirt from her skirt with as much dignity as she could muster. She glanced at the targets, certain she had missed. To her surprise, the bottle she'd aimed at was shattered. "I hit it?"

Mark nodded, a glimmer of respect in his eyes. "Dead center. Good shooting, despite the fall."

Emma's embarrassment gave way to pride. "Perhaps I could try again? With better preparation for the... kick, as you called it."

"That's the spirit," Mark said, and for the second time that day, Emma saw a genuine smile transform his face. "Brace yourself better this time. Lean slightly forward into the shot."

He loaded the rifle again and returned it to her, standing closer this time. "Ready for the recoil," he reminded her.

Emma positioned herself as instructed, planting her feet more firmly and leaning into the rifle. This time when she fired, she managed to absorb the recoil, though her shoulder still protested the impact.

"Better," Mark approved as another bottle shattered. "Much better."

They continued practicing until Emma could consistently hit targets, each shot building her confidence. When they finally finished, her shoulder was sore, but she felt a profound sense of accomplishment.

They walked back toward the house as the afternoon light began to soften toward evening. Emma felt a new confidence in her step, born from the day's accomplishments and the growing ease between herself and Mark.

"Would you like to stay for supper?" she asked impulsively. "I promise not to attempt bacon again."

Mark hesitated, clearly torn between politeness and his habitual solitude. "I should check the north pasture fence before dark," he said finally. "Another time, maybe."

Emma nodded, accepting his decision without showing disappointment. "Of course. Thank you for today's lessons—both riding and shooting. I feel more prepared already."

He turned to leave, then paused. "Keep that pistol close at all times. Just in case."

The warning sobered Emma immediately. "Do you expect trouble?"

"Hope not," Mark said, his expression grave. "But I've spotted Walker's men near the property lines. Better safe than sorry."

After he departed, Emma returned the pistol to her bedroom, placing it in the drawer of her nightstand where it would be easily accessible.

As evening approached, Emma prepared a simple meal of bread and cheese, lacking the confidence to attempt anything more complex after her morning disaster. She ate at the kitchen table, the Winchester rifle now propped in the corner within reach, a tangible reminder of her changing circumstances.

When darkness fell, Emma lit the lamps and settled in the study with her uncle's journals, determined to learn more. She selected volumes from the previous year when Thomas's health had been declining.

After an hour of reading, Emma found an entry that caught her attention:

June 12, 1884

Explored the north ridge today with M. Promising findings in the stream bed. Third such discovery this month. Need to document carefully. If confirmed, this changes everything. Must be cautious about who knows.

Emma frowned, turning the page to find more.

June 20, 1884

Walker came by again with another offer. Higher than before, but still, I refused. He has grown suspicious, I think. Asked pointed questions about the north ridge. Said he'd heard I'd been prospecting. Denied it, of course. M. thinks we should file a claim quietly, but that would only confirm suspicions. Better to wait, gather more evidence.

Emma's heartbeat quickened.

She continued reading, finding scattered references to "samples" and "tests" but nothing concrete enough to confirm her suspicions.

Thomas had been deliberately vague, perhaps fearing that his journals might fall into the wrong hands.

A sudden noise from outside pulled Emma from her reading. She froze, listening intently. Something—or someone—was moving near the barn.

Emma extinguished the lamp and moved cautiously to the window, peering out into the darkness. The moon was partially obscured by clouds, casting the ranch yard in deep shadows. For a moment, she saw nothing.

Then, a figure darted between the barn and the corral—a human shape, moving with purpose.

Emma's heart hammered against her ribs. She retreated from the window, retrieving the pistol from her nightstand. With trembling fingers, she checked that it was loaded.

Should she confront the intruder? Fire a warning shot? The prudent course might be to remain inside, secured behind locked doors. But what if the trespasser was damaging property or threatening the animals?

Emma crept back to the window, intent on getting a better look at the intruder. The clouds had shifted, allowing more moonlight to illuminate the yard. The figure was tall and lean, moving with a furtive caution that confirmed they didn't belong there.

As Emma watched, the intruder approached the barn door, checking something on the ground before slipping inside. A moment later, a faint glow suggested they had lit a lantern or candle within.

Emma made her decision. She couldn't allow someone to freely trespass and potentially threaten her home. Taking a deep breath, she slipped the pistol in her deep pocket and lifted the rifle from the corner—it would be more intimidating than the pistol—and moved quietly to the back door.

The night air was cool against her face as she stepped outside, straining her eyes to see any movement. The barn remained quiet, the small light inside visible through the cracks in the wooden structure.

Emma descended the porch steps, keeping to the shadows as she approached the barn. Her heart pounded so loudly she feared the intruder might hear it.

Reaching the barn door, Emma took a steadying breath. She could hear movement inside—the shuffle of feet, the soft murmur of a voice speaking to the horses. With the element of surprise on her side, she opened the door forcefully, raising the rifle.

"Don't move!" she commanded, her voice steadier than she felt.

The figure spun around, hands raised—and Emma found herself staring at Mark McKay's startled face.

"Mark?" she gasped, immediately lowering the rifle. "What on earth are you doing here at this hour?"

Relief flooded his features, quickly replaced by concern. "Checking the horses. Thought I heard something when I was riding the fence line." His eyes fell on the rifle in her hands. "You came out alone to confront what you thought was an intruder?"

Emma straightened, unwilling to be admonished despite her embarrassment. "I saw someone sneaking around my barn. What did you expect me to do?"

"Stay inside. Stay safe." Mark's voice held a mixture of exasperation and something that might have been reluctant admiration. "Could have been one of Walker's men."

"Which is precisely why I couldn't ignore it," Emma countered. "I won't hide in the house while someone threatens my property."

They stared at each other in the dim lantern light, an impasse of conflicting protective instincts. Finally, Mark's shoulders relaxed slightly.

"You did well with the approach," he conceded. "Kept to shadows. Didn't announce yourself until you had the advantage."

Emma hadn't expected the compliment. "Thank you. Though I'm sorry, I nearly shot you."

The corner of Mark's mouth twitched. "Wouldn't be the first time someone's pulled a gun on me."

Something in his tone suggested a history behind those words, but before Emma could inquire further, a sound from outside caught their attention—the unmistakable thud of retreating hoofbeats.

Mark extinguished the lantern immediately, plunging them into darkness. "Stay here," he whispered, moving toward the door with silent efficiency.

But Emma was already following, rifle ready. "It's my ranch," she reminded him softly. "We go together."

She sensed rather than saw his frustration, but he didn't argue. Together, they crept to the barn door and peered out into the night.

A lone rider was disappearing down the road toward town, moving too quickly and too distant now for identification. Beside her, Mark made a sound of frustration.

"Must have been watching the house. Saw you come out and decided to retreat."

"One of Walker's men?" Emma asked, the night suddenly feeling much colder.

"Likely." Mark turned to her, his expression grave in the dim moonlight. "They're getting bolder. Coming closer to the house."

Emma tightened her grip on the rifle. "What do they want? To frighten me into selling?"

"Maybe." Mark's voice held a note of doubt. "Or looking for something."

"What do you mean?"

Mark hesitated, clearly weighing his words. "Your uncle's journals. Did you read anything about the north ridge?"

"Yes."

"Inside," Mark said, gesturing toward the house. "Not safe to talk out here."

Once they were seated at the table inside, Emma couldn't contain her questions any longer. "The north ridge—there are minerals there? Gold... copper? That's why Walker wants this land so desperately."

Mark's expression remained guarded, but he nodded slowly. "Thomas found color in the stream there last spring. Not just traces—significant amounts."

"Gold," Emma breathed.

"Yes." Mark's eyes met hers directly. "He didn't want to file a claim. Said once word got out, everything would change. The land would be overrun. The quiet he valued would be gone."

"So he kept it secret," Emma concluded. "And Walker somehow discovered or suspected the truth."

Mark nodded. "Thomas believed someone was following him. Watching his movements. He also believed there were others out scouting the area."

"Why didn't you tell me this before?" Emma asked, unable to keep a note of accusation from her voice.

"Wasn't sure how much you knew," Mark admitted. "Or how much you needed to know right away. Thomas valued his privacy. Thought I should respect that."

Emma considered this, finding she couldn't fault his loyalty to her uncle's wishes. "I understand. But things have changed now. If Walker is willing to intimidate or threaten me for this land, I need to know exactly what I'm defending."

Mark studied her for a long moment, as if making a final assessment of her trustworthiness. "Soon," he said finally. "We'll go up on the north ridge."

"Thank you," Emma said sincerely. "And Mark? Thank you for checking on the horses tonight. I'm sorry I nearly shot you."

The ghost of a smile touched his lips. "Your aim's good. Might not have missed."

Emma laughed, despite the tension of the evening. "I'll take that as a compliment."

Mark rose to leave, his expression becoming serious once more. "Lock up after me. Keep the pistol close tonight."

"I will," Emma promised. "Will you be all right getting back to your cabin?"

"Used to moving in the dark," he assured her. "Nobody's catching me unawares."

At the door, he paused. "You handled yourself well tonight. Thomas would be proud."

The simple words filled Emma with unexpected warmth. "I'm trying to be worthy of his trust."

"You are," Mark said. Then he was gone, disappearing into the night with the same silent efficiency with which he did everything.

Emma secured the door behind him and checked that all windows were latched.

As she prepared for bed, Emma whispered a prayer for protection and guidance. "Lord, give me the strength and wisdom to protect what Uncle Thomas entrusted to me. And thank you for sending Mark to help me through these challenges."

Gold on the property. Secret prospecting. Walker's determination made perfect sense. The ranch wasn't just land to him—it was potential wealth beyond measure. And he wouldn't give up easily.

As she drifted toward sleep, Emma's mind filled with images of the day—Mark's patient instruction during their riding lesson, the satisfaction of shattering bottles with well-placed shots, the startled look on his face when she confronted him in the barn. Despite the dangers lurking on the periphery of her new life, Emma felt a growing confidence in her ability to face them.

"Thank you, Uncle Thomas," she whispered into the darkness. "For believing I could do this. For sending Mark to help me."

Chapter 13

Emma peered through the window as hoofbeats thundered across the yard. She recognized Clara's wagon approaching, the dust cloud billowing behind it like a sail caught in the wind. Stuffing the final pins into her hair, Emma grabbed her shawl and reticule, then hurried outside to meet her neighbor.

"Right on time!" she called, waving to Clara, who pulled the wagon to a stop.

Clara beamed from beneath her wide-brimmed bonnet, her honey-colored curls framing her face. "I was afraid I'd be late. Tommy decided today was the perfect day to find a toad and bring it into the house." She shook her head. "Mrs. Peterson will have her hands full, keeping him out of mischief."

Emma laughed as she climbed up beside Clara. "Your son has an adventurous spirit."

"That's a kind way of putting it." Clara clicked her tongue and set the horses in motion. "I'm just grateful Mrs. Peterson was available to watch him. It's feels like ages since I've had an evening out."

As they trundled down the road toward Blue Ridge, Emma breathed in the crisp evening air. The setting sun painted the landscape in rich amber hues, highlighting the distant mountains against the darkening sky.

"I've been looking forward to this all day," Emma admitted. "After the past week, an evening of female company sounds heavenly."

Clara cast her a sidelong glance. "I imagine so, especially if you've been spending your days with the likes of Mark McKay." She adjusted the reins in her gloved hands. "How are those frontier life lessons coming along?"

Emma felt a slight warmth rise in her cheeks. "Quite well, actually. He's a thorough teacher."

"Is he now?" Clara's tone carried a hint of mischief.

"He taught me to shoot a rifle yesterday," Emma continued, choosing to ignore Clara's playful insinuation. "I managed to hit most of my targets."

Clara's eyebrows rose. "McKay took time to teach you how to shoot a rifle?"

"He's not as taciturn as he seems," Emma found herself defending him. "Once you get to know him, he's quite... knowledgeable."

"Knowledgeable," Clara repeated, her lips twitching with suppressed amusement. "Is that what the young ladies are calling it these days?"

Emma felt the heat in her cheeks intensify. "Clara! I simply meant that he's been invaluable in helping me learn. Without his assistance, I'd be completely lost."

"Mmm-hmm." Clara nodded, her expression far too innocent. "And I'm sure his assistance has nothing to do with those pretty green eyes of yours."

"He's been helping me because he is loyal to my uncle," Emma insisted, though even as she spoke, she recalled the moment outside the barn when Mark had stood so close, teaching her to aim the rifle.

"If you say so," Clara replied, her tone making it clear she wasn't convinced.

They rounded a bend in the road, and Emma seized the opportunity to change the subject. "What can I expect at this sewing circle tonight?"

Clara allowed the diversion with a knowing smile. "Mostly conversation, some actual sewing. Lydia Williams hosts it at her house every week. She's a talented seamstress—she could make a burlap sack look fashionable. Tonight will give you a chance to meet some of the other women in town in a more relaxed setting."

"I did bring some of my dresses from Boston," Emma said. "I've been thinking they need adjustments to be more practical for ranch life."

"Let Lydia tackle them, and you'll leave with entirely new outfits," Clara said. "And speaking of practical matters, what are you planning to do about the minerals on your property?"

Emma nearly gave herself whiplash turning to face Clara. "How did you—?"

"Remember... Tommy's special rocks? I was also close to your uncle," Clara reminded her.

"Mark is taking me to see the north ridge soon. Apparently, Uncle Thomas discovered significant deposits there last spring."

"Hmm mmm," Clara murmured. "Walker's not going to continue taking your no as a final answer."

"Mark has spotted his men around the ranch property lines," Emma replied grimly.

Clara's expression sobered immediately. "Emma, that's serious. Did you report it to Deputy Lewis?"

"Not yet. I planned to mention it to him if I saw him in town tonight."

"Be careful what you do and say," Clara warned. "Walker has a lot of influence in these parts, and not everyone who works for him respects the law."

They fell silent as the wagon crested a hill, revealing Blue Ridge spread out below them. The town looked almost picturesque in the evening light, with lamps being lit in windows and smoke curling from chimneys. The Silver Spur Saloon stood prominently on Main Street, its windows ablaze with light.

"I'm assuming we won't be dining at Mr. Walker's establishment tonight," Emma remarked dryly.

Clara chuckled. "I'd sooner eat with the pigs. No, we're headed to the Blue Ridge Inn. Mildred Harper runs it. You met her at church, and she's one of the most sensible women you'll ever know. She came out here as a mail-order bride twenty years ago, but her intended died of fever just after she arrived and wed. Instead of going back East, she stayed and built the inn from nothing."

"She sounds like a remarkable lady," Emma said.

"She is. And she makes the best apple pie west of the Mississippi."

As they approached the town, Emma noticed a few people turning to watch their wagon pass. Some nodded in greeting, while others simply stared with undisguised curiosity.

"I'll remind you again, word travels fast in Blue Ridge," Clara said, noticing Emma's discomfort. "Everyone's probably heard about Boston Emma Abbott by now... trying her hand at ranching... such juicy gossip for the locals."

"And what's the verdict?" Emma asked, attempting a light tone.

"Mixed. Some think you're brave, others think you're foolish. Most are just waiting to see if you'll pack up and leave at the first sign of trouble." Clara pulled the wagon to a stop in front of the well-maintained two-story building with a swinging sign that read "Blue Ridge Inn."

"Well, they'll be waiting a long time," Emma said firmly. "I'm not going anywhere."

Emma climbed down from the wagon, smoothing her skirts and adjusting her hat. She'd worn one of her plainer dresses—a navy blue with minimal trimming—but still felt overdressed compared to Clara's practical attire.

The Blue Ridge Inn welcomed them with warm lamplight and the mouthwatering aroma of roasted meat and fresh bread. A bell tinkled overhead as they entered, announcing their arrival to the half-dozen patrons already seated at the tables.

Mildred, a tall, sturdy woman with silver-streaked dark hair, swept toward them, wiping her hands on her apron. Her face, lined with years of frontier living, broke into a genuine smile.

"Clara Jacobs! It's been too long since you've graced my dining room. And you, Emma Abbott, I'm so glad you came."

"Good evening, Mrs. Harper," Emma said, extending her hand.

"Mildred, please," the older woman corrected, giving Emma's hand a firm shake. "Mrs. Harper makes me sound like I'm expecting my husband to walk through that door, and he's been gone twenty years now."

She led them to a table near the window. "Best seat in the house. You can see who's coming and going."

Once they were settled, Mildred handed them each a napkin. "We've got beef stew tonight, fresh baked bread, and apple pie for dessert. The pie comes with the meal, so don't try to argue about it, Clara—I know how you pinch pennies."

Clara laughed. "No arguments here. Your pie is worth every cent."

"Good. I'll bring you both some coffee to start." Mildred disappeared toward the kitchen, her efficient movements suggesting years of practice.

"She's a lovely woman," Emma whispered to Clara once Mildred was out of earshot.

"Wait until you taste her cooking," Clara replied. "It's worth the trip to town all on its own."

The door to the inn opened again, and Deputy Sam entered, removing his hat as he crossed the threshold. His gaze swept the room before settling on Emma and Clara. With a nod of recognition, he approached their table.

"Evening, ladies," he greeted them, his manner polite but professional. "Mind if I join you for a moment?"

"Please do," Emma invited, gesturing to an empty chair.

He sat down, placing his hat on the table beside him. "How are you settling in, Emma?"

"As well as can be expected," Emma replied. "Though I did have an unwelcome visitor last night. Someone was prowling around after dark."

The deputy's expression sharpened. "Did you get a look at them?"

"Only a glimpse. They were riding off when Mark and I noticed them."

Lewis frowned. "McKay was there with you?"

"He'd come to check on the horses and property," Emma explained, noticing something flash briefly in the deputy's eyes. "He heard something while he was riding the fence line."

"I see." Lewis's tone remained neutral, but Emma sensed a subtle tension. "I've been meaning to tell you both—there have been reports of cattle rustlers operating in nearby towns. They've hit two ranches north of here in the past month."

Clara's hand tightened around her napkin. "Are you expecting trouble in Blue Ridge?"

"I'm not expecting it, but I'm preparing for it," Lewis replied. "I'll be increasing patrols near both your properties. If you see any strangers or anything suspicious, don't hesitate to send word immediately."

"That's very kind of you," Emma said sincerely.

A small, tight smile appeared on Lewis's face. "Just doing my job, Miss Abbott." He stood, replacing his hat. "I should let you ladies enjoy your meal. I'll be checking in on you both regularly in the coming days."

After he departed, Clara leaned forward. "Is it my imagination, or did our good deputy seem a bit... tense when you mentioned Mark?"

Emma sighed. "I noticed that too. I hope there's no bad blood between them."

"Men and their territorial instincts," Clara murmured. "I suspect our deputy has taken a shine to you, Emma."

Mildred returned with their coffee. "I saw the deputy chatting with you," she remarked, setting down the cups. "Official business, or was he making his interest known?"

Clara laughed. "Emma seems to be collecting admirers faster than I collect eggs from my hens."

"I am not," Emma protested, feeling her cheeks warm again. "The deputy was simply warning us about cattle rustlers in the area."

Mildred's expression turned serious. "He's right to be concerned. Times are tough for some folks. Makes honest men consider dishonest work." She glanced around to ensure no other patrons needed her attention, then surprised them by pulling up a chair. "Mind if I join you? The kitchen's under control, and I could use a few minutes off my feet."

"Please do," Emma welcomed her.

Mildred poured herself a cup of coffee from the pot she'd brought. "So, tell me about yourself, Emma Abbott. I knew your uncle—fine man, kept to himself mostly, but always had a kind word when he came to town."

"That sounds like him," Emma agreed. "I'm trying to honor his memory by maintaining the ranch, though I'm finding it more challenging than I anticipated."

"Nothing worth doing comes easy," Mildred said sagely. "Especially out here. When I first arrived and married my fiancé, and then he passed so suddenly, folks gave me two weeks before I'd be on the eastbound stage. Twenty years later, I'm still here."

Their conversation paused as a group of four men entered the inn, their clothes and faces bearing the unmistakable grime of hard labor. Miners, Emma guessed from their appearance and the tools hanging from their belts.

Mildred acknowledged them with a nod. "Evening, gentlemen. Take any table you like. I'll be with you directly."

She turned back to Emma and Clara. "Excuse me while I fetch your meals and see to these fellows."

As Mildred bustled away, Emma watched the miners settling at a table not far from theirs. They spoke in low voices, but in the small dining room, fragments of their conversation drifted over.

"... Walker says there's a mother lode just waiting to be found..."

"...offering three dollars a day, which beats breaking my back for Consolidated Mining Company..."

"...new claims all through this valley, once he secures the land..."

Emma and Clara exchanged glances, both clearly hearing the same thing. When Mildred returned with steaming bowls of stew and a basket of bread, Emma leaned in close.

"Those miners," she whispered, "they're talking about Walker's plans for mining claims."

Mildred set down the food and nodded discreetly. "He's been recruiting workers from as far as Virginia City, promising rich strikes once he 'consolidates his interests,' whatever that means."

"It means my ranch," Emma murmured, breaking off a piece of bread. "He knows there's gold on my land."

Mildred's eyes widened slightly, but she recovered quickly. "Eat your stew before it gets cold. We can discuss this after I've seen to my other customers."

Throughout their meal, Emma tried to focus on the delicious food and Clara's conversation, but her attention kept straying to the miners. They continued to discuss Walker's plans, mentioning surveys and test pits that indicated substantial deposits in the area.

When Mildred rejoined them after serving the miners, she brought slices of apple pie that looked too perfect to eat.

"Walker's been buying drinks for every miner and prospector passing through," she informed them, keeping her voice low. "Offering wages well above the standard rate. Says he's anticipating a boom larger than the one in Virginia City."

Emma set down her fork. "He's so certain of the gold on my property that he's already recruiting workers?"

"Seems that way," Mildred confirmed. "Though I doubt those men know exactly whose land Walker's planning to mine."

Clara touched Emma's arm. "What will you do?"

Emma considered the question carefully. "First, I need to see the north ridge for myself. Mark is taking me there tomorrow." She straightened her shoulders. "Then I'll decide whether to file a mining claim or keep it quiet, as Uncle Thomas did."

"Whatever you decide, do it quickly," Mildred advised. "Walker's not a patient man, especially when there's money involved."

"I appreciate the warning," Emma said sincerely.

Mildred glanced at the clock on the wall. "You should finish up if you're planning to make it to Lydia's sewing circle on time. I'll be joining you there myself once I finish up here."

They finished their dessert, with Emma savoring every bite of the exceptional pie. After settling their bill, despite Mildred's attempts to refuse payment, they gathered their belongings.

Chapter 14

Outside, the evening had deepened, with stars appearing in the indigo sky. Clara lit the wagon's lanterns before they climbed aboard. The short ride to Lydia Williams' home took them down a quiet residential street just outside of town, where lamplight spilled from windows and the occasional barking dog announced their passage.

Lydia's home was a modest cottage on the eastern edge of town, distinguished by a well-tended flower garden even in the fading light. Several horses and wagons were already tethered outside, indicating they weren't the first to arrive.

"Ready to face the Blue Ridge ladies' committee?" Clara asked with a smile as they gathered Emma's bag of dresses and sewing materials.

"As ready as I'll ever be," Emma replied, straightening her shoulders.

The door opened before they could knock, revealing a petite woman with blond hair twisted into an elegant knot. Despite the frontier setting, she wore a fashionable dress that might not have looked out of place in Boston, though Emma noted the practical modifications—shorter hemline, roomier sleeves, sturdy fabric.

"Clara! I was beginning to worry you wouldn't make it," the woman exclaimed, embracing Clara warmly before turning her bright gaze to Emma. "I'm so glad you came, Emma. Welcome to my home and our little sewing circle."

"Thank you for having me," Emma replied, immediately warming to Lydia's genuine smile.

"Come in, come in," Lydia ushered them inside. "Everyone's already set up in the parlor."

The cottage's interior was as charming as its exterior—simple but tasteful, with colorful quilts adorning the walls and fresh wildflowers in pottery vases. The parlor hummed with feminine voices and laughter as six women of various ages worked on sewing projects around a circle of chairs.

"Ladies," Lydia announced, "our final guests have arrived. This is Emma Abbott, Thomas Abbott's niece from Boston."

Emma found herself the center of attention as curious faces turned toward her. She recognized a few from church but couldn't recall the names of all of them.

"You remember Dr. Emily Hargrove," Lydia began, gesturing to a tall woman with intelligent eyes and capable hands currently threading a needle.

"Of course," Emma nodded. "Lovely to see you again, Doctor."

"And this is Abigail Adams, our schoolteacher. I believe you already met her at church as well," Lydia continued, indicating a younger woman with a sweet face and round spectacles.

"Miss Adams," Emma greeted her. "Good to see you again."

"Please, call me Abigail," the teacher replied with a warm smile. "I hope you'll visit the schoolhouse soon. The children would love to hear about Boston."

Lydia continued the introductions: Sophie Bennett, a pretty blonde who Emma was surprised to learn, worked at Walker's saloon; Mrs. Eleanor Granger, the blacksmith's wife; and Samantha Turner, a young woman who ran her family's farm independently after her parents' passing.

Emma exchanged pleasantries with each, feeling welcome among these frontier women.

"Now," Lydia said once the introductions were complete, "Clara mentioned to me that you needed good frontier clothing."

"Yes," Emma confirmed, opening her bag. "These dresses are suitable for Boston society, but they are rather impractical for ranch work. Would you be able to help me?"

"Let's see what we're working with," Lydia said eagerly, helping Emma spread the garments across a table.

The women gathered around, examining the fine fabrics and detailed stitching with appreciative murmurs. Emma had brought three-day dresses, each beautifully made but entirely unsuited to the demands of frontier life.

"Gorgeous work," Lydia commented, running her fingers along a seam. "But these skirts are far too long for ranch work—you'll be tripping and catching on everything."

"The sleeves need more room for movement," Samantha added practically. "And these fabrics, while beautiful, won't stand up to daily wear and washing."

"But we can use elements from each," Dr. Hargrove suggested. "The bodice from this one could be adapted and would work with a practical skirt made from sturdier fabric."

"I've brought some material," Emma said, pulling out several lengths of fabric she'd purchased from McGinty's store.

"Perfect," Lydia declared. "Now, let's take your measurements properly."

What followed was a flurry of activity as the women set to work. Emma stood patiently while Lydia took exacting measurements, calling out numbers that Abigail dutifully recorded in a small notebook. Meanwhile, the others examined Emma's dresses, discussing which elements could be salvaged and how they might be transformed.

"You'll need at least one riding outfit," Samantha insisted. "Skirts are well and good, but if you're serious about ranching, you'll want something practical for long days in the saddle."

"Like split skirts," Sophie suggested. "Not quite trousers, but they allow freedom of movement while maintaining some modesty."

"I've been considering that," Emma admitted. "Mark—Mr. McKay—has been teaching me to ride western-style, and my eastern riding habits are quite impractical."

The women exchanged knowing glances at the mention of Mark's name, which Clara didn't miss.

"Emma's been spending quite a bit of time with our mysterious Mr. McKay," Clara said with barely suppressed amusement. "He's giving her riding lessons, shooting lessons..."

"How interesting," Lydia commented, her eyes twinkling as she measured Emma's waist. "Mr. McKay is not known for his sociability, but he is rather easy on the eye."

Emma felt her cheeks warming. "He worked for my uncle and knows the ranch better than anyone. His assistance has been invaluable to me."

"I'm sure it has," Sophie said with a smile, cutting into one of Emma's dresses with confident snips of her scissors.

"You'll have to forgive us," Dr. Hargrove said more kindly. "Eligible bachelors are a subject of great interest in Blue Ridge, and Mr. McKay has been the subject of speculation since he arrived."

"Speculation?" Emma couldn't help asking.

The women exchanged glances again, and it was Abigail who spoke up. "He's rather… mysterious. Keeps to himself. Some people find that suspicious as well as intriguing."

"Deputy Lewis certainly seems to find him suspicious," Eleanor Granger added.

Emma frowned. "Has Mark done something wrong?"

"Not that anyone knows," Dr. Hargrove replied diplomatically. "He's always been honest in his dealings, hardworking, and respectful. But in small towns, being private is sometimes mistaken for being secretive."

"Some men come west to escape their past," Samantha said bluntly. "Not always because they've committed crimes, but because they're running from something."

"Or toward something," Lydia countered. "Not everyone's story is ours to know." She gave Emma a reassuring smile. "Mark McKay has proven himself a decent man during his time here, regardless of where he came from or why he landed here."

The conversation shifted to other topics as the women worked, their hands busy with pins, scissors, and fabric. Emma relaxed in their company, enjoying the easy flow of conversation that ranged from local gossip to practical advice about frontier life.

When Mildred arrived an hour later, she brought freshly baked cookies and joined in the work, her experienced hands quickly taking over the task of cutting a pattern for a new work dress from the fabric Emma had brought.

"Stand up straight, dear," Mildred instructed, as she held the fabric against Emma's frame. "No sense in making these clothes if they don't fit properly."

"This blue would look lovely with your eyes," Sophie suggested, holding up a length of sturdy cotton in a shade that complemented Emma's coloring.

"I think so too," Lydia agreed. "And we can use the lace from your Boston dress as a modest accent at the neckline—practical but still feminine."

As the evening progressed, Emma shared more about her life in Boston, her decision to come west, and her determination to make the ranch succeed. The women listened with interest, offering encouragement and practical advice drawn from their own experiences.

"My father was furious when I announced I was accepting the teaching position here," Abigail revealed. "He said the frontier was no place for an educated young lady."

"My medical professor said much the same," Dr. Hargrove added with a wry smile. "But there's greater need for doctors here than in cities already crowded with physicians."

"And greater freedom," Samantha pointed out. "When my parents died, neighbors expected me to sell the farm or find a husband to run it. Nobody thought I could manage alone."

"But you proved them wrong," Emma said admiringly.

Samantha grinned. "Every harvest season."

"That's what men don't understand about us frontier women," Mildred said, her tone matter-of-fact rather than bitter. "Out here, we're judged more by what we can do than by who we are. It's hard, but there's opportunity in that hardship."

"Especially for women," Clara agreed. "After my husband died, I had choices that wouldn't have been available back East. Difficult choices, but they were mine to make."

Emma nodded thoughtfully. "That's part of why I came. In Boston, my path was already determined—marriage to a suitable man, a life of social obligations and constraints. Here, I can create something of my own."

"Even if that something includes Mr. McKay?" Sophie teased gently.

Emma felt herself blushing again. "I didn't say that."

"You didn't have to, dear," Mildred chuckled. "Your expression whenever his name comes up says plenty."

"It's perfectly natural," Lydia assured her. "Mark McKay may be taciturn, but he's certainly handsome, and his devotion to your uncle speaks well of his character."

"We're merely business associates," Emma insisted, though even as she spoke the words, she recognized their inaccuracy. Something had shifted between her and Mark during the past few days, a tentative connection forming that went beyond mere cooperation.

"If you say so," Clara said, clearly unconvinced. "But I saw how you lit up discussing those riding lessons."

The other women laughed good-naturedly, and Emma joined in despite her embarrassment. There was something refreshing about their teasing—it lacked the malice or judgment she might have faced in Boston society.

By the time they began packing up their work around ten o'clock, significant progress had been made. Two of Emma's dresses had been completely dismantled and redesigned into more practical garments. Patterns had been cut for a riding outfit and two work dresses that Lydia promised to finish within the week.

"I can't thank you all enough," Emma said sincerely as she helped fold the remaining fabric. "You've been so welcoming and helpful."

"That's how we survive out here," Mildred replied. "By helping each other."

"We expect a full report on what you find at the north ridge tomorrow with Mr. McKay," Lydia said with a grin.

Emma startled. "How did you—"

"Small towns," Clara reminded her with a shrug and a smile. "No secrets. You're in good company here among us. We are your friends, and we always watch out for one another."

"Not everyone knows about the gold on your property. Only a few of us that your uncle trusted," Dr. Hargrove clarified in a lower voice. "And everyone knows about Walker's interest in your property."

"Just be careful," Samantha warned. "Gold makes people act foolishly, even dangerously."

"And Walker's influence in this town runs deep," Sophie added, her expression troubled. "Working at the saloon, I hear things. He's not above using force to get what he wants."

Emma nodded, appreciating their concern. "I'll be cautious. And I won't be alone—Mark will be with me."

"I'm sure he will," Mildred said with a knowing smile that set the other women chuckling again.

As they prepared to leave, Lydia pulled Emma aside. "I hope we haven't overwhelmed you tonight. We can be a bit... forward."

"Not at all," Emma assured her. "It's refreshing, actually. And I'm grateful to have found friends so quickly."

"You're one of us now," Lydia said simply. "A Blue Ridge woman, facing the frontier on her own terms."

The phrase stayed with Emma as she and Clara rode back through the quiet town toward their homes. A Blue Ridge woman. She found she liked the sound of it.

"You're awfully quiet," Clara observed as they left the town behind. "Thinking about tomorrow's expedition with Mr. McKay?"

"Among other things," Emma admitted. "I'm trying to decide what to do about the gold if it's as significant as my uncle believed."

"What are your options?"

Emma sighed. "I could file a formal claim, which would protect my rights but attract attention. Or I could follow my uncle's approach and keep it quiet, but that leaves me very vulnerable to Walker's schemes."

"What would your uncle want you to do?" Clara asked thoughtfully.

"I think he valued the peace and natural beauty of the ranch more than potential wealth," Emma replied. "His journals suggest he was reluctant to see the land transformed by mining operations."

Clara nodded. "Thomas always did prefer the company of his books and horses to people or profits. But circumstances change."

They rode in companionable silence for a while, the wagon creaking rhythmically over the road. The night sky spread above them like black velvet studded with diamonds.

"Whatever you decide," Clara said eventually, "you have allies now. Tonight proved that to you, I hope."

Emma smiled, grateful for the reminder. "Yes, it did. I never expected to find such a welcoming community, especially after some of the initial reactions to my arrival."

"People are cautious with newcomers," Clara explained. "But actions speak louder than words out here."

As they approached the turnoff to the ranch, Emma's thoughts drifted. What would they find at the north ridge tomorrow? Would seeing the gold deposits clarify her path forward, or only complicate her decisions?

And what of Mark McKay? The women's teasing had struck closer to home than Emma cared to admit. There was something about him—his quiet competence, his unexpected moments of kindness, the rare smiles that transformed his face—that intrigued her beyond mere professional appreciation.

"Here we are," Clara announced, pulling the wagon to a stop where the road forked. "Will you be all right from here? I can drive you all the way to the house if you'd prefer."

"I'll be fine," Emma assured her, gathering her bag of sewing materials and the bundles Lydia had sent home with her. "It's not far, and the moon is bright. I have my pistol," Emma patted her reticule, where the small firearm nestled among her belongings. "Mark insisted I carry it whenever I leave the ranch."

"Did he now?" Clara's tone regained its teasing lilt. "How considerate of him."

Emma shook her head, smiling despite herself. "Don't start that again."

"I'm just saying, a man doesn't teach a woman to shoot a rifle and insist she arm herself unless he cares for her safety."

"He worked for my uncle, and now he works for me," Emma reminded her. "He feels responsible."

"If that helps you sleep at night," Clara replied with a wink.

"Thank you for tonight, Clara. I enjoyed myself more than I expected to."

"It's good to see you making connections," Clara said more seriously. "Frontier life is hard enough without trying to face it alone."

With a final wave, Clara headed toward her homestead. Emma watched until the lantern light faded into the distance before starting down the road toward the ranch.

The night wrapped around Emma, peaceful but alive with sounds—the soft hooting of an owl, the rustle of leaves in the gentle breeze, the distant howl of a coyote. Emma breathed deeply, savoring every moment.

As her home came into view, Emma noticed a light burning in one of the windows. She hesitated, certain she'd extinguished all the lamps before leaving. Heart quickening, she reached for the pistol in her reticule.

Moving cautiously toward the house, Emma kept to the shadows. As she neared the porch, the door opened, spilling lamplight onto the steps.

Mark McKay stood in the doorway, rifle in hand, his tall figure silhouetted against the light.

"Emma?" he called softly, peering into the darkness.

Relief flooded through her. "It's me," she confirmed, emerging from the shadows. "You startled me. I wasn't expecting anyone to be here."

Mark lowered the rifle. "Rode by and saw your lamps were out, but no sign of you. Got concerned." He sounded almost apologetic, as if embarrassed by his worry. "Thomas gave me a key a while back, just in case."

"I see. Clara drove me into town," Emma explained, climbing the porch steps. "We had dinner at the inn, then attended the sewing circle at Lydia Williams' home."

Mark nodded, stepping back to let her enter. "Heard hoofbeats came to check. Better safe than sorry with rustlers about."

"Deputy Lewis mentioned them," Emma said, setting her packages on the table and removing her hat. "He's increasing patrols in the area."

"Good precaution."

An awkward silence fell between them. Emma suddenly felt acutely aware of how unusual this situation might appear—an unmarried woman and man alone in her home after dark. In Boston, it would have caused an irreparable scandal.

But this wasn't Boston, she reminded herself. This was the frontier, where different rules applied.

"I should get going," Mark said. "Just wanted to make sure you were safe."

"I am. Thank you," Emma said sincerely. "That was very thoughtful."

He moved toward the door, then paused. "Still planning to ride to the north ridge tomorrow?"

"Absolutely," Emma confirmed. "What time should we start?"

"After breakfast. It's a few hours' ride. Bring water and something to eat."

"I will." Emma hesitated, then added, "I heard something interesting at the inn tonight. Miners were discussing Walker's plans to recruit workers for new claims in this area. He's apparently promising them a 'mother lode' once he 'secures the land.'"

Mark's expression darkened. "He's getting bolder. We need to move quickly."

"Agreed. I also spoke with some of the women tonight. They seem to think Walker's influence in town runs deeper than I realized."

"They're right," Mark said grimly. "He owns more than just the saloon," Mark said grimly. "Holds loans on several businesses in town. People who cross him tend to find themselves in difficult situations."

Emma absorbed this troubling information. "Then we'll need to be especially careful when dealing with him."

Mark nodded. "I'll be here at eight in the morning. We should reach the ridge by midday."

As he turned to leave, Emma found herself reluctant to see him go. "Mark?"

He paused, looking back at her.

"Thank you again. For checking on me."

Something softened in his expression. "Get some rest. Tomorrow will be a long day."

After he departed, Emma secured the door and moved through the house, checking windows and drawing curtains. The pistol remained close at hand as she prepared for bed, Mark's warnings and the miners' conversation weighing on her mind.

Chapter 15

Emma rose early the next morning, determined to prepare a proper breakfast. This time, she watched the bacon carefully, turning it before it could burn, and managed to produce a respectable breakfast of bacon and biscuits.

She was just wrapping biscuits, cheese, and apples for a midday meal when she heard hoofbeats approaching. Through the window, she watched as Mark neared with Rusty, already saddled.

Emma stepped onto the porch, feeling a flutter of anticipation. "Good morning!"

Mark touched the brim of his hat. "Morning." His eyes moved over her appraisingly, taking in the practical outfit she'd cobbled together—one of her simpler skirts paired with a sturdy shirt waist and boots. "Ready to ride?"

"Nearly. Just finishing packing provisions." Emma gestured toward the house. "Would you like some coffee before we start? I made breakfast."

Surprise flickered across his face. "You cooked?"

"Successfully, this time," she assured him with a smile. "No fires, no charcoal."

A hint of amusement touched his eyes. "Impressive progress. I could eat a bite or two."

Inside, Emma poured coffee while Mark stood somewhat awkwardly in the kitchen. He accepted the cup and the simple biscuit and slice of bacon with a nod of thanks.

"I thought about some things," Emma said. "Walker's determination is tied to the gold on my property. I'm convinced of this. The miners I overheard last night mentioned he's already recruiting workers."

Mark's jaw tightened. "He's overconfident."

"Or desperate," Emma suggested. "If he's planning to invest in labor before securing the land, his finances are robust, and it means he's been actively scouting out properties he probably has no business being on."

Mark nodded as he looked at her with new appreciation.

"Which makes him even more dangerous," Emma concluded, finishing off her biscuit. "Shall we go? I'm eager to see this gold that's causing so much trouble."

Outside, Mark helped her mount Rusty, his hands steady on her waist as he assisted her into the saddle. Emma was grateful he couldn't see her face as heat rose in her cheeks at his touch.

"You remembered the pistol?" he asked, swinging onto his horse.

Emma patted her pocket. "And extra ammunition."

He nodded approvingly. "Stay close. The trail gets rough in places."

They rode at a steady pace, following the creek that wound through Emma's property. As they traveled, Mark pointed out landmarks and features of the land—good grazing areas, sheltered spots where cattle gathered during storms, a stand of trees that provided the best shade in summer.

"You know this ranch as well as if it were your own," Emma observed.

Mark was quiet for a moment. "Thomas let me explore every inch of it. Said a man should know the land he works on."

"He trusted you deeply," Emma said. "His journals make that clear."

Mark's eyes flicked toward her, then back to the trail.

As they rode, the terrain gradually changed, becoming more rugged. The gentle slopes gave way to steeper hills, and the vegetation grew sparser. After about two hours, they began climbing a more pronounced incline.

"Is this the north ridge?" Emma asked, noticing how the land rose before them.

Mark nodded. "Beginning of it. Gets steeper ahead. We'll need to walk the horses part way."

The ascent became more challenging as they continued. True to Mark's warning, they eventually dismounted, leading their horses up a narrow trail that wound between rocky outcroppings. Emma's boots slipped occasionally on loose stones, but she pressed on determinedly, unwilling to show weakness.

When Mark offered his hand at a particularly treacherous section, however, she accepted it gratefully. His grip was warm and secure, steadying her as they navigated the difficult terrain.

"Almost there," he encouraged as they reached a flatter area. "Ridge levels out ahead."

Emma paused to catch her breath, turning to look back the way they had come. The view stole her breath. From this elevation, she could see for miles—her property spreading out below them, the tiny shape of the ranch house in the distance, the town of Blue Ridge beyond, and the vast expanse of mountains and plains stretching to the horizon.

"It's magnificent," she whispered.

Mark stood beside her, his gaze taking in the panorama. "Worth the climb, for sure."

For a moment, they simply absorbed the view together, standing shoulder to shoulder in companionable silence. Emma was acutely aware of his presence beside her.

"We should continue," Mark said finally. "Stream's just ahead."

They mounted again for the last portion of the journey, following a relatively flat path along the ridge until they reached a small valley nestled between two peaks. A clear stream tumbled down from higher elevations, creating a series of small pools and rapids as it wound through the valley.

Mark dismounted at the stream's edge, tethering his horse to a sturdy pine. Emma followed suit.

"This is where Thomas found the first color," Mark explained, leading her to a bend in the stream where the water slowed and deepened. He crouched down, gesturing for Emma to join him. "Look there, in the gravel bed."

Emma knelt beside him, scanning the stream bottom. At first, she saw nothing unusual—just stones, sand, and the occasional glint of mica reflecting the sunlight. Then, as the water cleared after their disturbance, she spotted it: a tiny yellow fleck among the gray and brown pebbles.

"Is that...?" she began, not quite believing her eyes.

"Gold," Mark confirmed. "Small flake. But where there's flakes, there's sometimes more." He reached into his vest pocket and pulled out a small metal pan.

Mark scooped some gravel and sand from the streambed into the pan, then began swirling water through it with a practiced motion. Gradually, he washed away the lighter materials, leaving heavier elements behind. When he tilted the pan toward Emma, she gasped.

Several gold flakes glinted in the sunlight.

"This is from one small scoop," Mark explained. "Thomas tested all along this stream. Found richer deposits upstream, near the source."

"May I try?" Emma asked, fascinated.

Mark handed her the pan, showing her how to scoop the gravelly material and then swirl it properly. Her first attempt washed everything away, but on her second try, guided by Mark's patient instruction, she managed to retain a few tiny flakes of gold.

"I did it!" she exclaimed, delighted despite herself.

Mark's rare smile appeared, warming his features. "Natural prospector."

They spent the next hour testing different spots along the stream, with Mark showing Emma how to recognize promising locations. Each pan yielded at least a few flakes, and some produced impressive amounts.

"This isn't just a minor deposit, is it?" Emma asked as they rested on a boulder near the stream, sharing the provisions she'd brought.

Mark shook his head. "Thomas believed it's part of a larger vein. These are surface deposits, washed down from somewhere upstream." He pointed toward the rocky slope that rose above them. "Likely the source is up there, in the bedrock."

Emma considered this information as she bit into an apple. "How much would it cost to extract it properly?"

"Depends on the approach. Simple placer mining like we've been doing is cheap but slow. To get at the main vein would require tunneling, equipment, workers. Substantial investment."

"Which Walker could provide," Emma mused.

"Yes," Mark agreed grimly. "With his connections, he could have a full operation running within months."

Emma stared at the peaceful stream, trying to imagine it transformed by mining operations—the clear water muddied, trees cleared, the natural beauty destroyed in pursuit of wealth.

"What would you do?" she asked, turning to Mark. "If this land were yours?"

He considered the question seriously, his gaze sweeping across the valley. "Gold means security and financial freedom. But it also brings trouble. Changes things." He looked at her directly. "What are you thinking?"

Emma sighed. "Part of me wants to file a claim immediately, secure my rights to this discovery. But another part... I just don't know... mining would destroy this."

"Could file a claim but delay development," Mark suggested. "Protect your rights without immediate action."

"That might be the wisest course," Emma agreed. "At least until I decide what's best for the long term."

They finished their meal in thoughtful silence. After repacking their provisions, Mark led Emma further upstream, where the gold deposits grew richer. In one location, a small pool had formed where the stream bent sharply, creating an eddy that trapped heavier materials.

"Thomas's favorite spot," Mark explained, crouching beside the pool. "Called it his treasure chest."

He demonstrated, scooping material from the bottom of the pool. When he washed it in the pan, Emma was astonished to see not just flakes but small nuggets of gold among the sand.

"There must be twenty dollars' worth just there!" she exclaimed.

"At least, if not more. Thomas collected samples a lot in his last two years of life from this spot. He dug holes in different spots around your property and buried jars filled with nuggets as security for the future. I have the map of the locations where he buried the jars. We built a secret spot under the flooring of my cabin, much like the one your uncle created under the desk in the study. I keep the map and a few other things in my hidden spot. The maps yours by all rights. I'll bring it to you."

"I appreciate that. Did he ever sell any of what he found?"

Mark shook his head. "Kept it quiet. Only he and I knew the amount of gold he found here. It's quite significant."

Emma understood her uncle's caution better now, having seen both the beauty of this secluded valley and the wealth it contained. The discovery presented both opportunity and threat.

"We should head back soon," Mark said, glancing at the sun's position.

Emma nodded, taking one last look around the peaceful valley. "I appreciate you showing me this. It helps to understand what we're dealing with."

As they prepared to leave, Emma filled a small pouch with some of the gold-bearing sand and a few nuggets as a sample to examine later. The weight of it in her pocket was a tangible reminder of what was at stake.

The return journey was quiet, both of them lost in their own thoughts. The descent from the ridge required careful navigation, but felt easier than the climb up had been. As they reached the more familiar terrain of the lower ranch lands, Emma broke the silence.

"I'm going to file a claim," she announced. "To protect my rights, as you suggested."

Mark nodded. "Wise choice."

"I'll need to go to the county seat to file the proper paperwork. Would you be willing to accompany me? Your knowledge of the deposit locations would be valuable."

"Of course," Mark agreed. "Better to go soon, before Walker realizes what we're doing."

As they approached the ranch house, Emma noticed something wasn't right. The door stood partially open, though she was certain she'd closed it securely before leaving.

Mark noticed it too, immediately tensing. He raised a hand, signaling her to stop. "Stay here," he instructed, dismounting and drawing his pistol.

"I'm coming with you," Emma said, refusing to remain behind. She slid from her saddle and pulled out her own weapon.

Mark looked like he wanted to argue, but instead gave a short nod. "Stay behind me. Move quietly."

They approached the house cautiously, Mark leading the way with his pistol ready. The yard was silent except for the natural sounds of the afternoon—birds calling, a light breeze rustling the leaves.

At the porch steps, Mark paused, listening intently. Then he moved forward swiftly, opening the door wider with the barrel of his pistol.

The scene inside stopped them both cold. The main room had been methodically ransacked—drawers pulled out and emptied, furniture overturned, books scattered across the floor. Someone had systematically searched the house, leaving chaos in their wake.

"Uncle's study," Emma gasped, pushing past Mark to rush toward the small room that housed Thomas's desk and journals.

The study had received the worst treatment. Every book had been pulled from the shelves, their pages flipped through and discarded. The desk drawers hung open, their contents strewn across the floor.

Most disturbing of all, the floorboard that had concealed Thomas's secret compartment lay pried up.

Emma knelt beside it, heart racing. "The map is gone," she whispered, reaching into the space. "And the pouch of gold coins."

Mark's expression was grim as he surveyed the damage.

"Walker's men," he said flatly. "Must have been watching, and knew we were gone."

Emma rose shakily, anger replacing her initial shock. "The only people who knew about this hiding place were you and me, correct?"

He nodded. "Or whoever might have seen us accessing it."

"Through the window when you showed it to me?" Emma asked, trying to make sense of the violation.

"Possible," Mark conceded. "Or there could be a simpler explanation. These men know their business—probably checked for loose floorboards, and hollow sounds throughout the house until they literally... struck gold."

Emma surveyed the destruction surrounding them, feeling violated and angry. "They won't intimidate me," she said firmly. "This only confirms to me that I need to file that claim immediately."

Mark nodded, his expression resolute. "We'll ride to the county seat tomorrow. First light."

As they began the task of restoring order to the ransacked house, Emma's thoughts turned to the women at the sewing circle. They had warned her about Walker's influence and determination. Now she understood just how far he was willing to go.

"Mark," she said as they straightened the overturned furniture, "do you think I should tell Deputy Lewis about this?"

A shadow crossed Mark's face at the mention of the deputy. "Probably should. The law should know about break-ins, even if they can't do much."

"You don't sound convinced."

Mark hesitated. "Deputy Lewis is honest enough. But Walker has friends in official places. Information has a way of traveling."

"You don't trust the deputy?" Emma pressed, sensing an undercurrent of tension.

"Don't know him well enough to trust or not trust," Mark replied. "Just suggesting caution."

As they continued cleaning, Emma found her uncle's journals scattered across the floor. She gathered them reverently, checking each one for damage. Most were intact, though several pages had been torn from the most recent volumes—likely those containing references to the gold discovery.

"They tore out pages," she told Mark, showing him the damage.

Mark's expression darkened further.

Late at night, they had restored some semblance of order to the house. Emma felt exhausted but determined as she and Mark sat at the kitchen table, sharing a simple meal she'd managed to assemble.

"I'll stay close tonight," Mark told her. "Camp on the porch. Just in case they return."

"Thank you," Emma said sincerely, grateful for his steadfast presence in the face of this new threat. "I don't know what I would have done without your help this evening."

Mark's gaze met hers across the table, unexpectedly intense. "You'd have managed. You're stronger than you know."

The simple words warmed her more than they should have. For a moment, neither spoke, the air between them charged with unspoken emotions.

Emma broke the silence first. "We should get some rest. Tomorrow will be another long day."

Mark left to prepare his makeshift camp on the porch, and as she prepared for bed, pistol once again close at hand, Emma's determination hardened.

Chapter 16

Emma gripped her reins tighter as a gunshot cracked through the morning air. Her horse sidestepped nervously, but she held firm, steadying the animal.

"Down!" Mark commanded, already sliding from his saddle.

Emma dismounted quickly, heart pounding as she followed Mark's lead. They crouched behind a large fallen log as another shot rang out.

"Was that meant for us?" she whispered.

Mark shook his head, peering cautiously over the log. "Don't think so. It sound's too distant." He pointed toward a stand of trees about a quarter mile ahead. "Hunters, most likely."

The tension in Emma's shoulders eased slightly, but Mark's wary expression kept her on alert.

They had left the ranch at dawn, hoping to reach the county seat by early afternoon. The morning mist still hung in patches across the valleys they traversed, creating ghostly islands in the landscape.

"We should move on," Mark said after a moment of silence. "But stay alert."

As they remounted, Emma noticed Mark's hand never strayed far from his holster. The break-in at the ranch had heightened both their senses of caution. She had slept poorly, startling at every creak of the house settling and the occasional sounds of Mark shifting position on her porch.

"Did you sleep at all last night?" she asked as they urged their horses forward at a brisk trot.

Mark gave her a sidelong glance. "Enough."

"That's not an answer," Emma countered. "You look tired."

A hint of amusement flickered across his face. "Worried about me, Miss Abbott?"

"We have a long journey ahead," she replied practically, though she felt a flush rise to her cheeks. "And I need you alert enough to keep us both safe."

The path narrowed as they entered a wooded area, forcing them to ride single file. Emma followed Mark, studying his straight back and the easy way he moved with his horse. Despite his evident fatigue, there was a fluid grace to his movements that spoke of years in the saddle.

They emerged from the trees into rolling grassland, the trail widening enough for them to ride side by side once more. In the distance, Blue Ridge was just visible, a tiny cluster of buildings against the vast Montana landscape.

"We'll skirt around town," Mark said, nodding toward a path that branched eastward. "Faster route to the county seat."

As they followed the eastern trail, the terrain became more varied, with rocky outcroppings punctuating the grasslands. The morning sun burned away the last of the mist, revealing a crystal-clear day. Under different circumstances, Emma might have enjoyed the ride, the magnificent scenery, and the companionship.

Emma squinted against the sunlight. A small plume of smoke rose from behind a cluster of rocks about half a mile distant. As they drew closer, she could make out what appeared to be a crude cabin and an outdoor cook fire, sending tendrils of smoke into the clear morning air.

"Josiah Smith," Mark said. "Old trapper."

"Is he... friendly?" Emma asked cautiously.

"Eccentric," Mark replied. "But harmless. Knows these hills better than anyone."

As they approached, a figure emerged from behind the rocks—an elderly man with a long white beard and a weathered face. He wore buckskins that had seen better days and a fur cap, despite the warming day. A rifle rested casually in the crook of his arm, but he made no threatening moves as they drew near.

"McKay!" the old man called, raising a gnarled hand in greeting. "Thought that might be you. Eyes ain't what they were, but I'd know that horse anywhere."

Mark nodded in acknowledgment as they halted their horses a respectful distance from the camp. "Morning, Josiah. Good hunting?"

"Fair to middling," the old man replied, his sharp eyes moving to Emma with undisguised curiosity. "Who's your companion? Don't often see you riding with company."

"Emma Abbott," Mark introduced her. "Thomas Abbott's niece. She's taken over the ranch."

Emma nodded politely. "Pleased to meet you, Mr. Smith."

A strange expression crossed the old trapper's face—something between surprise and knowing satisfaction. "Abbott's niece, eh? Well, now, that's interesting." He gestured toward his fire. "Got coffee brewing. Care to share a cup before you continue on your way?"

Mark glanced at Emma, silently deferring to her decision. Despite their need to reach the county seat, something in the old man's manner piqued her curiosity.

"We have time for coffee," she decided, dismounting.

Josiah's camp was surprisingly neat, with furs stretched on outdoor frames to dry and various tools arranged methodically around the perimeter. He poured coffee into tin cups, offering them to his visitors with surprising courtliness.

"So, Thomas Abbott's niece," Josiah mused, studying Emma over the rim of his cup. "Come to claim your inheritance, did you?"

"Yes," Emma confirmed. "Did you know my uncle well?"

"Know him? I suppose you could say that." Josiah chuckled, a raspy sound like dry leaves rustling. "Man liked to keep to himself mostly, but we'd cross paths now and then. Same interests, you might say."

"What interests would those be?" Emma asked.

The old man's eyes twinkled with mischief. "Oh, this and that. Thomas had a curious mind. Always asking questions about the land, the rocks, the old stories."

"Old stories?" Emma prompted, sensing there was more to the trapper's words than simple reminiscence.

Josiah settled himself on a rock, clearly preparing for a tale. "This land speaks, Miss Abbott, if you know how to listen. Some folks hear it better than others. Your uncle, he had a good ear for the whispers among the rocks."

Emma exchanged a glance with Mark, whose expression remained carefully neutral.

"What sort of whispers, Mr. Smith?" she asked.

The old man leaned forward, lowering his voice as if sharing a secret. "Minerals have a voice all their own, Miss Abbott. Sings to those who can hear it. Your uncle spent many a day up on that north ridge, listening to that song."

Emma felt a chill despite the morning warmth. "You knew about the gold on my uncle's property?"

"Known about it for years," Josiah confirmed with a nod. "Never bothered with it myself. No interest in the mining life. But others—" his expression darkened, "—others have been listening to that song for a while now."

"Walker," Mark stated flatly.

"Him and his posse," Josiah agreed. "Men who would steal the very ground beneath your feet if they thought there was profit in it." He fixed Emma with a penetrating stare. "Your uncle protected that land. Kept the secret close. Now that burden falls on you."

Emma set down her coffee cup, unsettled by the trapper's words. "We're on our way to file a claim, to protect my rights to any minerals on the property."

Josiah nodded slowly, approval evident in his rheumy eyes. "Wise. But papers only mean so much out here. It's strength and allies that truly protect what's yours." His gaze shifted to Mark. "You've chosen well in that regard, at least."

Emma felt herself flush again. "Mr. McKay works for me. He's been invaluable in helping me understand the ranch operations."

A knowing smile creased the old man's weathered face. He turned to Mark. "How's that trouble of yours, son? Settled yet?"

Mark's expression closed like a shutter. "Not yet, but it's not as much a worry."

Josiah sighed. "Figured as much. Hard thing, being hunted for something you didn't do."

Emma looked sharply at Mark. "Hunted?"

Mark stood abruptly, handing his empty cup back to Josiah. "We should move on. Long ride ahead."

The old trapper accepted the cup without comment, though his eyes held sympathy. "She'll need to know someday if she's standing beside you."

"Thank you for the coffee," Mark said stiffly, already moving toward the horses.

Emma rose more slowly, her mind whirling with questions. "It was a pleasure meeting you, Mr. Smith," she said, offering her hand.

Josiah took it, his grip surprisingly strong. "Take care of that land, Miss Abbott. And remember—sometimes the greatest treasures aren't the ones that gleam in the sunlight." He lowered his voice. "Your uncle knew that."

Emma looked at him quizzically.

Josiah merely smiled mysteriously and released her hand. "You'll understand in time. Safe journey to you both."

As they rode away, Emma's thoughts churned with the trapper's cryptic words. Mark maintained rigid silence, his jaw set in a hard line that discouraged questioning.

Only when they were well beyond the trapper's camp did Emma speak. "What did he mean about you being hunted?"

Mark's shoulders tensed visibly. "It's complicated."

"We have plenty of time for complications before we reach the county seat," Emma pointed out.

For several long moments, she thought he would refuse to answer. Then he sighed, the sound heavy with resignation.

"A few years back, I was blamed for something I didn't do," he said finally, his voice low and controlled. "Man was killed during a robbery in a mining town in Colorado. I was in the wrong place at the wrong time."

Emma waited, sensing there was more to the story.

"I'd done some work for him—carpentry in his office. Was there late one night finishing up when someone broke in. Heard the commotion, went to investigate. Found him dead, safe open." Mark's knuckles whitened on the reins. "Sheriff arrived while I was still standing there. He drew the obvious conclusion."

"But surely, you explained," Emma protested.

A bitter smile touched Mark's lips. "Sure. Explained I was just a drifter passing through, working odd jobs. No family, no connections, no one to vouch for me except the dead man. Sheriff wasn't interested in my explanation."

"You escaped?"

Mark nodded. "Managed to get away during transport to the county jail. I've been moving around ever since. I feel safe here, even with a bounty on my head. The bounty isn't large enough to attract professional hunters, but any lawman who recognizes me would bring me in."

Emma processed this information, suddenly understanding his wariness around Deputy Lewis. "That's why you live so simply, so remotely."

"Partly," he acknowledged. "Also why your uncle hired me without too many questions. He understood what it meant to want a fresh start."

The revelation painted her uncle in a new light—not just a kindly gentleman rancher, but a man who had offered sanctuary to someone in need. It made his trust in Mark all the more significant.

"Do you think Josiah was trying to warn us about something specific?" Emma asked.

"Josiah hears things. Trappers move through the territory, share stories. If he's concerned, we should be cautious."

The landscape changed gradually as they continued eastward, the grass growing sparser and the rocky outcroppings more frequent. By mid-morning, they had climbed to higher ground that offered an expansive view of a valley below.

"There," Mark pointed to a cluster of buildings in the distance. "Pinecrest. County seat."

Emma studied the town—much larger than Blue Ridge, with more substantial buildings and a proper courthouse at its center.

"How well do you know Pinecrest?" she asked as they began their descent toward the town.

"Well enough," Mark replied. "Not as well as Walker does, though." He cast a sidelong glance at her. "County commissioner Owen Bradley is a regular at Walker's poker tables. Might be an issue when we file your claim."

Emma frowned. "Are you suggesting he might obstruct my filing because of Walker's influence?"

"Not openly," Mark clarified. "But paperwork can get lost. Processing delayed."

"Then we'll need to ensure everything is properly documented," Emma said firmly. "I won't be outmaneuvered by Walker's cronies."

Mark's expression softened slightly. "Your uncle would be proud of your determination."

The unexpected praise warmed her.

"He spoke of you often," Mark offered unexpectedly. "Had a photograph he kept in his desk drawer. Said you had your grandmother's spirit—the kind that couldn't be contained by drawing rooms and tea parties."

Emma smiled at the thought. "He was right about that. My parents were constantly scandalized by my preference for books over balls, and adventure over needlepoint."

"Can't picture you doing needlepoint," Mark admitted with the ghost of a smile.

"I'll have you know, I'm quite proficient," Emma retorted with mock indignation.

"Keep your pistol handy in town. Pinecrest isn't Blue Ridge. More strangers, less accountability," Mark said, his tone becoming serious again.

Emma nodded, as she checked the weapon was secured in her pocket. As they approached the town limits, she studied the people they passed—wondering which might be allied with Walker, which might be reporting their presence back to him.

Pinecrest was indeed larger and more developed than Blue Ridge. The main street was lined with various businesses—hotels, several saloons, a couple of banks, a large hardware store, and numerous other establishments. People moved purposefully along the boardwalks, barely sparing them a glance as they rode through.

"We'll go to the courthouse first," Mark said, guiding them toward the imposing building at the end of the main street. "Then find somewhere to eat. Long ride back ahead of us."

The courthouse was a two-story brick structure with white columns framing the entrance. Emma smoothed her skirt as best she could after dismounting, conscious of her travel-worn appearance. Mark secured their horses at a hitching post and scanned the street with wary eyes before accompanying her inside.

The interior was cool and dim after the bright sunlight, with a central corridor leading to various offices. A directory board listed "County Records and Claims" on the second floor. They climbed the wooden staircase, their boots echoing on the polished steps.

The claim office was a large room with several desks, only two of which were occupied. A bored-looking clerk glanced up as they entered, his expression sharpening with interest when he saw Emma.

"May I help you, ma'am?" he asked, straightening his vest.

"Yes, I need to file a mining claim," Emma responded.

The clerk's eyebrows rose. "A mining claim? That's somewhat unusual for a..." he hesitated, apparently rethinking his words, "...for a property owner such as yourself."

Emma maintained a pleasant smile despite the implied critique. "Nevertheless, that's why I'm here. I'm Emma Abbott, owner of the Abbott Ranch in Blue Ridge. I've discovered gold deposits on my property and wish to secure my rights to them."

At the mention of gold, the clerk's manner changed subtly.

"I see," he said, pulling a form from a drawer. "You'll need to complete this documentation, providing the exact location and nature of the discovery. There's a filing fee of five dollars."

Emma took the form and scanned it quickly. "Is Commissioner Bradley available? I understand he oversees mining claims in this county."

The clerk hesitated. "The commissioner is quite busy today, but I can certainly see that your paperwork reaches his desk."

"I'd prefer to speak with him directly," Emma pressed. "It's a matter of some importance."

Before the clerk could respond, a door at the rear of the office opened, and a portly man in an expensive suit emerged. He paused when he noticed them, his gaze moving from Emma to Mark with obvious recognition.

"McKay," he acknowledged with a curt nod.

Mark touched the brim of his hat. "Commissioner."

The man's attention shifted to Emma, his expression warming considerably. "And who might this lovely lady be?"

Emma stepped forward before Mark could introduce her. "Emma Abbott, Commissioner Bradley. I've inherited the Abbott Ranch from my late uncle Thomas and have come to file a mining claim on the property."

Bradley's eyebrows lifted in surprise, much as the clerk's had. "Abbott's niece? Well now, this is interesting." He gestured toward his office. "Please, come in. We can discuss your claim more comfortably."

As they followed him into the private office, Emma caught Mark's warning glance. Be careful, his eyes seemed to say.

Bradley's office was well-appointed, with a large desk, comfortable chairs, and a window overlooking the town square. He settled behind his desk and motioned for them to sit.

"So, Miss Abbott, you've discovered minerals on your property?" he prompted, steepling his fingers.

"Yes," Emma confirmed, deciding directness was her best approach. "Gold deposits. My uncle was aware of them but chose not to develop them during his lifetime."

"Fascinating," Bradley murmured. "Thomas was always a private man. Never showed much interest in mining ventures, despite the obvious opportunities." His gaze sharpened. "What are your intentions regarding these deposits?"

"For now, I simply wish to secure my legal rights to them," Emma explained. "I haven't decided whether to develop them immediately or wait."

Bradley nodded slowly. "Very prudent. Mining operations require significant investment and expertise." He glanced at Mark. "I'm surprised our mutual acquaintance hasn't encouraged immediate development. There's substantial profit to be made."

"Miss Abbott makes her own decisions," Mark replied evenly.

A smile that didn't reach his eyes crossed Bradley's face. "Of course." He returned his attention to Emma. "I'll be happy to process your claim personally, Miss Abbott. Though I must warn you, there are certain... interested parties who might contest it."

"You mean Jedediah Walker," Emma stated bluntly.

Bradley looked momentarily taken aback by her directness, then chuckled. "You're well-informed for a newcomer. Yes, Mr. Walker has expressed interest in acquiring properties in that area. He's been a significant contributor to this county's development."

"Has he filed any claims that would conflict with mine?" Emma asked, refusing to be intimidated.

"No," Bradley admitted. "But he does have certain mining rights on adjacent properties."

"Then there should be no issue with my claim," Emma concluded firmly.

Bradley studied her for a long moment, seeming to reassess his initial impression. "Very well. Complete the forms the clerk provided, and I'll see that everything is processed properly." He rose, signaling the end of the meeting. "Welcome to Montana Territory, Miss Abbott. I hope you find it to your liking."

Chapter 17

As they exited the commissioner's office, Emma felt Mark's hand lightly touch her elbow, guiding her toward the staircase rather than back to the clerk's desk.

"We'll complete the forms elsewhere," he murmured once they were out of earshot. "I don't trust Bradley."

They found a small café across from the courthouse where they could sit and complete the necessary documentation while having lunch. The establishment was modest but clean, with checkered cloths on the tables and the aroma of fresh bread filling the air.

After ordering, Mark spread the claim forms on the table between them. "We need to be precise about the location," he explained, producing a small map from his pocket. "Thomas made this. Shows the exact boundaries of the deposit as he surveyed it."

Emma studied the carefully drawn map with appreciation for her uncle's foresight. "He prepared for this possibility, didn't he? That someone might try to claim the gold."

Mark nodded. "Thomas was cautious but thorough. Knew the value of proper documentation."

As they worked through the forms, Emma found herself increasingly aware of Mark's presence beside her at the table—the way he bent over the papers, the careful precision of his handwriting, the occasional brush of his fingers against hers as they exchanged documents. There was something intimate about the shared task, this joint effort to protect what she was beginning to think of as theirs, not just hers.

"You're staring," Mark observed without looking up from the form he was completing.

Emma blinked, embarrassed at being caught. "I was just thinking about how lucky I am that you stayed on at the ranch. I couldn't have done any of this without your help."

Now he did look up, his blue eyes meeting hers with an intensity that made her breath catch. "You'd have managed. Like I said before—you're stronger than you know."

"Perhaps," she conceded. "But I'm grateful, nonetheless."

"Your uncle said you had a fire in you that reminded him of himself in his younger days."

Mark returned his attention to the form, but his voice held a warmth she rarely heard. "He was very proud of you. Said you had the backbone for Montana."

The waitress arrived with their food—simple fare of stew and freshly baked bread—interrupting the moment. As they ate, Emma found herself studying Mark with new eyes, seeing beyond the reserved exterior to the thoughtful, observant man beneath.

"What about your family?" she ventured, realizing how little she knew of his past beyond what Josiah had inadvertently revealed.

Mark stiffened almost imperceptibly, then deliberately relaxed his shoulders. "Gone. Fire took them all when I was sixteen. Missouri farm."

The stark simplicity of his answer made Emma's heart ache. "I'm so sorry."

He shrugged, the gesture clearly meant to dismiss the topic, but Emma wasn't ready to let it go.

"Did you have siblings?" she asked.

"Sister and brother. Younger. Kate was fourteen, Daniel twelve when they died." His voice remained steady, but Emma noticed his hand had tightened around his spoon.

"What were they like?" she prompted, sensing that perhaps no one had asked him about them in a very long time.

Mark set down his spoon and looked at her, a complex mixture of emotions in his eyes—pain, yes, but also a flicker of something like gratitude for the question.

"Kate was smart. Always had her nose in a book when she wasn't helping Ma with chores. Wanted to be a teacher." A ghost of a smile touched his lips. "Daniel was all energy. Couldn't sit still for more than a minute. Good with animals, though. Had a way with even the most contrary mules."

"They sound wonderful," Emma said.

Mark nodded, the brief openness in his expression slowly receding. "They were."

Understanding he had shared as much as he could bear, Emma returned to the forms. "I think we've covered everything here. The boundaries are clearly marked, and I've included reference to Uncle Thomas's original discovery."

Mark seemed grateful for the return to practical matters. "Good. Best file these and be on our way before word of our presence spreads further."

They finished their meal quickly and returned to the courthouse. This time, Emma insisted on dealing directly with the clerk, ensuring that every document was properly stamped and copies provided for her records. She paid the filing fee, obtained a receipt, and made a point of noting aloud that Commissioner Bradley had agreed to personally oversee the processing.

"That should prevent any convenient 'misplacement' of the paperwork," she observed as they left the courthouse.

Mark's approval was evident in his slight nod. "Smart move. Bradley won't risk open corruption, even for Walker."

As they retrieved their horses, Emma noticed a man watching them from across the street—a hard-faced individual leaning against the wall of the telegraph office. When he caught her looking, he straightened and sauntered inside.

"Mark," she said quietly, nodding toward the office.

"Saw him," Mark confirmed grimly. "Walker's man. Sending word back, no doubt."

"Then we should expect trouble," Emma concluded.

"Yes," Mark replied, helping her mount.

They left Pinecrest at a brisk pace, both aware of the need to put distance between themselves and the town. The afternoon sun was warm on their backs as they retraced their route, though Mark chose a slightly different path to avoid predictability.

"We'll need to be vigilant when we return to the ranch," Emma said as they rode. "Walker won't be pleased with my claim."

Mark nodded. "Might be best if I stay at the main house for a while, rather than in my cabin. More defensible position."

The thought of Mark's continued presence at her home produced a flutter in Emma's stomach that she chose to attribute to practical relief rather than anything more personal.

"That would be sensible," she agreed, trying to keep her voice neutral. "I will prepare the loft for you."

If Mark noticed any undercurrent in her suggestion, he gave no sign.

As they continued their journey, the shadows lengthened, and Emma reviewed the events of the day. The encounter with Josiah Smith had been interesting and unsettling, Commissioner Bradley's calculated interest concerning, and Mark's revelations about his past unexpectedly moving.

"Do you think Josiah was right?" she asked suddenly. "About there being something more valuable than gold on the property?"

Mark considered the question. "Thomas believed the land itself was the true wealth. He once said that gold comes and goes, but good earth endures."

"That sounds like something he would say," Emma mused, remembering passages from her uncle's journals that expressed similar sentiments.

The terrain grew more familiar as they approached the area where they had met Josiah that morning, though there was no sign of the old trapper now.

They increased their pace, the horses responding eagerly. Emma watched Mark as he rode—the easy confidence he had in the saddle, the alert way he scanned their surroundings, the strength evident in every movement. She had kept him on at the ranch initially for his knowledge, but increasingly she valued his steadfast presence for entirely different reasons.

Chapter 18

Emma spread the quilt across the narrow bed in the loft, smoothing the wrinkles with quick, efficient strokes. She had spent the past hour transforming the dusty space into something habitable—sweeping away cobwebs, laying fresh linens, and arranging a washstand with a basin and pitcher in the corner.

She sensed movement behind her and whirled around, her heart leaping to her throat.

Mark stood at the top of the ladder, his tall frame filling the narrow space. "Sorry," he said, ducking his head slightly beneath the sloped ceiling. "Didn't mean to startle you."

Emma pressed a hand to her chest, willing her pulse to slow. "It's fine. I was just finishing up." She gestured to the bed. "It's not much, but it should be comfortable enough."

Mark surveyed the space, his expression unreadable. His eyes lingered on the quilt—a colorful patchwork that Emma had found in a trunk—before scanning the rest of her preparations.

"This is too much trouble," he said, his voice gruff. "I can sleep downstairs by the hearth or on the porch."

"Nonsense," Emma replied, folding her arms across her chest.

He shifted uncomfortably, his hat in his hands. "Miss Abbott—Emma—I want to be clear about something."

The formal tone made her pause. "Yes?"

"Having a man stay in your home, even in these circumstances... I know how it might appear to others." He met her eyes directly. "I need you to know that you have nothing to worry about from me. I'll respect your privacy and your reputation."

A flush crept up Emma's neck. The impropriety of their arrangement hadn't fully registered until he mentioned it. In Boston, such an accommodation would have been scandalous, but here on the frontier, practicality often superseded social conventions.

"I trust you, Mark," she said simply. "And I'd rather risk gossip than face danger alone if it should come."

Something flickered in his eyes. He nodded once, decisively.

Emma smiled, relieved that the awkward moment had passed. "I've put some soup on to warm. Are you hungry after our ride?"

"Always," he admitted, the corner of his mouth quirking up.

They descended the ladder one after the other. Mark paused at the bottom, surveying the main room of the cabin with a careful eye. "You've made changes," he observed.

Emma glanced around, seeing the space through his eyes—the books she'd arranged on the shelves, the fresh curtains at the windows she had brought with from Boston and hemmed to fit the windows, the vase of wildflowers on the table. Small touches that transformed her uncle's bachelor quarters into her home.

"Just a few," she acknowledged. "Nothing dramatic."

"Thomas would approve," Mark said quietly. "Always said the place needed a woman's touch."

The casual reference to her uncle sent a pang through Emma's heart. "Our contact was limited to letters over the years... but I loved him very much."

Mark moved to the hearth, checking the soup that simmered in the cast-iron pot suspended over the coals. "He kept every letter you sent him."

"He did?" Emma's voice caught with surprise.

Mark nodded, stirring the soup with a wooden spoon. "In that desk drawer. Third one down on the left. Tied with a blue ribbon."

Emma crossed to the small desk in the corner and opened the drawer he'd indicated. Sure enough, a bundle of letters tied with a faded blue ribbon rested inside. She lifted them reverently, recognizing her own handwriting on the envelopes.

"I had no idea he saved them," she murmured, touching the ribbon gently.

"Said your letters brought the outside world to him," Mark replied, his attention seemingly on the soup but his voice holding a note of tenderness. "He read them aloud to me sometimes."

Emma tried to picture it—her reserved uncle reading her words to this equally reserved man, sharing stories of Boston society and her small rebellions against convention. The image warmed her unexpectedly.

"Soup's ready," Mark announced, breaking into her thoughts. "Smells like you've improved on Thomas's recipe."

Emma smiled, setting the letters aside carefully. "I added a few herbs from Clara's garden. She's been teaching me which wild plants are edible and which are medicinal."

They settled at the table, and Mark waited for Emma to serve herself before filling his own bowl. His manners remained impeccable despite their informal setting.

"Where did you learn such proper table manners?" she asked impulsively.

Mark glanced up, surprised by the question. "My ma," he answered after a moment. "She was particular about such things. Said dignity was free, and we should claim our share of it."

"Wise woman," Emma commented, breaking off a piece of bread.

"She was." His voice held a quiet finality that discouraged further questions on that topic.

They ate in companionable silence for a time, the only sounds the clink of spoons against bowls and the occasional pop from the fire. Outside, the twilight deepened, and Emma lit another oil lamp and placed it on the table, casting a brighter light over their meal.

"I've been reading more of Uncle Thomas's journals," Emma said when they had both eaten their fill. "He documented everything so meticulously."

Mark nodded. "Thomas believed in keeping records. Said history had a way of repeating itself."

"I found several more entries about you," Emma ventured, watching his reaction. "About when you first came to work for him."

A shadow seemed to cross Mark's face before his expression returned to its usual stoic calm. "Did you now?"

"He respected you immensely," she continued. "Wrote that you were the most capable man he'd ever employed, and that he valued your judgment above most."

"Thomas gave me a chance when others wouldn't."

"Because of what happened in Colorado?" Emma asked gently.

He met her gaze steadily. "Yes."

Emma rose and retrieved one of her uncle's journals from the study. "Would you mind if we read some of these together? I've been trying to understand his vision for the ranch, and I suspect you could provide context that I'm missing."

Mark hesitated, then nodded. "If you'd like."

They moved to the chairs by the hearth, the journal between them. Emma opened it and began to read aloud.

April 15, 1884.

Spring has finally taken hold, though the nights remain cold. McKay and I rode the north boundary today to check fences after the winter. Found three breaks where snow drifts had pushed the rails down. Repaired what we could, marked the rest for tomorrow. McKay spotted a wolf pack in the distance—five of them, moving east. He has the sharpest eyes I've known.

Emma looked up at Mark, who was staring into the fire. "He noticed details about you. Small things."

"Thomas noticed everything," Mark replied. "Nothing got past him."

Emma turned a few pages and continued reading.

May 3, 1883.

McKay finished the new corral today. Fine workmanship, as always. We sat on the porch this evening, discussing books. Was surprised to find he's never read Melville. Offered to lend him my copy of Moby Dick. He declined, then admitted he struggles with reading. Have offered to help improve his skills. He accepted, though reluctantly. Suspect there's more education there than he lets on, but circumstances have intervened.

Mark shifted in his chair. "He taught me properly. Patient man, your uncle."

"So you couldn't read before you came here?" Emma asked.

"Could read some," Mark clarified. "Basics. School was sporadic on the farm, and after the fire..." He trailed off. "Didn't seem important during those years."

Emma nodded, understanding what he left unsaid—that survival had taken precedence over education. "But it became important to you here."

A hint of a smile touched his lips. "Hard to refuse Thomas when he got an idea in his head. Said a man who couldn't read was at the mercy of those who could."

Emma flipped through more pages, finding an entry from the following winter.

December 12, 1883.

Blizzard has us housebound for the third day. McKay has proven a quick study with his reading. Finished Great Expectations yesterday and had much to say about Pip's journey. See much of myself in McKay—a man carved by circumstance rather than birth. Would like to think I might have shown his resolve had life dealt me his challenges.

"He admired you," Emma said softly, looking up from the journal.

Mark's expression remained guarded, but his eyes held a depth of emotion that his face didn't reveal. "Feeling was mutual."

Emma closed the journal, setting it aside. "Will you tell me more about what happened in Colorado? The real story, not just the outline."

Mark was silent for so long that Emma thought he might refuse. When he finally spoke, his voice was low and measured, as if carefully controlling what emotions might escape.

"I'd been drifting for a few years after my family died. Picking up work where I could—ranch hand, livery stable, carpentry when I found someone willing to teach me the trade." He paused, collecting his thoughts. "Ended up in a mining town called Silver Creek. Found work with a man named Harrison Pierce—assayer's office needed repairs, and I'd learned enough from a carpenter in Wyoming to handle basic jobs."

He leaned forward, elbows on his knees, eyes fixed on the fire. "Pierce was a decent employer. Paid fair, treated me with respect. I worked late one night, finishing cabinets in his back office. Heard a commotion in the front room after hours. Went to investigate."

His jaw tightened at the memory. "Found Pierce on the floor, bleeding from a head wound. Safe was open, empty. I went to help him, but he was already gone. Sheriff and two deputies arrived while I was still kneeling beside him, my hands covered in his blood."

Emma's heart ached at the image. "They assumed you killed him."

"Wouldn't listen to anything else," Mark confirmed. "Town had seen a string of robberies. They were looking for someone to blame. Drifter with no connections made an easy target."

"But surely there was evidence that someone else had been there?" Emma pressed.

Mark shook his head. "My word against what they wanted to believe. Sheriff found money in my bunk at the boarding house I was staring at—planted, but who'd take my word for it? Trial was set, but everyone knew the outcome before it began."

"How did you get away?" Emma asked, leaning forward in her chair.

"Transport to county jail," Mark explained. "Two deputies, one wagon. Ambush on the road—stagecoach robbery happening at the same time. Deputies distracted. I took my chance and ran."

"And you've been running ever since," Emma said quietly.

Mark's shoulders lifted in a slight shrug. "Not exactly running these days. More like... staying purposefully lost. My bounty is small—five hundred dollars. Not enough to attract serious hunters. Figured most have forgotten by now."

"Until Josiah Smith mentioned it today," Emma pointed out.

"Josiah knows many things," Mark acknowledged. "But he keeps his own counsel. Won't betray me."

"And Uncle Thomas? He knew your story?"

Mark nodded. "Yes, I told him everything, offered to leave if he wanted. He said a man's past was his own business as long as his present was honest."

Emma smiled faintly. "That sounds like something he would say."

The lamp cast a warm glow over the room, creating a sense of intimacy that made it easier to share confidences.

"What about you?" Mark asked. "Your letters to Thomas painted quite a picture of Boston society, but I'd like to hear your version."

Emma laughed softly. "I wasn't exactly suited to the life expected of a young woman in my position in Boston."

"How so?" Mark's interest seemed genuine.

Emma considered how to explain. "Boston society operates according to very specific rules. The right families associate with other right families. Young women are educated just enough to be interesting conversationalists, but not so much that they develop inconvenient opinions. Marriage is a strategic alliance between families rather than a union of hearts."

"And you rebelled against this," Mark surmised.

"Yes," Emma admitted. "I read books my parents considered inappropriate—philosophy, science, novels they deemed too realistic. I asked questions at dinner parties that made the gentlemen uncomfortable. I preferred adventures to needlework, debate to dancing."

"Thomas said you had a mind that wouldn't stay within the boundaries others set for it."

Emma smiled at the description. "My mother despaired of finding me a suitable husband. She said I thought too much and spoke too directly to ever catch a proper gentleman's interest."

"Yet someone was arranged for you," Mark prompted, remembering her earlier mention of an unwanted match.

Emma's smile faded. "Yes. Edward Sinclair III, heir to a shipping fortune and thoroughly convinced of his own importance. My parents were delighted with the match. His family connections were impeccable, his finances sound, and most importantly, he seemed willing to overlook my 'peculiarities,' as my mother called them."

"But you weren't willing to overlook his," Mark guessed.

Emma shook her head. "Edward was... conventionally handsome, well-educated, and utterly devoid of any original thought or genuine feeling. His conversation consisted entirely of his club activities, his business prospects, and his opinions on how I might improve myself to better reflect his status."

Mark's mouth twitched. "Sounds insufferable."

"He was," Emma confirmed with feeling. "But more than that, he was... controlling. Even during our chaperoned courtship, he attempted to dictate what I should wear, whom I should befriend, and which books I should read. He spoke of our future as if I would be merely an extension of himself, with no will or desires of my own."

"What changed? What made you decide to leave?" Mark asked.

Emma rose from her chair and walked to the window, looking out at the darkness. "A letter arrived, informing me of my inheritance and Thomas's death. The timing was… providential. Edward had formally proposed, and my parents were already planning the wedding."

She turned back to face Mark. "I had always felt like a stranger in my own life in Boston—as if I were playing a role in a production I hadn't auditioned for. When I read the letter that notified me of Uncle Thomas's death, it was as if someone had finally offered me a different script, a different stage."

"So you chose freedom," Mark said quietly.

Emma nodded. "A few months later, after careful planning, I told my parents I was declining Edward's proposal and intended to claim my inheritance in Montana. They were… less than supportive."

"I imagine that's putting it mildly," Mark commented.

"My father threatened to disown me," Emma admitted. "Said if I left, I shouldn't expect to be welcomed back. My mother wept and predicted I would be murdered by savages within a week."

Despite the painful memory, Emma found herself smiling at the absurdity of it now. "Edward was perhaps the worst. He actually suggested that I was mentally unbalanced and offered to overlook this 'temporary insanity' if I would reconsider."

Mark's expression darkened. "Generous of him."

"Indeed," Emma agreed dryly. "When I remained firm in my decision, he warned that I would regret refusing him—that no proper man would want a woman who had lived unchaperoned on the frontier."

"His loss," Mark said simply, his gaze steady on hers.

The direct statement and the quiet intensity behind it sent a flutter through Emma's chest.

"I withdrew my savings from the bank… money my grandmother had left me and my allowances that I had been carefully saving and purchased a ticket west," she continued as she sat back down. "The journey here was... educational. I thought I knew what to expect from uncle's letters, but reading about the frontier and experiencing it are entirely different matters."

"And now that you're here?" Mark asked. "Any regrets?"

Emma considered the question seriously. "No. For the first time in my life, I feel as though I'm precisely where I'm meant to be."

As she spoke the words, Emma realized their truth. Despite the threats from Walker, despite the hardships of ranch life so far, and despite the social isolation—she felt more authentic, more alive here than she ever had in Boston.

Mark nodded, as if her answer confirmed something he'd already suspected. "Thomas believed the same thing—that some people aren't meant for the lives they're born into. That they have to find their true place in the world, even if it's far from where they started."

"A journey of self-discovery," Emma mused, thinking of her uncle's own path from Boston to Montana.

"Something like that," Mark agreed. He reached for the journal she had set aside. "May I?"

Emma nodded, and he opened it, turning pages until he found what he was looking for.

September 8, 1883

Received a letter from Emma today. She writes of feeling constrained by Boston society, of yearning for something more meaningful than the endless round of social obligations. I recognize in her words the same restlessness that drove me west years ago. Perhaps it runs in our blood, this need for open spaces and genuine purpose.

Mark closed the journal gently. "He understood you, even from a distance."

"I wish I had come sooner," Emma said softly. "While he was still alive."

"He knew you would come eventually," Mark replied. "Said as much to me in his final days. Made me promise to look after the place until you arrived."

Emma's eyes widened.

"Said his niece had the Abbott spirit, and sooner or later, that spirit would bring her west. Asked me to stay on, help you get established."

"And yet, you seemed surprised when I arrived," Emma pointed out.

"Surprised by the timing, maybe," Mark admitted. "Not by the fact itself."

Emma studied him in the lamplight—the strong planes of his face, the watchful blue eyes, the careful way he held himself, as if always prepared for whatever might come.

"Thank you for keeping your promise to him. For staying."

Their eyes met across the small space between their chairs, and something shifted in the atmosphere—an exhilarating tension that hadn't been there before, or perhaps had always been present but unacknowledged.

Mark set the journal aside and stood, moving to add another log to the fire. The simple domestic action seemed to emphasize the intimacy of their situation—alone in this cabin.

"Thomas's journals," he said. "There's an entry you should read. About the gold claim."

He walked into the study and selected a specific volume, turning pages until he found what he was seeking as he returned. "Here," he said. "Might explain a few things about Walker's interest."

Emma took the journal, their fingers brushing in the exchange. She looked down at the page, focusing on her uncle's neat handwriting to steady herself.

May 3, 1884.

Confirmed today what I've suspected for some time—the gold deposit on the north ridge is more substantial than initial findings suggested. Followed the vein into the hillside and discovered it widens considerably. Had McKay with me, and we agreed that this knowledge must be protected. Too many men have been destroyed by gold fever, too many communities torn apart by the greed it engenders.

Walker approached me again last week with an offer for the ranch—the third such proposal this month. The man's persistence suggests he knows or suspects what lies beneath this land. His methods grow increasingly less subtle. Found one of his men near the north ridge yesterday, claiming to be tracking a stray horse. McKay escorted him firmly off the property.

Have decided against filing an official claim for now. To do so would invite attention we cannot afford. Have instead mapped the deposit carefully and hidden these records where only family might find them. Should anything happen to me, Emma must be made aware of both the opportunity and the risk this discovery presents.

Emma looked up from the journal, her expression troubled.

"Thomas wasn't naïve. He understood what men would do for the kind of wealth that is on this property."

"And soon, if not already, Walker will know I've filed a claim," Emma said.

"We'll be ready for him," Mark assured her, his voice calm but determined.

The plural pronoun—we—struck Emma forcefully. This wasn't just her fight alone; it was theirs. Somewhere in these past few days, they had become allies.

She closed the journal carefully. "Uncle Thomas was right to be cautious. Gold does change people. Makes them forget what truly matters."

"And what matters to you, Emma Abbott?" Mark asked, his voice low and intent.

The directness of the question caught her off guard. She considered it seriously, gazing into the fire as she gathered her thoughts.

"Independence," she said finally. "The freedom to choose my own path. The ranch itself—not just for what wealth it might contain, but for what it represents. A home where I belong, land that responds to care and effort. The chance to build something lasting."

She looked up to find Mark watching her with an expression she couldn't quite read—respect, certainly, but something more complex beneath it.

"What about you?" she asked. "What matters to Mark McKay?"

He didn't answer immediately, seeming to weigh his words carefully. "Peace," he said at last. "A place where the past is forgotten. Work that has meaning. The trust of people who matter."

Their gazes held across the space between them, and Emma felt something shift again—a deepening of understanding, a recognition of how closely their values aligned despite their vastly different backgrounds.

"It's getting late," Mark observed, though he made no move to rise from his chair.

"Yes," Emma agreed, equally reluctant to end the evening.

Neither spoke for a time, content in the companionable silence. Emma studied Mark's hands—strong, calloused from work, yet gentle when handling delicate objects, as he had been with her uncle's journals.

"Tell me about the chess set," she said suddenly, remembering the entry in Thomas's journal.

Mark looked surprised by the question. "Chess set?"

"Uncle Thomas wrote that you carved it for him," Emma explained.

A faint flush touched Mark's cheeks. "It wasn't that special. Just something I made to pass the time during evenings in my cabin."

Emma rose, moving to the study to retrieve it.

Mark nodded, as she returned, a hint of embarrassment in his expression.

Emma opened it, revealing the chess pieces nestled in individual compartments lined with velvet. She lifted one—a king, carved from dark wood, his robes flowing in intricate detail despite the small scale.

"This is exquisite," she said, examining the piece with genuine admiration. "Where did you learn to carve like this?"

"My father taught me," he said, his voice holding a note of remembered affection. "Said whittling kept idle hands busy."

Emma lifted each piece in turn—the proud queen with her crown, the bishop with his flowing robes, the knight's horse with its arched neck, the castle with its tiny crenellations, down to the simplest pawn, each with individual character despite their uniform role.

"These must have taken months to create," she said, marveling at the craftsmanship.

Mark nodded. "Thomas taught me the game, so it seemed fitting to make him a set."

Emma carefully arranged the pieces on the inlaid board that formed the top of the box when opened fully. "Would you teach me to play?"

Mark hesitated, then nodded. "If you'd like. Not tonight, though. It's a game that deserves a fresh mind."

Emma replaced the pieces in their compartments with reluctance. "Another evening, then."

As she closed the box, her fingers traced the pattern on the lid—an intricate border of leaves and vines surrounding a central design that, she now realized, incorporated her uncle's initials: T.A.

"You included his initials in the design," she observed, glancing up at Mark.

"Seemed right," he replied simply. "It was his set."

"And now it's mine," Emma said softly. "Something I'll treasure forever."

Their eyes met, and Emma was acutely aware of how close they were sitting, how intimate the circle of lamplight felt around them, how much of themselves they had revealed to each other this evening.

Mark must have felt it too, for he straightened in his chair, his expression becoming more guarded. "It's late," he said again, more definitively this time. "You should rest. Tomorrow will bring new challenges."

Emma nodded, reluctantly acknowledging the wisdom of his words. She stood, gathering the journals they had been reading.

"I'll check the doors and windows," Mark said, rising as well.

They moved around the cabin together, securing it for the night—Mark testing latches and locks, Emma banking the fire and turning down the lamp. The domestic ritual felt natural, as if they had been performing it together for years rather than for the first time.

When all was in order, they stood awkwardly in the center of the room.

"Thank you," Emma said finally. "For sharing your story. For trusting me with it."

Mark nodded, his expression softening.

"Good night, then," Emma said, but made no move toward her bedroom.

"Good night," Mark replied, equally stationary.

In the dimmed lamplight, his features seemed both stronger and more vulnerable—the hard lines of his face balanced by the openness in his eyes. Emma stepped closer, drawn by something she couldn't name but felt with increasing certainty.

Mark remained still as she approached, his breathing visibly quickening. When she stood before him, close enough that she could feel the warmth radiating from his body, his gaze dropped briefly to her lips before returning to her eyes.

For a heart-stopping moment, Emma thought he might kiss her. The air between them seemed charged with possibility, with unspoken words and unfamiliar yearnings.

Mark stepped back, breaking the spell. "I'll sit on the porch for a piece," he said, his voice rougher than usual. "Keep watch for a while. You should turn in."

Emma nodded, suddenly feeling foolish.

"Don't stay out too long," she said, striving for normalcy.

"I won't," he promised, already moving toward the door.

As he stepped outside, closing the door softly behind him, Emma breathed in deeply. She pressed her fingers to her lips, wondering what might have happened if he hadn't stepped away—if they had given in to the impulse that had so clearly passed between them.

Shaking her head at her own fanciful thoughts, she retreated to her bedroom. Yet as she prepared for sleep, Emma pondered on the question Mark had asked: What matters to you, Emma Abbott?

Chapter 19

A sharp crack jolted Emma from sleep. Her eyes flew open in the darkness, heart hammering against her ribs. She lay perfectly still, straining to identify the sound that had awakened her.

There it was again—a distinct popping noise from outside, followed by a distant crash.

Emma flung back her quilt and rushed to the window, peering through the curtains. The moon provided just enough light to make out shadowy figures moving near the barn. A faint orange glow flickered.

Fire.

"Mark!" she called, grabbing her robe and throwing it over her nightgown as she burst from her bedroom.

The loft ladder creaked, and Mark appeared halfway down, gun already in hand. "Stay inside," he ordered, his voice taut. "Lock the door behind me."

"The barn's on fire," Emma said, reaching for her boots. "I'm not staying inside while you face this alone."

Mark's jaw clenched. "Stay behind me," he conceded, checking his weapon before moving to the door.

Emma grabbed the rifle from the corner of the room and followed. Mark eased the door open, scanning the yard before stepping out onto the porch. Emma's breath caught at the scene before them—flames licked at the corner of the barn. Two horses were circling nervously in the corral, while muffled whinnies of distress came from those inside the barn.

"Get water," Mark instructed, already running toward the barn.

Emma dashed to the well, her heart pounding with fear and anger. As she cranked the bucket up, she caught a movement in her peripheral vision—a figure darting along the tree line. She hesitated, torn between following Mark's instruction to bring water and the need to prevent whoever had set the fire from causing more damage.

The decision was made for her when a frightened whinny pierced the air, followed by Mark's shout. Emma grabbed the bucket and raced toward the barn, where flames now climbed halfway up the wooden wall.

Mark had thrown open the barn doors and was leading the horses out. Smoke billowed around him, making him cough as he worked.

As Emma hurried back with a second bucket, she spotted more movement—not at the tree line this time, but closer to the house. Without hesitation, she set down the water and raised her rifle, aiming at the shadowy figure.

"Stop right there!" she commanded, her voice carrying across the yard.

The figure froze momentarily, then bolted around the house toward the trees. Emma considered firing a warning shot, but decided against it. The horses were already panicked enough, and her priority had to be extinguishing the fire.

She grabbed the bucket and ran to Mark.

"Someone's still out there," she warned, passing him the water.

"Get the rest of the horses," Mark replied, his face grim in the firelight. "I'll handle this."

Emma nodded and slipped into the barn, immediately assaulted by smoke that made her eyes water and lungs burn. She found the last two horses at the far end, pressing themselves against their stall doors in terror. Speaking softly through her coughs, Emma managed to lead them out, her eyes stinging from the smoke.

By the time she returned to help Mark, he had managed to contain the worst of the fire. Together, they made trip after trip from well to barn, throwing water on the smoldering timbers until finally, the last flame hissed into steam and darkness.

They stood side by side, breathing heavily, clothes soaked with water and sweat, faces streaked with soot. The eastern horizon showed the first pale hints of dawn.

"Are you all right?" Mark asked, his voice raspy from smoke.

Emma nodded, though she could still feel her heart racing. "The horses?"

"All accounted for, though spooked." He surveyed the damage. "Could have been much worse if we hadn't caught it early."

"It wasn't an accident," Emma stated flatly.

"No," Mark agreed, his expression hardening. "Walker's work, no doubt."

"I saw someone running away—toward the east trail."

Mark's head snapped toward her. "You should have told me immediately."

"You were busy saving the barn and the horses," Emma countered. "I made a choice."

He studied her face for a moment, then gave a grudging nod. "Fair enough. But next time—"

"Next time, I'll shoot first and explain later," Emma interrupted, surprising herself with the vehemence in her voice.

Mark's eyebrows rose, but a hint of approval crossed his face. "Let's hope there won't be a next time." He glanced toward the tree line. "Though I'm not counting on it."

"We need to report this to Deputy Lewis," Emma said, already moving toward the house.

Mark caught her arm gently. "Later. Right now, we need to secure the property and check for other damage."

They walked the perimeter of the ranch buildings together, finding no other signs of sabotage. The horses had settled in the corral, though they remained skittish, clustering together near the gate. The damage to the barn was significant but repairable—one corner blackened and weakened, part of the roof compromised.

Back at the house, Emma filled the washbasin while Mark stoked the fire in the stove in the kitchen. They took turns cleaning the worst of the soot from their faces and hands.

"You should go lay down and try to get more sleep," Mark suggested.

Emma shook her head. "I couldn't possibly sleep now." She moved to the stove. "I'll make coffee."

They sat at the kitchen table as the light of day filtered through the windows, both cradling cups of strong coffee.

"This changes things," Emma said. "Walker's escalating. First searching the house, now arson." She met Mark's gaze directly. "What's next?"

"Nothing good," Mark admitted. "Filing that claim has backed him into a corner. He's desperate now."

"All the more reason to involve Deputy Lewis," Emma insisted. "This is a criminal matter."

Mark looked unconvinced. "Lewis is one man. And we still don't know how far Walker's influence extends."

"So, what do you suggest? That we just wait for the next attack?" Emma's frustration sharpened her tone.

"No," Mark replied evenly. "I suggest we give Walker something else to think about."

Emma's eyebrows rose. "What do you mean?"

"A man like Walker has enemies. People he's cheated, threatened, or worse." Mark took a slow sip of coffee. "Maybe it's time we found some allies."

"You're suggesting we fight fire with fire?" Emma asked skeptically.

"I'm proposing we gather information," Mark clarified. "Find out who else might have reason to stand against Walker. There's strength in numbers, Emma."

She considered this, turning her cup thoughtfully between her hands. The idea had merit, though it wasn't without risk. "Where would we start?"

"Town," Mark said. "I'll go today, ask around. Carefully."

"We'll go," Emma corrected him. "I'm not staying behind."

Mark opened his mouth as if to argue, then sighed. "You're the most stubborn woman I've ever met, you know that?"

"I believe the term is 'determined,'" Emma replied with a small smile. "And thank you."

A reluctant chuckle escaped him. "Wasn't entirely a compliment."

"I'll take it as one, nonetheless." Her expression grew serious again. "We should still report the fire to Deputy Lewis. He needs to know what happened, even if he can't do much about it."

Mark nodded his assent.

Emma rose to prepare a simple breakfast, grateful for the mundane task to occupy her hands. As she worked, she stole glances at Mark, who sat at the table cleaning his revolver with methodical precision. The events of the night had shifted something between them yet again—deepening their partnership, cementing their alliance against a common enemy.

But there was something else, too. In those fraught moments battling the fire, she had glimpsed yet another side of Mark McKay—his selfless courage, his quick thinking under pressure, his instinct to protect what mattered. The same qualities that had drawn her uncle to him were steadily working their influence on her as well.

Chapter 20

McGinty's bustled with mid-morning activity when Emma and Mark entered. Conversations paused momentarily as heads turned toward them, curious gazes taking in their appearance. Though they had both changed clothes and washed as thoroughly as possible, faint smudges of soot and the lingering smell of smoke still clung to them.

"Miss Abbott! Mr. McKay!" Patrick McGinty called from behind the counter. "What brings you to town today?" His friendly expression faltered as they drew closer. "Good heavens, what happened to you two?"

"Someone tried to burn down my barn last night," Emma replied, her voice deliberately carrying to the store's other occupants.

A murmur rippled through the gathering. Emma noticed several people exchange glances, while others pointedly avoided eye contact.

"Burn your barn?" McGinty repeated, visibly shocked. "Who would do such a thing?"

"That's what we intend to find out," Mark said, his quiet voice somehow more imposing than if he had shouted.

"Is there anything you need?" McGinty asked, looking genuinely concerned. "Materials for repairs?"

"We'll need lumber and roofing nails," Mark confirmed. "And information, if anyone has any to share."

This last was addressed to the store at large. A weighted silence followed his words, broken only by the sound of someone shifting uncomfortably near the dry goods.

"I need to visit Deputy Lewis," Emma said to McGinty. "Is he in his office this morning?"

"Should be," the shopkeeper confirmed. "Saw him heading that way about an hour ago."

Emma nodded her thanks. "Mark, why don't you arrange for the supplies while I speak with the deputy? I'll meet you back here."

Mark's eyes narrowed slightly at the suggestion they separate, but he gave a curt nod. "Don't go anywhere else alone," he said.

"I won't," she promised, touched by his concern.

Outside, Emma took a deep breath of fresh air. The curious stares and hushed whispers had been uncomfortable in the store, but expected. News of the fire would spread quickly.

The sheriff's office was a small, neat building at the end of the main street. Emma knocked once before entering, finding Samuel Lewis at his desk. Paperwork spread before him.

He looked up with surprise that quickly turned to concern. "Miss Abbott! Are you all right?" He rose immediately, gesturing to a chair. "Please, sit down."

"Thank you, Deputy," Emma said as she took the offered seat. "I'm afraid I'm here to report a crime."

Lewis's expression turned grave as Emma recounted the events of the night before. He took notes in a small ledger, asking occasional questions about timing and details.

"And you're certain you saw someone fleeing the scene?" he asked when she had finished.

"Absolutely certain," Emma confirmed. "Though it was too dark to identify who it was."

Lewis set down his pencil with a sigh. "This is serious business, Miss Abbott. Arson is a hanging offense in this territory."

"Then I trust you'll investigate thoroughly," Emma said, meeting his gaze directly.

A flicker of discomfort crossed the deputy's face. "I'll certainly try. But without witnesses or evidence pointing to a specific person..."

"We both know who's behind this," Emma said flatly.

Lewis shifted in his chair. "Suspicion isn't the same as proof, Miss Abbott. And Jed Walker is a powerful man in this town."

"Are you saying you won't investigate because you're afraid of Walker?" Emma asked, disappointment coloring her tone.

"No, ma'am," Lewis replied firmly. "I'm saying I need to be careful about how I proceed. Making accusations without evidence would only make matters worse."

Emma studied him for a moment, measuring his sincerity. "So, what will you do?"

"I'll come out to the ranch today," he promised. "Look over the damage, see if I can find any evidence left behind. And I'll have some discreet conversations with individuals."

"Thank you," Emma said, somewhat mollified. "That's all I can ask."

As she rose to leave, Lewis said, "Miss Abbott, may I speak frankly?"

Emma paused. "Of course."

"You're in a dangerous situation," he said earnestly. "Walker doesn't take kindly to opposition, and he's not known for restraint."

"I'm aware of the risk, Deputy," Emma replied.

"Then you should also be aware that McKay's presence at your ranch is..." he hesitated, clearly choosing his words carefully, "...potentially complicating matters."

Emma tensed. "I'm not sure what you are referring to, deputy. Mr. McKay works for me. He's been invaluable, especially last night. And he will remain on my ranch."

"I don't doubt his capabilities," Lewis said quickly. "But his history with Walker isn't straightforward. There's bad blood there, beyond what you might know."

This was new information, and Emma filed it away carefully. "What kind of bad blood?"

Lewis seemed to regret having raised the topic. "I cannot speak further about it. Just... be cautious, is all I'm saying."

"Mark McKay has my complete trust," Emma stated firmly. "If you have specific concerns about him, I'd prefer you voice them directly rather than hint at mysteries."

The deputy raised his hands in a placating gesture. "I only mean to caution you."

Emma softened her stance slightly. "I appreciate your concern, Deputy Lewis. Truly. But I need allies right now, not words of caution."

He nodded. "I'll be out at your ranch this afternoon. And Miss Abbott—" he added as she reached for the door, "—please be careful."

"Always," she assured him, offering a small smile before departing.

Outside, Emma paused on the boardwalk, Deputy Lewis's words of warning echoing in her mind. What history existed between Mark and

Walker that the deputy thought she should know? And why hadn't Mark mentioned it himself?

She was so deep in thought that she nearly collided with Lydia Williams coming around the corner.

"Emma!" Lydia exclaimed, steadying her with a hand on her arm. "I heard about the fire. Are you all right?"

"I'm fine," Emma assured her. "The damage could have been much worse."

Lydia looked genuinely distressed. "This has gone too far." She glanced around and lowered her voice. "Listen, some of us are meeting at Clara's this afternoon. You should come."

"Some of us?" Emma questioned.

"People who are concerned," Lydia explained vaguely. "About what's happening. About Walker's influence in Blue Ridge." She squeezed Emma's arm meaningfully. "Three o'clock. Tell no one except those you absolutely trust."

Before Emma could ask more questions, Lydia hurried away with a meaningful look. The mysterious invitation intrigued Emma—perhaps Mark had been right about finding allies against Walker.

She made her way back to the general store, where she found Mark completing the order for lumber with McGinty. He glanced up as she entered, relief evident in his expression.

"Everything settled with the deputy?" he asked as she approached.

"He's coming out to the ranch this afternoon to investigate," Emma confirmed.

Mark's expression revealed his skepticism, but he merely nodded. "McGinty says he can have the lumber delivered by tomorrow morning."

"Excellent," Emma said. "Thank you, Mr. McGinty."

The shopkeeper leaned forward across the counter. "Miss Abbott, I want you to know that not everyone in town supports what's happening. Some of us remember when Blue Ridge was a decent place, before Walker got his hooks in so deep."

"I appreciate that," Emma said, touched by his loyalty.

"If there's anything else you need," McGinty added, "you just let me know."

As they left the store, Emma pondered how to tell Mark about Lydia's invitation. Before she could formulate the right words, a familiar voice called her name.

"Emma! Thank goodness!" Clara hurried toward them, Tommy trailing behind her. "I just heard about the fire. Are you both all right?"

"We're fine," Emma assured her, embracing her friend briefly. "The barn is damaged, but repairable."

Clara's expression was a mixture of relief and anger. "This has to stop. Walker's gone too far this time."

"You sound like Lydia," Emma commented. "She mentioned something about a meeting at your house this afternoon?"

Clara darted a glance at Mark, then back to Emma. "Yes. Just a few neighbors gathering to discuss recent events." Her tone was deliberately casual, but her eyes conveyed a deeper message.

Mark, ever observant, caught the exchange. "I should check on a few things while we're in town," he said, tactfully offering to give the women privacy. "I'll meet you at the livery in half an hour."

After he walked away, Clara drew Emma aside. "The meeting is important," she said urgently. "And discreet. There are people who want to help, but fear Walker's retribution if he finds out."

"What kind of help can they offer?" Emma asked.

"Information, for one thing," Clara replied. "And safety in numbers. Walker's power comes partly from keeping people isolated, afraid to stand together against him."

Emma thought about Mark's suggestion that morning—to find allies against Walker. "I'll be there," she promised.

"Good." Clara squeezed her hand. "And Emma... there are some who might be uncomfortable with Mark's presence. Not because of anything he's done," she added quickly, seeing Emma's expression. "But because of what Walker might do if he learns, Mark is involved."

"What do you mean?" Emma asked, increasingly frustrated by these vague warnings.

Clara hesitated, clearly uncomfortable. "It's not my story to tell. But there's history between them—personal history. You should ask Mark directly."

Tommy, who had been patiently waiting nearby, tugged at his mother's skirt. "Ma, can I go see the candy jars in McGinty's?"

Clara smiled down at her son. "Just for a minute, and don't touch anything." As Tommy dashed off, she turned back to Emma. "Will you come alone this afternoon?"

Emma considered the request. Her instinct was to include Mark in any plans, yet both Deputy Lewis and Clara seemed to think there were complications she didn't fully understand.

"I'll come alone," she decided. "But I won't keep secrets from Mark for long. He deserves my honesty."

Clara nodded in understanding. "Three o'clock, then."

As Clara collected Tommy and departed, Emma felt a growing unease. What was this history between Mark and Walker that everyone seemed to know except her? And why had Mark never mentioned it?

She found him at the livery stable, examining a new saddle with Russ Miller. Both men looked up as she approached.

"Miss Abbott," Miller greeted her. "Terrible news about your barn. If you need any help with repairs, just say the word."

"Thank you, Mr. Miller," Emma replied warmly. "I may take you up on that offer."

After a few more minutes of conversation, Emma and Mark started back toward the ranch. Emma was acutely aware of the curious gazes following them—some sympathetic, others wary or calculating.

"Something on your mind?" Mark asked when they were beyond the town limits.

Emma gave him a startled glance. "Is it that obvious?"

"Yes," he replied, his tone light but his eyes serious.

Emma debated how to broach the subject. Direct questions seemed the only way forward. "Mark, what's the history between you and Jedediah Walker?"

He stiffened visibly, his expression closing. "What do you mean?"

"Both Deputy Lewis and Clara hinted at some personal conflict between the two of you."

Mark was silent for so long that Emma thought he might refuse to answer. When he finally spoke, his voice was carefully controlled.

"Silver Creek," he said. "The mining town in Colorado where I was accused of murder."

Emma waited, letting him continue at his own pace.

"The man who died—Harrison Pierce—wasn't just an employer. He was investigating corruption in the mining operations." Mark's jaw tightened. "Walker was one of the men he was building a case against."

Emma drew in a sharp breath. "Walker was in Colorado?"

"Under a different name," Mark confirmed. "James Wallace. Running the same schemes he's doing here—intimidation, fraud, manipulation."

"And you think he was behind Pierce's murder?" Emma asked, the pieces falling into place.

Mark nodded grimly. "I'm certain of it. Pierce told me he was close to proving Wallace—Walker—had been stealing from the mining company, fixing assay results, and skimming profits. The next day, Pierce was dead, and I was the convenient scapegoat."

"Why didn't you tell me this before?" Emma asked, hurt by his omission.

Mark's expression softened slightly. "At first, I didn't trust you enough. Later, I didn't want to put you in more danger. Knowledge is dangerous, Emma. Especially knowledge that could incriminate a man like Walker."

Emma processed this information, understanding dawning. "So Walker knows who you are. He knows you're the one who was accused of the murder he likely committed."

"Yes," Mark admitted.

"No wonder Deputy Lewis and others are concerned," Emma murmured.

Mark's head snapped toward her. "What did Lewis say?"

"Nothing specific," Emma assured him. "Only that there was bad blood between you and Walker, and that I should be cautious."

Mark grunted. "Lewis is sharp. I suspect he knows a lot about the Colorado incident. I believe he knows I am innocent."

They rode in silence for a few minutes, each lost in thought. Finally, Emma asked, "Does Walker know that you know a lot about his past?"

"I'm not sure," Mark stated flatly.

The full weight of the situation settled on Emma's shoulders. Not only was she fighting Walker for her land and its gold, but she was harboring a man who represented a direct threat to Walker's carefully constructed identity.

"This changes how we need to approach things," she said finally.

Mark looked at her questioningly.

"If we're going to stand against Walker effectively, we do need more allies," Emma explained. "Clara and Lydia have invited me to a meeting this afternoon—people who oppose Walker but have been afraid to act openly."

"And they didn't invite me," Mark concluded, his tone neutral.

"They're worried about Walker's reaction if he learns you're involved," Emma admitted. "But I think we need all the help we can get."

Mark considered this in silence. "You should go," he said finally. "Alone. Find out what they know and what they're willing to do."

Emma studied his profile. "You're not upset that they want to exclude you?"

A ghost of a smile touched his lips. "I've been excluded from most things for years, Emma. I'm used to it. I understand my presence makes some people uncomfortable."

The simple statement struck Emma deeply—a reminder of how isolated Mark's life had been, how much he had sacrificed in his flight from injustice.

"I'll go to the meeting this afternoon," she said. "But everything I learn, I'll share with you. We're partners in this."

Mark's eyes met hers, something warm and unguarded in their depths. "Partners," he agreed.

Chapter 21

Clara's home buzzed with subdued conversation when Emma arrived promptly at three o'clock. She counted eight people gathered in the small front room—Clara, Lydia, Dr. Emily Hargrove, Mildred Harper from the inn, Professor Harold Barclay, a new face to Emma, Eli Granger the blacksmith, Sophie Bennett from the Silver Spur Saloon, and to Emma's surprise, Patrick McGinty.

Conversations halted as Emma entered, and Clara quickly made introductions to those Emma hadn't formally met.

"Thank you all for coming," Clara said once everyone was settled with cups of tea. "I think we all understand why we're here."

"Walker's gone too far this time," Eli stated bluntly, his blacksmith's hands curled tightly around his teacup. "Arson isn't something we can just look away from."

"He's been going too far for years," Mildred countered. "We've just been too afraid to do anything about it."

"With good reason," Sophie added quietly. Her position at Walker's saloon made her attendance particularly risky. "You don't know what he's capable of like I do."

"That's precisely why we need to act now," Dr. Hargrove said firmly. "Before someone gets seriously hurt—or worse."

Emma listened intently, gauging each person's level of commitment and their reasons for opposing Walker.

"What exactly are you proposing?" she asked when there was a lull in the conversation.

The group exchanged glances, and it was Professor Barclay who finally spoke. "Information, primarily. Each of us has pieces of the puzzle regarding Walker's operations, his plans, his vulnerabilities. Together, we might find a way to legally threaten his power."

"I've been documenting irregularities in land transfers since Walker arrived in Blue Ridge," Clara explained, retrieving a leather-bound journal from a nearby shelf. "Properties that changed hands under suspicious circumstances, often after the owners experienced a run of bad luck."

"Like fires?" Emma suggested grimly.

"Exactly," Clara confirmed. "Or sudden illness, accidents, theft—anything that might force someone to sell quickly and cheaply."

"I've treated some of those 'accidents,'" Dr. Hargrove added. "Too many to be coincidence."

"And I've overheard Walker's men discussing their assignments," Sophie contributed. "Usually, after they've had too much to drink. They're careful, but not careful enough."

"What about the law?" Emma asked. "Is Deputy Lewis aware of all this?"

Another exchange of glances between the group members.

"Lewis is... complicated," McGinty said carefully. "He tries to do right, but he's one man against Walker's organization. And the sheriff is rarely in town—conveniently absent whenever Walker's activities might warrant investigation."

"So we're on our own," Emma concluded.

"Not entirely," Professor Barclay interjected. "I've been corresponding with colleagues at the territorial capital. There's growing concern about corruption in outlying areas like Blue Ridge. With enough documented evidence, territorial authorities might be persuaded to intervene."

"And that's where you come in, Miss Abbott," Lydia said, leaning forward earnestly. "Your case—the gold claim, the attacks on your property—could be the catalyst that finally brings Walker's activities under official scrutiny."

Emma absorbed this, understanding the weight of responsibility they were placing on her shoulders. "My situation alone isn't enough," she said thoughtfully. "We need to connect it to the broader pattern of Walker's behavior."

"Exactly," Professor Barclay agreed. "If we can demonstrate that your experience is part of a systematic approach Walker has used repeatedly, it strengthens the case considerably."

The conversation continued for over an hour, with each person sharing what they knew about Walker's operations. Emma was impressed by the thoroughness of their observations, despite their cautious approach until now.

"There's one more thing you should know," Emma said when the initial information exchange had concluded. "About Walker's past."

She hesitated, aware that sharing Mark's information potentially put him at risk. Yet, these people had trusted her with their opposition to Walker; they deserved to know what they were truly facing.

"Walker wasn't always Jedediah Walker," she began carefully. "He operated in Colorado under the name James Wallace, where he was involved in similar schemes of fraud and intimidation in mining operations."

The revelation caused a stir among the group.

"How do you know this?" Professor Barclay asked, his academic interest clearly piqued.

Emma chose her words carefully. "I have a reliable source who was in Colorado during that time. Walker left under suspicious circumstances—possibly connected to a murder."

"This changes everything," Mildred declared. "If we can prove he's using a false identity..."

"It won't be easy," McGinty cautioned. "Walker's careful about his past. There's a reason none of us knew this until now."

"We need more information from your source," Professor Barclay said to Emma. "Specific details that could be verified."

Emma nodded, though she felt uncomfortable committing Mark to further involvement without his consent. "I'll see what else I can learn," she promised.

As the meeting drew to a close, Clara distributed tasks—McGinty would quietly check shipping records for patterns related to Walker's businesses; Sophie would continue gathering information at the saloon; Professor Barclay would consult territorial law regarding fraudulent identities; and Dr. Hargrove would compile medical evidence of "accidents" befalling Walker's opponents.

"What about me?" Emma asked.

"Stay safe," Clara said firmly. "Document everything that happens at your ranch, but don't provoke Walker further. Your safety is paramount—both for your own sake and because your testimony will be crucial."

Emma understood the logic but chafed at the passive role. "I can do more than just wait for the next attack."

"Actually," Professor Barclay interjected, "there is something specific you might help with. I've been surveying geological formations in the region, including the area near your property. With your permission, I'd like to examine the gold deposit Walker is so interested in. Scientific documentation of the site could strengthen your claim and provide context for Walker's aggressive interest."

"Of course," Emma agreed. "When would you like to go?"

"Tomorrow afternoon?" the professor suggested. "I have surveying equipment to map the extent of the deposit."

With plans made and a commitment to meet again in three days, the group dispersed carefully—leaving at different times to avoid drawing attention to their gathering.

As Emma rode back toward the ranch, her mind whirled with all she had learned. The shared purpose of the group had invigorated her, providing hope that Walker's influence could indeed be challenged. Yet, she couldn't help feeling that they were still missing crucial pieces of the puzzle—that Walker's full history and the extent of his operations remained obscured.

Mark was waiting on the porch when she returned, his posture alert but his expression carefully neutral. Emma knew him well enough now to recognize the tension beneath his calm exterior—he had been worried about her.

"How was the sewing circle?" he asked as she dismounted, using the cover story they had agreed upon in case anyone lurked nearby.

"Quite enlightening," Emma replied, glancing around to ensure they were truly alone before continuing. "Let's talk inside."

Once the door was closed, Emma recounted the meeting in detail—the participants, their knowledge of Walker's activities, and the plans they had made.

Mark listened intently, asking occasional questions, but mostly absorbing the information with thoughtful silence. When Emma mentioned sharing what she knew about Walker's Colorado identity, his expression darkened momentarily before returning to careful neutrality.

"It was necessary," Emma explained, seeing his reaction. "They needed to understand what kind of man they're dealing with."

"I know," Mark acknowledged. "It's just—" He broke off, running a hand through his hair in a rare gesture of frustration. "The more people who know, the greater the risk to everyone involved."

"They're already at risk," Emma pointed out gently. "Walker has been intimidating this town for years. At least now they're finding the courage to stand together."

Mark nodded reluctantly. "Professor Barclay's idea is sound. Documenting the gold deposit scientifically could provide even more protection against Walker."

"Will you come with us tomorrow?" Emma asked. "I'd feel safer having you along, and you know the location better than I do."

"Of course," Mark agreed without hesitation. "Though I'll keep my distance if the professor seems uncomfortable with my presence."

Emma wanted to protest this self-imposed isolation, but Mark continued before she could speak.

The sound of approaching hoofbeats alerted their attention. Emma moved to the window, relieved to see Deputy Lewis dismounting in the yard.

The deputy's investigation was thorough, but yielded little concrete evidence. He examined the burned section of the barn carefully, noting the pattern of the fire damage.

"Coal oil, most likely," he commented, holding up a shard of glass that still carried the distinctive odor. "Probably a bottle of it, tossed on the ground here at this corner post."

"Can you tell who did it?" Emma asked.

Lewis shook his head. "No footprints left in this dry soil. No witnesses except for yourselves." He straightened, tucking the glass shard into a small evidence pouch. "But it's definitely arson, no question about that."

"And what happens now?" Emma pressed.

"I'll file a report. If we get more evidence, or if someone comes forward with information..."

"So nothing happens," Mark concluded flatly.

Lewis flushed. "I'm doing my job, McKay. But the law requires evidence, not just suspicion."

"Even when the suspicion points directly at the most powerful man in town?" Emma asked.

"Especially then," Lewis replied firmly. "Making accusations against Walker without proof would only make things worse for everyone."

Chapter 22

After the deputy departed, promising to increase his patrols near the ranch, Emma and Mark returned to assessing the barn damage. The afternoon sun beat down as they worked, clearing away debris.

"The lumber McGinty's sending will cover most of the repairs needed," Mark said.

Emma nodded, wiping sweat from her brow. "At least the horses weren't harmed."

They worked side by side until the sun began to dip toward the horizon, settling into a rhythm that required few words between them. Emma found herself increasingly aware of Mark's presence—the strength in his movements, the intensity of his focus, the occasional glance in her direction when he thought she wasn't looking.

When they finally took a break, sitting on a hay bale with canteens of water, Emma studied his profile. The strong line of his jaw, the slight furrow between his brows as he contemplated the work ahead, the way his hands—capable of such precise, delicate work with horses—now rested loosely on his knees.

"Something on your mind?" Mark asked, catching her gaze.

Emma felt a flush creep up her neck, embarrassed at being caught staring. "I was just thinking about how much has changed in such a short time."

"Having second thoughts about Montana?"

"Not at all," she assured him with a smile. "Quite the opposite, actually. For all the challenges, I feel more alive here than I ever did in Boston."

Mark took a slow drink from his canteen, considering her words. "Your uncle said the East was where a man existed, but the West was where he lived."

"And my father used to say the opposite."

"Your uncle was proud of your independent spirit."

"I understand why he stayed here, why this place meant so much to him." She gestured to the wide expanse of land spreading out from the ranch. "It's not just the beauty or the freedom—though those are part of it—it's the chance to build something that's truly your own. To really live instead of existing."

Mark nodded, his eyes tracking the same view. "That's what he valued most. The chance to shape his own destiny and live."

"Is that what you value, too?" Emma asked.

Mark seemed surprised by the question, taking a moment before answering. "I spent so long just surviving, moving from place to place, that I never gave much thought to building anything permanent in the past." He paused, his gaze still at the distant horizon. "Your uncle changed that for me. He showed me what it meant to put down roots, to care for something beyond yourself."

Mark turned to look at her then, his blue eyes meeting hers with an intensity that made her breath catch. "Now I'm finding more reasons to stay in one place than I ever expected."

The moment stretched between them, charged with unspoken meaning. Emma felt her heart beating faster.

The spell was broken by the distant sound of a coyote, reminding them of the approaching evening. Mark stood, offering Emma his hand. "We should head back to the house. It'll be dark soon."

Emma took his hand, allowing him to help her up. His palm was warm and callused against hers, and he held on a moment longer than necessary before releasing her.

"I'll check on the horses one more time," he said. "You go on ahead."

Emma nodded, sensing he needed a moment alone. As she walked back to the house, she wondered about the life Mark might have led if circumstances had been different—if he hadn't been falsely accused, if he hadn't been forced to become a fugitive. Would he have found his way to Montana, anyway? Would their paths still have crossed?

***

Emma prepared a simple supper while Mark tended to outdoor chores. They ate together at the kitchen table, discussing the day's events and plans for tomorrow's visit from Professor Barclay.

"Do you think he can be trusted?" Mark asked, helping himself to another serving of beans. "The professor, I mean."

Emma considered the question. "He seems genuinely concerned about Walker's influence, and his scientific interest in the gold deposit appears legitimate."

"It's not his interest in the gold that concerns me," Mark clarified. "It's what he might do with information about me."

Emma understood immediately. "I didn't give him your name when I mentioned my source about Walker's Colorado identity. But you're right to be cautious." She hesitated before continuing. "If you'd prefer not to come tomorrow—"

"No," Mark interrupted. "I'll be there. I just need to be careful about how much I reveal."

After supper, they moved to the study. Emma lit the lamp and settled into one of the worn chairs, while Mark took the other.

"There's something I've been wondering about," Emma said. "That day at the north ridge, when we found the gold—you seemed to know exactly where to look. You went there often with my uncle."

Mark nodded, leaning forward with his elbows on his knees. "Several times."

"And you never considered...?" Emma let the question hang in the air.

"Taking the gold for myself?" Mark finished, a faint smile touching his lips. "The thought crossed my mind for about five seconds the first time Thomas showed me. But your uncle had given me something more valuable than gold."

"What was that?"

"Trust," Mark said simply. "When you've lived the way I have, moving from place to place, always watching your back—having someone trust you completely is worth more than any mineral in the ground."

Emma was struck by the sincerity in his voice. "My uncle was a good judge of character."

"Usually," Mark agreed. "Though he did have a blind spot where Walker was concerned, at least initially. Walker can be charming when it serves his purpose."

"What is your impression of Walker?" Emma asked.

Mark's expression darkened. "Ambitious. Calculating. The kind of man who sees people as either useful tools or obstacles to be removed." He paused. "He owned a mining supply business in the town where I was working back in Colorado. Always friendly to your face, always ready with a deal or an opportunity. But men who crossed him had a way of encountering bad luck."

"Like being accused of murder," Emma said softly.

Mark nodded. "The man I supposedly killed was also an investigator for a mining company that was considering buying several claims in that area. He'd been asking questions about property transfers, record-keeping discrepancies. The kind of questions Walker wouldn't have wanted to be answered."

"And you were a convenient scapegoat."

"I was new to town, kept to myself, had few connections," Mark confirmed. "Easy to frame, easy to condemn."

"But you escaped," Emma prompted.

A grim smile crossed Mark's face. "Pure luck. I spent weeks hiding in the mountains before I could travel safely. Then I kept moving—Colorado to Wyoming, to Montana."

"Until you met my uncle," Emma concluded.

"Until I met your uncle," Mark agreed. "I'd been in Blue Ridge for about a month, working odd jobs, when Thomas hired me to help with spring branding. We got to talking, and somehow... I ended up telling him everything. I still don't know why. There was just something about him that made you want to be honest."

"I felt that in his letters," Emma said. "Like he could see right through any pretense."

"He offered me work and a place to stay, no questions asked. Said a man deserved the chance to rebuild his life."

Emma felt a rush of pride at her uncle's compassion. "And now Walker's, threatening that life you've rebuilt."

"It's not just my life I'm worried about," Mark said, his gaze meeting hers intently.

The weight of his words hung in the air between them. Emma was acutely aware of how close they were sitting, of the lamplight highlighting the strong lines of his face, of the subtle shift in his posture as he leaned slightly toward her.

"Mark, I—" she began, but was interrupted by a sharp knock at the door.

They both tensed, exchanging an alert glance. Mark rose quickly. Emma followed, her heart racing as she approached the door.

"Who's there?" she called firmly.

"Sophie Bennett," came the strained reply. "From the saloon. Please, Miss Abbott, I need to speak with you."

Emma unlocked the door, revealing Sophie's anxious face. The young woman's clothes were disheveled, and she was breathing hard as if she'd been running.

"I'm sorry to come so late," Sophie gasped, "but it couldn't wait. They're planning something for tomorrow—Walker's men. I overheard them talking toward the end of my shift at the saloon."

"Come inside," Emma urged, guiding Sophie to a chair. Mark remained standing, pistol now concealed behind his back, but still at the ready.

"What did you hear exactly?" he asked once Sophie had caught her breath.

"They know about Professor Barclay coming to your ranch tomorrow," Sophie explained. "One of Walker's men overheard him in town discussing the trail from your property. They're planning to intercept him on his way here."

"Intercept how?" Emma asked, alarmed.

"I don't know the details," Sophie admitted. "But they mentioned making sure he never reaches the Abbott Ranch. One of them said something about 'accidents happen all the time.'"

Mark and Emma exchanged grim looks.

"We need to warn him," Emma said immediately. "Where is the professor staying?"

"At Mildred's inn," Sophie replied. "I thought of going there directly, but I was afraid of being followed in town. Walker doesn't know I was at Clara's meeting today, but he's been suspicious of me lately."

"You took a risk coming here," Mark acknowledged.

Sophie nodded, twisting her hands in her lap. "I couldn't just say nothing. Not after seeing what Walker's done to others who stood in his way."

"You did the right thing," Emma assured her, placing a hand over Sophie's restless ones. "And we're grateful."

Mark moved to the window, checking the darkness outside. "How did you get here? Did anyone follow you?"

"I borrowed a horse from Russ Miller at the livery," Sophie explained. "Told him I needed to visit my sister on the Johnson farm. I took the long way around and doubled back twice to make sure no one was trailing me."

"Smart," Mark commented, still scanning the night for any sign of watchers.

"I should go," Sophie said, rising from her chair.

"It's not safe for you to return alone," Emma protested.

"I'll escort her," Mark decided. "We'll take a different route back to town."

"What about Professor Barclay?" Emma asked. "We need to warn him tonight."

Mark considered for a moment. "I'll stop at the inn after I make sure Sophie gets home safely. Mildred will let me speak with the professor discreetly."

The plan decided. They moved quickly. Mark saddled his horse, while Emma provided Sophie with a long coat to conceal her distinctive saloon attire. Within minutes, they were ready to depart.

"Be careful," Emma urged, standing on the porch as they prepared to leave. Her eyes met Mark's, conveying all the concern she couldn't express aloud.

"We will," he promised. "Lock the doors behind me. I'll be back as soon as I can."

Emma watched them disappear into the darkness, the sound of hoofbeats fading until all was silent except for the night insects and the distant call of an owl. She secured the house as Mark had instructed, placing the pistol within easy reach as she settled down to wait.

Chapter 23

The hours stretched long as Emma moved restlessly through the house, alternating between watching at the windows and reviewing her uncle's journals for any additional insights about Walker. Shortly after midnight, she heard the approach of a horse at a careful walk rather than a trot—someone trying to move quietly.

Heart pounding, Emma took up the pistol and moved to a position where she could see the door without being immediately visible to anyone entering. The soft sound of boots on the porch was followed by a distinctive pattern of knocks—three quick, two slow—the signal she and Mark had established.

Relieved, Emma removed the wooden crossbar from the brackets on either side of the door and turned the lock, finding Mark looking weary but unharmed.

"Everything all right?" she asked immediately, ushering him inside.

"Sophie's safely at home," he reported, removing his hat. "And I spoke with Professor Barclay. He's alarmed but grateful for the warning."

"Is he still coming tomorrow?" Emma asked, relocking the door and placing the wood crossbar back in place.

Mark nodded, dropping into a chair. "He's determined not to be intimidated. Says the documentation of your claim is too important to delay."

"What about Walker's men?"

"That's where it gets complicated," Mark said, rubbing a hand across his jaw. "The professor insists on keeping his appointment, but we've modified the plan. He'll announce publicly at breakfast tomorrow while speaking with Mildred that he's heading to the Stevens property to conduct geological surveys—it's in the opposite direction from your ranch. Meanwhile, I'll meet him at Josiah Smith's camp in the morning and bring him here by a roundabout route."

Emma considered this. "Will that be enough to fool Walker's men?"

"It's our best option," Mark said. "Josiah's place is isolated enough that they won't be watching it."

"Did you tell the professor about yourself and the Colorado incident?" Emma asked.

Mark shook his head. "Not yet. I wanted to discuss that with you first. If we share that information, we need to be prepared for the questions it will raise."

"About your knowledge of Walker's identity," Emma surmised.

"Exactly." Mark's expression was guarded. "Once that door is opened, it may be difficult to control where it leads, and we don't know the professor well enough yet."

Emma moved to sit opposite him, their knees nearly touching in the small space.

"Emma," he began, his voice lower than usual, "there's something I should—"

A distant crash from the direction of the barn interrupted him. They both jumped to their feet, instantly alert.

"Stay here," he ordered, reaching for his pistol.

"Really?" Emma countered, already moving to retrieve her rifle from its place beside the door.

Mark looked like he wanted to argue, but recognized the determination in her stance. "Stay behind me. And if I tell you to run, you run—no questions."

They moved cautiously from the house, using the shadows for cover as they approached the barn. The structure was dark and seemingly undisturbed, but Mark's raised hand halted Emma as they drew closer.

"Listen," he whispered.

Emma strained her ears, detecting a faint rustling and the nervous shuffling of horses inside the barn.

"Someone's in there," she breathed, tightening her grip on the rifle.

Mark nodded, gesturing for her to move to the side of the barn door while he took position on the other side. With practiced efficiency, he checked his pistol, then held up three fingers, counting down.

Three.

Two.

One.

Mark yanked the barn door open, leveling his pistol into the darkness. "Come out slowly with your hands where I can see them," he commanded.

There was a moment of silence, then a small voice replied, "Please don't shoot, Mr. McKay. It's just me."

"Tommy?" Emma exclaimed, recognizing Clara's son's voice. She lowered her rifle as the small figure emerged from the darkness.

The boy looked frightened but determined, his young face streaked with tears and dirt. "I'm sorry, Miss Abbott. I didn't mean to scare you."

Mark holstered his pistol and knelt at the boy's level. "What are you doing here, Tommy? Does your mother know where you are?"

Tommy shook his head miserably. "She's gonna be awful mad. But I had to come. They took Ranger!"

"Ranger?" Emma questioned, joining Mark beside the distressed child.

"My dog," Tommy explained, his voice trembling. "Those men from the saloon—they said if my ma and I want to see Ranger again, she needs to give them her journal. The one with all the writing about Mr. Walker in it."

Mark and Emma exchanged alarmed glances.

"When did this happen, Tommy?" Mark asked urgently.

"Tonight, after supper," Tommy sniffled. "Ma told me to go to bed, but I heard voices downstairs and peeked through the railings. Those men said she had until morning to decide. Then they left, and Ma was crying, and I thought—" he hiccupped, "I thought maybe Mr. McKay could help get Ranger back."

"So you snuck out of your house and walked all the way here by yourself?" Emma asked, amazed at the boy's courage despite his foolishness.

Tommy nodded. "I know these trails good. Pa showed me before he died. But it took longer in the dark, and I got scared, and then I heard you coming and hid in the barn."

Mark placed a gentle hand on the boy's shoulder. "You were very brave, Tommy, but also very foolish."

Fresh tears welled in Tommy's eyes. "I just want Ranger back. He's my best friend. I need your help."

Emma felt her heart breaking for the child. "We'll help you, Tommy. But first, we need to let your mother know you're safe."

"I'll ride to Clara's," Mark decided, standing. "Clara needs to know where her son is."

"What about Ranger?" Tommy asked anxiously.

Mark's expression softened. "We'll figure out how to help Ranger too, I promise. But your mother comes first."

As Mark prepared to leave, Emma led Tommy into the house, settling him at the kitchen table with a cup of milk and some leftover biscuits. The boy was exhausted, his eyelids drooping despite his attempts to stay alert.

"You can rest in my room until your mother arrives," Emma told him gently. "I'll wake you when she gets here."

Tommy nodded sleepily, allowing Emma to guide him to the bedroom. She covered him with a blanket, and within minutes, his breathing had deepened into sleep.

Emma returned to the kitchen, her mind racing with the implications of Walker's latest move. Targeting Clara was a clear escalation—and using the boy's dog as leverage was cruel.

Nearly an hour passed before Emma heard the approach of horses. She moved to the window, relieved to see Mark returning with Clara riding beside him, her face etched with worry.

Emma met them at the door. "Tommy's asleep in my room," she said quietly. "He's safe, just exhausted."

Clara rushed past her, making directly for the bedroom. Emma and Mark followed, watching as Clara knelt beside her sleeping son, her fingers tenderly brushing the hair from his forehead.

Once assured that her son was truly okay, Clara followed Emma and Mark outside the bedroom. They sat at the table, each with a cup of coffee in hand.

"Walker's men came to your house?" Mark confirmed, sitting across from Clara at the table.

Clara nodded grimly. "Two of them. Burke and that new one—Reynolds. They said they'd heard I was 'collecting stories' about Mr. Walker, and that such activities could be dangerous for a widow with a young child. I refused to give them my journals."

"And they took Tommy's dog as insurance," Emma concluded, her anger rising.

"They said it was just 'looking after the mutt' while I reconsidered my 'misguided notions,'" Clara's voice was bitter.

"What will you do about the journals?" Mark asked.

Clara's hands tightened around her cup. "I won't hand them over. Those journals contain evidence of Walker's wrongdoing over years—property transfers that never should have happened, 'accidents' that weren't accidental. It's the only record of what he's done to this town and the people here that I'm aware of."

"But Ranger—" Emma began.

"I love that dog," Clara interrupted, "and it will break Tommy's heart if something happens to him. If Walker gets away with this intimidation, what's next? I can't live in fear of what he might take from us each time we stand up to him."

"There's nothing we can do about this now," Emma said firmly. "Clara, you and Tommy will stay here with us. There's safety in numbers."

Mark nodded, his face resolute in the dim light. "I agree. I'll keep watch through the night. It's late—the rest of you should get some proper sleep."

Emma gestured toward her bedroom. "There's no need to wake Tommy. Let him sleep. Clara, you take the bed in the loft." She settled into a chair by the hearth, the firelight casting long shadows across her tired face. "I'll stay here with Mark and try to get some rest."

Chapter 24

Mark jolted awake at the sound of hoofbeats approaching the ranch. Dawn had barely broken, casting long shadows across the yard as he moved swiftly to the window, pistol in hand. His muscles ached from spending the night in the wooden chair by the hearth, but alertness surged through him as he identified three riders approaching at a steady pace.

"Emma," he said, his voice low but urgent.

She stirred immediately from where she'd been dozing in the chair opposite him, her auburn hair tumbling loose around her shoulders. "What is it?"

"Riders. Three of them." He recognized the lead figure with a grimace. "Burke, and Reynolds—Walker's men."

Emma was on her feet instantly. "And the third?"

Mark narrowed his eyes at the early morning light. "Can't tell yet."

"I'll wake Clara," Emma said, already moving toward the stairs to the loft.

"No need," came Clara's voice as she descended, fully dressed and alert. "I've been awake for some time."

The three stood together at the window, watching as the riders approached. The third man became visible as they drew closer—a heavyset figure with a thick beard.

"That's Donovan," Clara said, her voice tight. "He tends bar at Walker's saloon."

"Stay inside," Mark instructed, checking his pistol. "Both of you."

Emma shook her head firmly. "No. They won't try anything with witnesses."

Emma retrieved the Winchester and checked the chamber. The look she gave him brooked no argument.

"Stay on the porch. Let me do the talking."

The three riders halted their horses about twenty yards from the house. Burke, a lean man with a pockmarked face, dismounted first. He carried a small burlap sack in one hand.

"Morning, McKay," he called, his tone falsely cheerful. "Didn't expect to find such a gathering here."

Mark stepped onto the porch, positioning himself slightly in front of Emma and Clara. "State your business, Burke."

Burke's smile remained, but his eyes were cold. "Just delivering a message from Mr. Walker. Seems Mrs. Jacobs wasn't home when we called on her earlier. Lucky for us, we found her here."

"What have you done with my dog?" Clara asked.

In answer, Burke lifted the burlap sack, which suddenly moved and emitted a muffled whine.

"Ranger!" Clara gasped.

"Still alive and well, good pup, I might add," Burke confirmed. "Mr. Walker's a reasonable man, Mrs. Jacobs. All he wants is those journals of yours—the ones with all those interesting stories you've been collecting. Hand them over, and the mutt goes free, no harm done. I'm not wanting to dog sit forever."

Mark felt Emma tense beside him, her rifle shifting slightly in her hands. He gave her a warning glance, and she stilled, though her eyes blazed with anger.

"And if I refuse?" Clara asked, lifting her chin.

Reynolds, a burly man with a scar bisecting his left eyebrow, spoke up. "Then you best start thinking about what you're going to tell that boy of yours when his dog doesn't come home."

"That's enough," Mark said, his hand resting on his holstered pistol. "You're trespassing on Miss Abbott's property."

Burke's eyes glinted with malice. "Funny thing about property in these parts—ownership can change mighty quick. Mr. Walker asked me to remind Miss Abbott about the incident with her barn. Terrible shame. So many accidents can happen on a ranch. Fire, stampedes, sick cattle..."

"Is that a threat?" Emma demanded, stepping forward despite Mark's attempt to keep her behind him.

"Just neighborly concern, ma'am," Burke replied with a mock tip of his hat. "Montana can be dangerous."

Mark moved subtly, placing his body between Emma and the men. "You've delivered your message. Now get off this land."

"Not without Mrs. Jacobs' answer," Donovan spoke for the first time, his deep voice gravelly. "Journals for the dog. Simple trade."

Clara took a deep breath. "I have a counter-offer. Let Tommy's dog go, and I won't send my notes or the journals to the territorial marshal's office."

Burke's smile faltered. "What notes would those be?"

"The ones documenting Mr. Walker's activities in Colorado," Clara bluffed smoothly. "When he went by a different name. Notes about a murder investigation that was never properly concluded."

Mark kept his expression neutral, impressed by Clara's quick thinking. She had no such notes, but Walker's men wouldn't know that.

Burke exchanged an uncertain glance with his companions. "You're bluffing."

"Am I?" Clara challenged. "Mr. Walker isn't the only one with connections. Set the dog free, leave us alone, and those notes stay private."

A tense silence followed as Burke considered her words. The burlap sack moved again, Ranger's muffled whines becoming more insistent.

"Mr. Walker won't be happy about this," Burke finally said.

"That's not our concern," Mark replied evenly. "What'll it be, Burke? You want to go back and tell Walker his identity might be exposed to territorial authorities?"

Another moment of hesitation, then Burke shrugged, dismounted and set the sack on the ground. "Take the mutt. But this isn't over, not by a long shot." He remounted his horse. "Mr. Walker always gets what he wants, one way or another."

The three men wheeled their horses around and rode away, dust billowing behind them. Mark remained vigilant until they disappeared from view, then nodded to Emma, who rushed forward with Clara to retrieve the sack.

Clara's hands trembled as she untied the drawstring. A small brown and white dog burst out, yipping frantically and leaping into her arms.

"Oh, Ranger," she whispered, burying her face in the dog's fur. "You're all right, boy. You're all right."

Emma knelt beside them, gently checking the dog for injuries. "He seems unharmed, just frightened."

Mark scanned the horizon once more, then joined them. "That was quick thinking, Clara. Walker's going to be furious."

Clara nodded, her face grim as she continued to stroke the trembling dog. "I know. But it bought us time, and it gave me back a piece of my son's heart."

"Let's get inside," Mark suggested, glancing at the brightening sky. "We have plans to make before the professor arrives."

The dog trotted happily ahead of them as they returned to the house, clearly relieved to be free. Inside, Mark secured the door while Emma stoked the fire and set water to boil for coffee.

"You think they bought it?" Clara asked, settling at the kitchen table with Ranger at her feet.

Mark considered. "Temporarily. Burke isn't the brightest, but he'll report back to Walker, who'll want proof of these supposed notes."

Emma placed cups of steaming coffee before them. "Then we need to make the most of that time. Professor Barclay will document the gold deposit today, giving us concrete evidence of why Walker wants this land."

"And we need to move your journals to a safer location," Mark added. "Where are they now?"

"Under a loose floorboard in my kitchen," Clara admitted. "Not terribly original, but effective so far."

Mark nodded. "We'll retrieve them when it's safe to return to your house. In the meantime—"

Tommy appeared in the doorway, rubbing sleep from his eyes. His gaze fell on the dog, and his entire face transformed with joy.

"Ranger!" he cried, launching himself across the room. The dog bounded up, meeting the boy halfway in an exuberant reunion of wet kisses and childish laughter.

Clara's eyes welled with tears as she watched her son roll on the floor with his beloved pet. "Worth any risk," she whispered.

Emma squeezed Clara's hand.

Mark felt something warm and unfamiliar expand in his chest as he observed the scene—Tommy's uninhibited joy, Clara's maternal love, and Emma's steadfast loyalty to a friend she'd known only a short time. It had been so long since he'd been part of something like this, a circle of people who cared for and protected one another.

As if sensing his thoughts, Emma glanced up at him, her green eyes meeting his with understanding. A silent communication passed between them.

Tommy's voice broke the spell. "Mr. McKay! Did you save Ranger? Ma said you would help!"

Mark crouched to the boy's level, ruffling his tousled hair. "Your mother did most of the saving, Tommy. She was very brave."

Tommy beamed at Clara. "That's 'cause she's the bravest person in all of Montana! That's what Pa always said."

Clara blushed, gathering her son into a tight embrace. "Your father would be so proud of you, Tommy. But next time you're worried about something, come talk to me instead of sneaking out in the middle of the night. You nearly frightened me to death."

"Yes, ma'am," Tommy agreed solemnly, though his attention was already returning to Ranger.

"How about some breakfast?" Emma suggested, moving to the stove. "We have a busy day ahead."

As Emma prepared a simple meal of flapjacks and bacon, Mark outlined the plan for meeting Professor Barclay at Josiah Smith's cabin.

"I'll leave shortly to ensure I reach Josiah's place before the professor. You three will stay here."

"I should return home," Clara objected. "I have chores that need tending, and I don't want to impose—"

"It's not safe," Mark interrupted. "Not yet. Walker's men will be watching your place."

Emma set plates of food on the table. "He's right, Clara. Stay here today, at least until we know more about Walker's next move."

Clara hesitated, then nodded reluctantly.

"And I could use your help here," Emma added. "I'm still learning the finer points of managing a household. Having an experienced homesteader to advise me would be invaluable."

Mark recognized Emma's diplomatic approach—framing Clara's stay as helpful rather than a burden—and admired her sensitivity. As she set a plate in front of him, he set his hand on top of hers, stilling her, sending an unexpected jolt through her system. Her cheeks colored slightly.

The meal passed with Tommy chattering excitedly about Ranger's heroic return, blissfully unaware of the danger that still surrounded them. When they finished eating, Mark prepared to depart for Josiah's cabin.

"Be careful," Emma said as she walked him to the door. "Walker's men could be watching the trails."

"I know these hills better than they do," he assured her. "But keep the rifle handy while I'm gone. And remember—"

"Don't open the door for anyone except you or the professor," she finished. "I know, Mark. We'll be fine."

He hesitated, wanting to say more, but conscious of Clara watching from across the room. "I'll be back soon," he said instead, settling his hat on his head.

Emma laid her hand on his arm, her touch light but steady. "God go with you."

Mark nodded, momentarily unable to speak past the tightness in his throat. With a final glance at the three people gathered in the warmth of the kitchen, he stepped outside into the cool morning.

Chapter 25

The ride to Josiah's took Mark on a winding route through dense forest and across shallow streams—paths unlikely to be observed by Walker's men.

As Mark approached, Josiah emerged from the trees beside the cabin, rifle in hand. Despite being well into his sixties, the trapper moved with the silent agility of a much younger man, his weathered face partially hidden beneath a grizzled beard.

"McKay," Josiah called, lowering his weapon. "Heard tell there's trouble brewing."

Mark dismounted, leading his horse to the small corral beside the cabin. "News travels fast, even in the wilderness."

Josiah chuckled, the sound like dry leaves rustling. "Your message was delivered to me discreetly. I wasted no time getting word to that professor how to find us here," His expression sobered. "While I was in town yesterday, I overheard some of Walker's men asking about you. Got some of my traps from the mercantile, heard them questioning McGinty."

"They're getting bolder," Mark acknowledged, loosening his horse's saddle. "Did McGinty tell them anything?"

"That Irishman?" Josiah snorted. "He sent them on a wild goose chase toward the territorial border."

Mark smiled grimly. "Good man."

Josiah shook his head. "I left markers on the trail—for the professor. He should find his way here if he's half as smart as he seems."

They settled on the porch, Josiah producing a pot of coffee that had been kept warm by the fire inside. As they drank the strong brew, Mark filled the old trapper in on the latest developments—the confrontation with Walker's men that morning, Clara's bluff about Walker's Colorado identity, and more about the plan to document the gold deposit.

Josiah listened without interruption, his keen eyes tracking the horizon as if he could see the threads of these events weaving together across the distance.

"Walker's a snake," he said when Mark finished. "But even snakes have their purpose in the greater design."

Mark raised an eyebrow. "What purpose could someone like Walker serve?"

The older man stroked his beard thoughtfully. "Sometimes the Lord uses the wicked to reveal what's in the hearts of the righteous. Tests of character, you might say."

"I'm not sure if I qualify as righteous," Mark replied dryly.

Josiah fixed him with a penetrating gaze. "You're a good man, McKay. That Abbott girl sees it clear enough."

Mark stared into his coffee cup. "Emma's got a kind heart. She sees the best in people."

"Maybe so," Josiah acknowledged. "Or perhaps she just sees the truth."

A movement on the trail caught their attention. Professor Barclay appeared, riding a placid-looking mare and leading a pack mule laden with equipment. His city clothes had been supplemented with practical frontier additions—a wide-brimmed hat against the sun and leather gloves for protection.

Mark rose to greet him. "Professor. Glad you made it safely."

Barclay dismounted somewhat awkwardly, adjusting his spectacles. "Mr. McKay. Your friend's directions were most helpful, if somewhat cryptic."

Josiah cackled. "Had to make sure you weren't followed, Professor. These hills have eyes, and not all of them are friendly."

The professor nodded earnestly. "Indeed. I encountered two rather unsavory characters near town this morning. They seemed quite interested in my destination."

"Walker's men?" Mark asked sharply.

"I believe so. One had a distinctive scar across his eyebrow."

"Reynolds," Mark confirmed. "What did you tell them?"

"Exactly what we agreed upon," Barclay said, straightening his shoulders with a hint of pride. "That I was conducting geological surveys at the Stevens' property. I even showed them falsified paperwork to that effect."

"Did they follow you?"

"Not that I could discern. I took the precaution of detouring through the creek bed for a mile, as suggested."

Mark nodded, satisfied. "Good. We should move quickly, though. Once they realize you're not at the Stevens' property, they'll start searching."

They transferred the most essential surveying equipment from the pack mule to their horses, leaving the animal with Josiah. The old trapper provided them with a hand-drawn map showing a little-used trail to the Abbott ranch that would keep them hidden from observation.

"This route adds time to your journey," Josiah explained, "but it'll keep you out of sight from the main trails where Walker's men patrol."

"We appreciate your help," Mark said, extending his hand.

Josiah clasped it firmly. "Been watching Walker too long not to do my part when the opportunity comes. Thomas Abbott was a good man. His niece deserves a fair chance at the life he built."

The professor shook Josiah's hand with equal enthusiasm. "Your knowledge of local geography is remarkable, sir. I'd be most interested in consulting with you further about the natural features of this region."

"Anytime, Professor," Josiah replied with amusement. "This land speaks clearer than any book once you learn its language."

With final thanks, Mark and Professor Barclay departed, following Josiah's route through dense stands of pine and across rocky outcroppings that offered no tracks to follow. As they rode, Barclay questioned Mark about the gold deposit—its location, approximate size, and surrounding geological features.

"Miss Abbott's claim could be significant," the professor explained, his academic enthusiasm evident. "Not just personally, but scientifically. The mineral composition in this region has unique characteristics that could advance our understanding of geological formations throughout the territory."

Mark listened with half an ear, his attention divided between the professor's explanations and vigilant observation of their surroundings. A snapped twig, a disturbed bird—any sign that might indicate they were being followed.

They were about halfway to the ranch when Mark detected movement to the west—too deliberate to be wildlife. He raised his hand for silence, then guided his horse behind a large boulder, motioning for the professor to follow.

"What is it?" Barclay whispered.

"Riders," Mark murmured. "Two of them, moving parallel to us about a hundred yards west."

Through the trees, they could make out the shapes of mounted men traveling at a steady pace along the main trail.

"Walker's men?" the professor asked, his voice hushed.

Mark nodded grimly. "Burke and someone I don't recognize. They're headed toward the ranch."

Concern flashed across Barclay's face. "Miss Abbott—"

"Emma can handle herself," Mark assured him. "And Clara's with her. They won't open the door to strangers."

They waited until the riders had passed, then continued their journey with increased urgency, Mark leading them on an even more circuitous route to ensure they weren't spotted. Despite the detour, they made good time, arriving at the ranch shortly before noon.

Mark's tension eased somewhat at the sight of smoke rising steadily from the chimney—a sign that all was well within. As they approached the house, he noted that the curtains were drawn, but a slight movement indicated someone watching their arrival through a gap.

The door opened as they dismounted, revealing Emma with her rifle in hand. Her expression shifted from wariness to relief when she recognized them.

"Praise God," she said, lowering the weapon. "We saw Walker's men earlier. Clara was worried they might intercept you."

"We spotted them," Mark confirmed, securing the horses. "They passed within a hundred yards of us, but we stayed hidden."

Emma ushered them inside, where Clara was setting the table for lunch, Tommy and Ranger playing quietly in the corner with a set of wooden blocks.

"I hope you gentlemen are hungry," Clara said. "We've prepared a hearty stew and biscuits. You'll need your strength for the expedition to the north ridge."

Over lunch, Mark described their journey from Josiah's cabin, while Emma updated them on events at the ranch—a quiet morning with no further visits from Walker's men.

"Though we did see a rider watching the house from that rise to the east," she added, gesturing toward the window. "He stayed for about an hour, then left."

"Surveillance," Mark said grimly. "Walker's trying to monitor all movement to and from the ranch."

Professor Barclay dabbed at his mouth with a napkin. "Which makes our documentation of the gold deposit all the more urgent. If we could begin as soon as possible..."

"Of course," Emma agreed. "What will you need for your assessment?"

The professor detailed his requirements—samples from various locations, measurements of the stream bed, observations of surrounding rock formations. Mark listened attentively, mentally calculating how long the process would take and the safest route to the deposit.

"We should be able to complete the basic documentation in one afternoon," Barclay concluded, "though a comprehensive assessment would require multiple visits."

"One visit will have to suffice for now," Mark said. "Once Walker realizes you're here, he'll increase his efforts to interfere."

They finalized their plan—Mark, Emma, and the professor would visit the north ridge that afternoon, while Clara and Tommy remained at the ranch house. Though Emma initially suggested that Clara accompany them, Mark convinced her it was safer for Clara to stay behind with Tommy.

As Clara cleared the lunch dishes, assisted by an eager Tommy, Emma led the professor to the study to gather more writing materials for his notes. Mark followed, using the moment to speak with Emma privately.

"I'd prefer if you stayed at the ranch as well," he said quietly.

Emma's eyebrows rose. "This is my property, Mark McKay. My claim. I need to be present for the documentation."

"It could be dangerous," he persisted. "If Walker's men are watching—"

"All the more reason for me to go," she interrupted. "I won't hide in my house while others take risks on my behalf."

The stubborn set of her jaw told Mark further argument would be futile. He changed tactics. "At least stay close to me at all times. And bring your rifle."

A smile tugged at the corner of her mouth. "I had every intention of doing both."

Their eyes met, and Mark felt that same inexplicable connection he'd experienced that morning—a wordless understanding that seemed to flow between them like an electric current. In a moment of courage, he cradled Emma's face between his palms and brushed his lips against hers in a kiss so tender it made his heart stutter. When he pulled back, his hands still framing her face, his gaze locked with hers. The intensity in her eyes nearly undid him.

"You're something else," he whispered, his voice carrying the weight of everything he couldn't yet say.

The professor's voice broke the moment.

"These journals are remarkable," Barclay said, examining one of Thomas Abbott's leather-bound volumes. "Your uncle's observations about the local geology are surprisingly accurate for a layman."

Emma turned toward him, still a little started by Mark's tender kiss. "Uncle Thomas was... a keen observer. His journals documented everything from weather patterns to wildlife movements."

"Including the gold deposit," Mark added.

While the professor glanced over the journals, Mark took the opportunity to check his pistol, ensuring it was loaded and ready.

***

By early afternoon, they were prepared to depart. Clara and Tommy stood on the porch to see them off, Ranger sitting alertly at the boy's feet.

"We'll be back after sundown," Emma assured Clara, mounting her horse with ease.

"Be watchful and God be with you all," Clara cautioned. "I'll keep the rifle handy, just in case."

The three riders set out, Mark taking the lead, with Emma beside him and the professor following. Rather than taking the direct route they had used on their previous visit to the north ridge, Mark led them on a winding path that utilized natural features for cover—stands of trees, rocky outcroppings, and shallow ravines.

"Walker's men will be watching the obvious trails," he explained when the professor questioned the circuitous route. "This way takes longer, but keeps us out of sight."

Emma rode with alert confidence, her rifle secured in a scabbard beside her saddle, her eyes constantly scanning their surroundings. Mark found his attention divided between watching for potential threats and observing Emma—the determined set of her shoulders, the way she handled her horse with gentle firmness, the slight furrow between her brows as she concentrated.

Their progress was steady but cautious. Twice, Mark halted the group when he detected movement in the distance, but both times it proved to be deer rather than human observers.

As they approached the north ridge, the landscape changed gradually—more exposed rock, fewer trees, the ground rising steadily toward the ridge line. They dismounted in a small copse of pines to conceal their horses, continuing the final portion of the journey on foot.

"The deposit is just ahead," Mark told Professor Barclay, pointing toward the stream that cut through the rocky terrain. "The water has exposed veins of quartz containing gold."

The professor nodded eagerly, adjusting his spectacles. "Classic alluvial deposition. Very promising."

They worked methodically for the next two hours. The professor collected samples, made detailed sketches of the area, and dictated notes which Emma recorded in her neat handwriting.

"The concentration is remarkable," Barclay commented, examining a pan of sediment through his magnifying glass. "Much higher than typical placer deposits in this region."

"Valuable enough to explain Walker's interest?" Emma asked.

"Without question," the professor confirmed. "Based on these samples, even a modest mining operation could yield significant returns. A full-scale operation—" he gestured toward the ridge rising above them, "—particularly if the vein extends into the hillside, as I suspect it does, could be extraordinarily profitable."

Emma's expression was thoughtful as she took notes. "Yet my uncle chose not to develop it."

"Thomas understood what mining would do to this land," Mark said, gesturing to the pristine wilderness surrounding them. "The trees cleared, the stream diverted or polluted, dynamite blasting away the hillside. He couldn't bring himself to destroy it."

"A preservationist ahead of his time," Professor Barclay mused. "Admirable, though unusual for this era of expansion."

"My uncle valued beauty and balance," Emma said, her voice soft with pride. "He believed God created this land with intention—that there was purpose in every tree and stone."

Mark watched her as she spoke, struck by how similar her values were to her uncle's. Thomas Abbott's spirit lived on in his niece.

As the professor continued his examination of the site, Mark felt a growing unease. They had been at the location longer than he had intended, and the afternoon was advancing toward evening.

"We should finish up soon," he suggested.

Barclay nodded, gathering his samples and notes. "I have sufficient data for an initial assessment. Most impressive, Miss Abbott. This claim alone will secure your financial future."

"If I can maintain ownership against Walker's schemes," Emma replied, her expression resolute.

"The documentation we've compiled today will strengthen your legal position significantly," the professor assured her. "Combined with your formal mining claim, it establishes your intent to develop the resource legitimately, which territorial courts generally uphold."

They packed the samples and equipment, preparing for the return journey. As Mark secured the last of the professor's tools, a sharp crack echoed across the ridge—unmistakably a rifle shot.

Mark reacted instantly, pulling Emma down behind a large boulder. "Stay down!" he ordered, drawing his pistol.

The professor dropped to the ground beside them, his face pale beneath his beard. "What in heaven's name—?"

Another shot rang out, striking the rock above their heads, sending chips of stone flying.

"Ambush," Mark said grimly, peering carefully around the edge of the boulder. "At least two shooters, positioned on the ridge above us."

Emma had already unslung her rifle and was checking the chamber. "Walker's men?"

"Most likely." Mark surveyed their position with a tactical eye. They had reasonable cover from the boulder, but were effectively pinned down with limited options for retreat. The horses were hidden in the trees about a hundred yards behind them, but reaching them would require crossing exposed ground.

"They must have followed us after all," the professor said, his voice remarkably steady despite the danger.

"Or they've been watching the deposit, knowing we'd return to it eventually," Mark suggested. A third shot struck nearby, confirming the shooters were trying to keep them pinned in place rather than hitting them directly.

"They want to hold us here until reinforcements arrive," Mark concluded. "We need to move before more of Walker's men join them."

Emma nodded, her face calm despite the danger. "What's the plan?"

Mark quickly outlined their options. "The stream bed provides some cover for about sixty yards. If we can reach it, we can follow it down toward where the horses are hidden."

"I'll go first," Emma volunteered. "I'm the smallest target."

"Absolutely not," Mark objected. "I'll go, draw their fire, and you two follow when I signal."

Emma's expression hardened. "This is my property, my fight. I won't let you take all the risk."

Another shot interrupted their debate, this one closer than before.

"There's no time to argue," Mark said firmly. "Professor, are you able to run when necessary?"

Barclay nodded grimly. "I may not look athletic, sir, but I assure you I can move when motivated. And current circumstances are exceedingly motivating."

Despite the gravity of their situation, Emma gave a small smile at the professor's gallows humor.

"On my signal, then," Mark decided. "Emma, you go second, helping the professor. I'll cover your retreat."

She looked as if she wanted to protest further, but a fifth shot, striking alarmingly close to their position, silenced her objection.

Mark removed his hat, placing it on the barrel of his pistol, and carefully raised it above the boulder. Immediately, two shots rang out, confirming the location of both shooters.

"Now!" he shouted, sprinting from behind the boulder toward the stream bed. As expected, the gunmen tracked him, firing rapidly but inaccurately as he zigzagged across the uneven ground.

Mark dove into the shallow stream, using its banks for cover. He glanced back to see Emma guiding Professor Barclay toward him, moving swiftly despite the older man's less agile pace. They reached the stream just as another volley of shots kicked up dirt around them.

"Stay low," Mark instructed, helping the professor down into the water. "Follow the stream bed. I'll be right behind you."

Emma hesitated. "Mark—"

"Go!" he urged, turning to fire two shots toward the ridge to discourage pursuit.

Emma nodded, taking the professor's arm to steady him as they began moving downstream, crouching below the bank.

Mark followed, periodically stopping to return fire and assess the situation. The shooters appeared to be repositioning, trying to gain a better angle on the stream bed. Their movements would eventually give them a clear line of sight, but Mark hoped to reach the horses before that happened.

They had covered about forty yards when a shout from ahead brought them to a halt. Mark peered cautiously over the bank to see two riders emerging from the trees where their horses were concealed.

"They've got men at our exit point," he reported grimly.

"We're surrounded?" the professor asked, his earlier composure slipping slightly.

Mark assessed their position. The stream continued downhill, eventually widening into a small marsh area dense with cattails and brush. It wasn't their planned escape route, but it offered concealment.

"This way," he decided, directing them downstream. "Stay in the water to hide our tracks."

They moved as quickly as possible, splashing through the shallow stream while keeping their heads below the banks. The shots from the ridge continued.

As they approached the marsh, Mark felt a surge of hope. The dense vegetation would provide excellent cover, and he knew from hunting in the area that the marsh connected to a dry creek bed that could lead them back toward the ranch by a roundabout route.

They had just reached the edge of the cattails when Emma suddenly stumbled, her face contorting in pain as she clutched her arm.

"Emma!" Mark was at her side instantly, supporting her weight.

"I'm all right," she insisted through gritted teeth. "Just grazed me."

Mark quickly examined her arm. A bullet had torn through her sleeve, leaving a bloody furrow across her upper arm—painful but not serious.

"We need to keep moving," he urged, tearing a strip from his shirt to bind the wound. "Can you continue?"

Emma nodded determinedly. "Of course."

Professor Barclay removed his neckerchief, offering it as an additional bandage. "Courage, Miss Abbott. We'll get you to safety."

The marsh proved to be their salvation. Its dense vegetation and muddy terrain discouraged pursuit on horseback, while the complex network of small waterways made their trail difficult to follow. Mark led them through the thickest parts, helping Emma when necessary, though she refused to show any further sign of pain.

After nearly an hour of cautious progress, they reached the dry creek bed Mark had remembered. From there, they could circle back toward the ranch while avoiding the main trails where Walker's men might be watching.

"What about our horses?" Emma asked as they trudged along the dusty creek bed.

"We'll have to retrieve them later," Mark replied. "Or they'll find their way back to the ranch, eventually. Horses are smarter than people give them credit for."

"And my samples?" the professor inquired, his scientific concerns reasserting themselves despite their danger.

Mark patted the saddlebag he had managed to grab during their retreat. "I have the most important ones here. The documentation should be sufficient for your report."

The sun was dipping toward the horizon by the time they sighted the ranch. Mark halted them behind a stand of trees for a final assessment before approaching.

"Wait here," he instructed. "I'll make sure it's safe."

Emma caught his arm before he could move away. "Be careful," she said softly.

Their eyes met, and Mark felt that same connection that had been growing between them—deepened now by shared danger. "Always," he promised.

He scouted the perimeter of the ranch carefully, alert for any sign of Walker's men. The house appeared peaceful, smoke rising steadily from the chimney, Clara's silhouette visible through the kitchen window as she moved about inside.

Satisfied, Mark signaled for Emma and the professor to join him, and they approached the house together.

Chapter 26

Clara flung open the door before they reached the porch steps, her face etched with worry.

"Thank the Lord!" she exclaimed, ushering them inside. "We've been beside ourselves with worry."

Tommy peered around Clara's skirts, eyes widening at their bedraggled appearance. Ranger barked once in greeting, then sniffed cautiously at their mud-caked boots.

"You're hurt!" Clara gasped, noticing Emma's bloodstained sleeve.

"It's just a bullet graze," Emma assured her, though the pain had intensified during their long trek back to the ranch.

Mark guided Emma to a chair by the fire. "We need hot water and clean bandages."

Clara moved with efficient speed, putting a kettle of water on to warm and retrieving medical supplies. The professor collapsed into another chair, removing his spectacles to wipe them with a trembling hand.

"Walker's men ambushed us," Mark explained tersely as he removed the makeshift bandage from Emma's arm that was soaked through with blood.

"How many?" Clara asked, returning with a wooden box of medical supplies.

"At least four that we saw," Mark replied.

Professor Barclay cleared his throat. "I believe, Miss Abbott, that your uncle's gold deposit has been quite definitively confirmed as valuable by Mr. Walker's determined efforts to obtain it."

Despite her pain, Emma managed a wry smile. "A rather excessive way to validate your scientific assessment, Professor."

Tommy's eyes were fixed on Emma's bloody sleeve. "Are you gonna die, Miss Abbott?"

"Tommy!" Clara admonished.

Emma shook her head. "No, sweetheart. It looks worse than it is."

"My pa got shot once," Tommy confided. "In the leg. Ma fixed him right up."

"And I'll do the same for Miss Abbott," Clara assured him.

Clara cut off Emma's sleeve to expose her injured arm. She cleaned the wound with practiced hands. "You're fortunate," she pronounced after careful examination. "The bullet carved a path through the flesh without striking bone. It'll be painful for a while, but should heal cleanly if we prevent infection."

Emma winced as Clara applied a stinging antiseptic. "I'm more concerned about our lost horses and equipment."

"The horses are secondary," Mark said firmly. "You could have been killed."

Something in his voice, a roughness, made Emma look up. His shoulders were tense beneath his mud-stained shirt, his hands clenched at his sides.

Mark's expression was carefully composed, though his eyes betrayed his concern as he assessed Emma's arm. "We need to decide our next steps," he said. "Walker is escalating matters. Today's ambush crossed a line."

"Attempted murder, in fact," Professor Barclay noted grimly. "A prosecutable offense, if we had witnesses."

"Which we don't," Mark pointed out. "And Walker will ensure his men have alibis."

Emma straightened in her chair, ignoring the throbbing in her arm. "Then we need to be more proactive. I refuse to remain besieged on my own property."

A knock at the door silenced further discussion. Mark drew his pistol, motioning for everyone to stay still as he moved silently to the window. Peering through a gap in the curtains, his posture relaxed slightly.

"It's Deputy Lewis," he announced, holstering his weapon.

He opened the door to reveal the deputy, whose eyes widened at Mark's disheveled state.

"McKay," Lewis nodded curtly before his gaze moved past to Emma, his expression shifting to alarm. "Miss Abbott! You're injured?"

"A minor wound," Emma assured him. "We had an encounter with Walker's men at the north ridge."

Lewis removed his hat as he entered, his face grim. "That's partly why I'm here. Mr. McGinty sent word that Walker's men were boasting in town about 'taking care of trespassers' on land they claimed belonged to Walker."

"Trespassers?" Emma's voice rose in indignation. "On my own property?"

"Walker's been telling folks he purchased the north section of your ranch," Lewis explained. "Even produced some paperwork claiming Thomas Abbott sold it to him before his death."

"That's preposterous!" Emma exclaimed. "My uncle would never—"

"It's a forgery," Mark interjected. "But a convincing one, I'd wager."

Lewis nodded. "Convincing enough to create confusion. I came to warn you they might try something desperate." His gaze swept over their mud-streaked clothing. "Though it appears I'm too late."

"Not entirely," Mark said. "We need to formalize a statement about today's events—and quickly, before Walker's version becomes the accepted truth."

For the next few minutes, Deputy Lewis took detailed notes as they recounted the ambush. Professor Barclay provided scientific documentation of the gold deposit, establishing a clear motive for Walker's aggressive tactics.

"This helps," Lewis said, reviewing his notes, "but it's still your word against theirs. Walker has influence with Judge Henderson, who'll likely preside over any case brought against him."

"What about the territorial marshal?" Emma suggested. "Surely, he's beyond Walker's influence."

"Marshal Collins is investigating a stage robbery near Helena," Lewis replied. "He won't return for at least two weeks."

"By which time Walker could escalate further," Mark observed grimly.

An uncomfortable silence fell over the room as the implications sank in. They were largely on their own.

"I should take the professor back to town," Lewis finally said. "He'll be safer there, and I can place his documentation in the safe at the sheriff's office."

"I'll prepare my report immediately," Professor Barclay assured them, gathering his notes and samples. "The scientific evidence is irrefutable, Miss Abbott. Your claim to the gold deposit is legitimate and documented."

Emma thanked him, rising carefully to escort their guests to the door.

"Deputy," she said quietly as they stood on the porch, "please ask Dr. Hargrove to visit at her earliest convenience. Clara has tended my wound admirably, but professional assessment would be prudent."

Lewis nodded, settling his hat back on his head. "I'll send her out first thing tomorrow. And I'll increase patrols past your property, though I can't spare men for constant guard duty."

"We understand," Emma said. "You're doing all you can."

Chapter 27

After Lewis and the professor departed, Emma returned to find Mark and Clara engaged in urgent discussion at the kitchen table. Tommy had fallen asleep on a small pallet near the fireplace, Ranger curled protectively at his feet.

"We need to move Clara and Tommy to town for safety," Mark was saying. "Today's events prove Walker won't hesitate to use violence."

Clara shook her head firmly. "No, I want to stay here."

"It's not forever," Mark insisted. "Just until—"

"Until what?" Clara challenged. "Until Walker gives up? You know he won't." She turned to Emma. "We homestead women don't abandon our land. It's all we have."

Emma sank into a chair beside them, feeling the day's events settling into her bones with leaden weight. "Clara's right. Retreat only emboldens men like Walker."

Mark's jaw tightened. "Your arm—"

"Will heal," Emma finished.

He studied her face intently, as if searching for signs she might waver. Finding none, he exhaled slowly. "You're as stubborn as your uncle was."

"I take that as a compliment," Emma replied, the ghost of a smile touching her lips.

A plan began to take shape as they talked into the evening. Clara was adamant about returning to her homestead in the morning but would check in daily. Mark would recover their horses and remaining equipment from the north ridge, being careful to avoid detection. Emma would continue normal ranch operations while adding prudent security measures.

"Walker wants us frightened and isolated," Emma reasoned. "So we'll show that we're undaunted. I'll attend Sunday services with my arm proudly bandaged and my head held high."

"A fine strategy," Clara approved. "Let everyone see Walker as the aggressor he truly is."

Mark remained skeptical. "Public opinion won't stop bullets."

"Perhaps not," Emma conceded, "but it might limit Walker's freedom to act with impunity. Even corrupt men need some public support to maintain their position."

As the evening deepened, Clara prepared a simple supper from Emma's pantry stores. They ate quietly, the day's stress and physical exertion leaving them too drained for conversation.

After the meal, Clara took Tommy to the loft to sleep, leaving Emma and Mark alone downstairs. Emma studied his profile as he stared into the fire, noticing the lines of fatigue etched around his eyes and the stubble darkening his jaw.

"You should rest," she said. "You've done more than enough today."

Mark shook his head, not looking away from the flames. "I failed you at the ridge. You could have been killed."

"Failed me?" Emma moved closer, incredulous. "Mark, you saved our lives. Without your quick thinking and knowledge of the terrain, we might never have escaped."

"I should have anticipated the ambush." Self-recrimination hardened his voice. "I knew Walker would be watching the gold deposit."

"As did I," Emma countered. "We took a calculated risk for necessary documentation. The decision was mutual."

His eyes finally met hers, burning with an intensity that caught her breath. "When I saw you fall, when I saw the blood on your sleeve..." He fell silent, unable to complete the thought.

Emma's heart quickened. She reached out, placing her hand over his where it rested on the arm of his chair. "But I'm here. We all are. Safe."

Mark's hand turned beneath hers, his callused fingers lacing with her smaller ones. The simple contact seemed to release something in him, his next words emerging with raw honesty.

"When Thomas died, I felt I'd lost the only person who truly knew me—the only one who believed in the man I could be despite my past. He was the only person in this world that cared about me." His gaze held hers steadily. "I never expected to find that again, least of all in his Boston-bred niece."

Emma felt warmth bloom in her chest, spreading outward until, surely, it must be visible on her face. "And I never expected to find understanding in a taciturn cowboy who seemed determined to maintain his solitude."

The firelight played across his features, softening them. For a moment, she glimpsed the vulnerability behind his rugged exterior—the loneliness that mirrored her own.

"God works in unexpected ways," he said quietly.

"Indeed He does." Emma smiled, feeling suddenly shy despite their shared perils. "My uncle believed you were sent to him for a purpose."

"And what purpose was that?"

"To become the son he never had," Emma replied. "He wrote that you renewed his faith in humanity during a time when he feared he'd grown too cynical."

Mark's expression softened with memory. "He renewed mine as well." He glanced down at their still-joined hands. "Thomas had a gift for seeing beyond appearances—beyond mistakes and failures. He saw possibilities where others saw only the past."

"A trait we shared," Emma said. "Though I've only recently come to appreciate it fully."

Their conversation paused as a log settled in the fireplace, sending sparks dancing up the chimney. In the momentary silence, Emma became acutely aware of the warmth of Mark's hand in hers, the steady rhythm of his breathing, the intimate space they occupied in the fire lit room.

"What possibilities do you see for the ranch now?" Mark asked, his voice lower than before. "Given what we know about the gold deposit."

Emma considered the question seriously. "I see a future where the land remains unspoiled, yet provides sufficiently for those who respect it. Perhaps limited mining carefully managed to preserve the beauty Uncle Thomas cherished. No destruction. All done by hand."

Mark nodded approvingly. "He would have appreciated that balance."

"And what do you see, Mark?" Emma asked. "For yourself, beyond the current conflict with Walker?"

The question seemed to catch him off guard. He was silent for so long, Emma thought he might not answer.

"For years, I've lived day to day," he finally said. "Planning a future seemed... presumptuous. When you're running from the past, tomorrow is as far ahead as you dare look."

"And now?" she prompted gently.

His eyes met hers, revealing emotions he rarely allowed to surface. "Now I find myself thinking about what it might mean to stop running. To clear my name. To build something lasting." He paused, his voice dropping to little more than a whisper. "To belong somewhere. To someone."

Emma's heart thundered in her chest. "I think we all yearn for belonging," she managed, her voice unsteady.

"Do you miss Boston at all? The comforts of it?" he asked unexpectedly.

"Not truly," Emma answered without hesitation. "I miss specific people—my friend Charlotte, who supported my decision to leave, my childhood nursemaid, who taught me kindness and love. But Boston itself was a beautiful cage. Here, despite the dangers, I feel alive for the first time."

Mark's thumb traced a gentle pattern on the back of her hand. "Thomas worried you might find ranch life too harsh. In his last months, he spoke often of making the house more comfortable for you."

Emma glanced around the simple but welcoming room. "He needn't have worried. This house already holds more genuine warmth than the mansion I left behind."

"Because of what he put into it," Mark said. "His character, his values." His eyes held hers. "His heart."

"Yes," Emma agreed softly. "And now it holds a piece of mine as well."

Mark's gaze dropped briefly to her lips before returning to her eyes, a question in his expression that made her breath catch.

Slowly, giving her every opportunity to withdraw, he leaned forward. Emma found herself meeting him halfway, drawn by a force both foreign and familiar. His free hand rose to gently brush her cheek, his touch reverent.

"Emma," he whispered, her name a prayer on his lips.

Their kiss was gentle, almost tentative—an exploration of newfound territory. Emma felt a tremor pass through Mark's frame as her uninjured arm slipped around his neck, drawing him closer. His restraint was evident in the careful way he cradled her face, mindful of her injured arm, yet the emotion behind his touch was unmistakable.

When they separated, both slightly breathless, Mark rested his forehead against hers.

"You are a woman with courage, Emma Abbott," he said, brushing a strand of hair from her face. "And compassion. And faith strong enough to match her determination."

A noise from above—Clara shifting in the loft—reminded them they weren't truly alone. Mark straightened reluctantly, though he kept hold of Emma's hand.

"You should rest," he said.

Emma nodded, feeling the day's exertions in every muscle. "As should you?"

Mark glanced at the door. "I should check the perimeter first."

"Of course," Emma agreed, understanding his caution was born of genuine concern rather than excessive worry.

While Mark made his rounds outside, Emma banked the fire and prepared for bed, her mind replaying their kiss with a warmth that defied her physical fatigue. She'd known attraction before—had even fancied herself in love with a young man in Boston before. But this feeling was different—deeper, more substantial, grounded in mutual respect and shared values.

When Mark returned, she was waiting with a quilt and pillow.

"All secure," he reported. "No sign of unwelcome visitors."

Emma handed him the bedding, their fingers brushing in a contact that now held new significance.

"Emma," Mark said softly, his expression earnest in the low lamplight. "What happened tonight... I want you to know I don't take it lightly."

"Nor do I," she assured him.

"Your reputation in town—"

Emma placed her fingers gently against his lips, silencing his concern. "Is secondary to the truth of what I feel for you." She lowered her hand, meeting his gaze steadily. "I've spent my life conforming to others' expectations, Mark. I came west to live authentically, according to my own heart and God's guidance."

Something eased in his expression. "And what is your heart telling you now?"

"That some journeys are meant to be shared," she replied simply. "That perhaps God brought me to Montana for more reasons than I initially understood."

Mark took her hand, pressing a kiss to her palm with surprising tenderness. "Sleep well, Emma Abbott. Dream of better days ahead."

"I shall," she promised. "And of the strength we find together."

Chapter 28

Emma woke to morning light streaming through her curtains and the mouthwatering aroma of frying bacon. For a moment, she lay still, orienting herself. Her arm ached. The events of yesterday flooding back in vivid detail—the ambush, their desperate escape through the marsh, the evening's revelations by firelight.

A smile touched her lips at the memory of Mark's kiss, so gentle yet so assured. Then reality intruded—the ongoing threat from Walker, the complexity of their situation, the careful balance they must maintain while resolving the conflict.

Rising carefully to avoid jarring her injured arm, Emma dressed in practical clothing and pinned up her hair in a simple twist.

In the kitchen, Mark was at the stove, competently turning bacon in a cast-iron skillet while coffee perked on the back burner. Clara sat at the table showing Tommy how to fold paper into animal shapes, the boy's face intense with concentration.

"Good morning," Emma greeted them, unexpectedly shy as Mark turned toward her.

His eyes softened as they met hers. "How's the arm?"

"Stiff, but manageable," she replied, accepting the cup of coffee he offered. Their fingers brushed during the exchange, a small contact that nonetheless sent warmth through her.

"You're just in time," Clara announced, standing to help Mark serve breakfast. "We've been discussing plans for the day."

Over a hearty meal of bacon, biscuits, and preserves, they finalized their strategy. Clara and Tommy would return to their homestead with Mark as escort, allowing Clara to tend to neglected chores and retrieve her journals of Walker's misdeeds. Mark would then attempt to recover their horses from the north ridge, taking a circuitous route to avoid detection.

"What about you?" Mark asked Emma, concern evident in his voice. "I don't like leaving you alone."

"I'll be fine," Emma assured him. "Dr. Hargrove is coming today to check my wound. And I have plenty of indoor tasks to occupy me."

Mark remained unconvinced. "Walker could—"

"By now, Walker probably believes any of us may have been wounded or possibly dead after yesterday," Emma reasoned. "He'll likely wait to see the outcome before making another move. He's likely got his men watching all of us very closely."

"Emma's right," Clara agreed. "Men like Walker are calculating. He won't risk further action until he assesses the results of yesterday's ambush."

Though clearly reluctant, Mark eventually conceded the point. "Keep your rifle within reach," he instructed. "And don't leave the house until I return."

"Yes, sir," Emma replied with a mock salute that drew a reluctant smile from him.

***

As they prepared to depart, Mark took Emma aside on the porch. "I'll be back by midafternoon," he promised, his voice low. "Sooner if possible."

"Take whatever time is necessary," she replied. "Clara's safety and retrieving the horses are the priorities."

He studied her face intently. "About last night—"

"I have no regrets," Emma said softly, meeting his gaze directly.

Relief washed over his features. "Nor do I. But the timing..." He glanced toward the distant hills, where danger still lurked. "There's much to resolve before we can truly explore what's between us."

"We have time," Emma assured him, touching his arm gently. "First, we secure our safety and our future here. The rest will follow as God leads."

Mark covered her hand with his own. "You've brought hope back into my life, Emma Abbott."

"And you've helped me find courage I didn't know I possessed," she replied.

He nodded, his expression softening. Then, with a quick glance to ensure Clara and Tommy were occupied with loading their belongings, he leaned down and pressed a brief, tender kiss to her lips.

"Until I return," he murmured.

Emma watched them ride away—Mark vigilant at the front, Clara and Tommy following with Ranger trotting alongside. Only when they disappeared from view, did she return inside, closing the door securely behind her.

Alone in the quiet house, Emma turned to practical matters. First, she checked her wound, carefully removing the bandage to examine the angry red furrow across her upper arm. The bullet had gouged a path through the flesh without striking bone, as Clara had noted. Though painful, it showed no signs of infection.

After re-bandaging her arm, Emma moved to her uncle's study, determined to continue her review of his journals and records. There might be additional information about the gold deposit or Walker's previous attempts to acquire the land—details that could prove useful in their current situation.

Hours passed as Emma immersed herself in detailed accounts of ranch life. Her uncle's meticulous nature extended to his record-keeping, with precise notes on everything from cattle purchases to weather patterns. Emma found herself smiling at occasional personal observations that revealed his wry humor and thoughtful perspective.

An entry from nearly two years prior caught her attention:

March 15, 1883

Jedediah Walker called on me again today with another offer for the north ridge property. Increased his bid by 20%, claiming he wishes to expand his grazing land. His interest in that particular section remains suspicious, as it offers poor pasturage compared to the eastern meadows. When I declined again, his manner turned briefly menacing before he recovered his affable facade. Must warn Mark to be vigilant during his patrols of that area.

Emma continued reading, finding several more mentions of Walker's persistent interest in the north ridge, each offer increasing in value. Her uncle had clearly grown more suspicious over time, noting in one entry:

July 8, 1883

Observed unfamiliar men examining the creek bed on the north ridge while returning from Pinecrest. They departed hastily upon noticing my approach. Suspect they were testing for mineral deposits under Walker's direction. My own discreet panning confirms what I've long suspected—there is gold in that stream, and in quantities sufficient to explain Walker's persistent interest. Will document the find privately, but make no official claim. This land's true wealth lies in its unspoiled beauty, not in metals that would bring destruction in their extraction.

A knock at the door startled Emma from her reading. Checking the mantel clock, she realized it was past noon—likely Dr. Hargrove arriving as promised. Still mindful of Mark's caution, Emma retrieved her rifle before approaching the door.

"Who is it?" she called, positioning herself to the side of the entrance as Mark had taught her.

"Dr. Emily Hargrove," came the reply. "Deputy Lewis asked me to check on you, Miss Abbott."

Relieved, Emma set aside the rifle and opened the door to reveal the doctor standing on the porch, medical bag in hand. Behind her, a buggy waited, driven by a young man Emma recognized as Dr. Hargrove's assistant.

"Please come in," Emma welcomed her. "I appreciate your making the journey out here."

Dr. Hargrove entered, her keen eyes immediately noting Emma's bandaged arm. "Deputy Lewis mentioned you'd been injured. A gunshot wound, I understand?"

Emma nodded, closing the door behind them. "A graze rather than a direct hit, thankfully."

"Let's have a look, shall we?" The doctor gestured toward the table, where the light was better.

As Dr. Hargrove examined the wound, she listened to Emma's account of the ambush, her expression growing increasingly concerned.

"This town has tolerated Walker for too long," she said as she applied a fresh bandage. "What began as questionable business practices has escalated to outright violence."

"How many have you treated that were harmed by Walker's tactics?" Emma inquired.

Dr. Hargrove nodded grimly. "Several. Most too frightened to formally accuse him. Last year, Michael Hayes—a miner who disputed Walker's claim to a promising site—was beaten so severely he couldn't work for months. The official story was that he fell down a mine shaft while intoxicated."

"And no one challenged this version of events?"

"Judge Henderson dismissed the case for lack of evidence," the doctor replied. "As he's done with every complaint against Walker."

Emma absorbed this information, her resolve strengthening. "Things cannot continue this way."

"No," Dr. Hargrove agreed, securing the bandage. "They cannot. Which is why many in town were heartened by your stand against him. You've become something of a symbol, Miss Abbott—the newcomer who refuses to be intimidated."

"I'm simply protecting what's rightfully mine," Emma demurred.

"Which is precisely what others have been afraid to do." Dr. Hargrove packed her supplies with efficient movements. "Your wound is clean and should heal nicely if you keep it dry and change the bandage daily. I'll leave additional dressings and antiseptic ointment."

Emma thanked her, walking her to the door. Before departing, the doctor paused. "We're having a community gathering tomorrow evening at the church—ostensibly to plan the summer festival, but in truth, to discuss Walker's growing threat. Your presence would be valued, Miss Abbott."

"I'll be there," Emma promised.

After Dr. Hargrove left, Emma returned to the study, her mind processing the doctor's revelations about Walker's previous victims. The pattern was clear—intimidation followed by violence against those who resisted, then official dismissal of any complaints. The system was stacked in Walker's favor, making legal recourse unlikely to succeed.

What they needed was irrefutable evidence of Walker's criminal activities—something that even a sympathetic judge couldn't ignore. Thomas's journals contained suspicions, but not proof. Professor Barclay's documentation established the value of the gold deposit but didn't connect Walker to the ambush.

Emma's thoughts were interrupted by the distant sound of approaching hoofbeats. Moving to the window, she peered out cautiously, relieved to see Mark riding alone toward the house. His expression was grim as he dismounted, and Emma hurried to meet him on the porch.

"What's happened?" she asked, immediately sensing something was wrong.

Mark removed his hat, running a hand through his hair in frustration. "Clara's house was ransacked while she was here with us. They turned over furniture, emptied drawers—searching for her journals."

"Did they find them?"

He shook his head. "No. They are safe."

Emma sighed with relief. "Thank God for that. And Clara and Tommy?"

"Shaken but resolute. I helped Clara put her home back in order." Mark's jaw tightened. "I offered to bring her and Tommy back here, but she refused."

Emma nodded. "What about our horses?"

"I found tracks indicating they were led away—probably back to town or to Walker's property."

"I sense Walker is becoming more desperate."

"Or confident," Mark countered. "Each action with no consequences emboldens him further."

They moved inside, where Emma shared Dr. Hargrove's invitation to the community meeting. Mark listened thoughtfully, considering the implications.

"It could be valuable to gauge town sentiment further," he acknowledged. "Though gathering openly might provide Walker an opportunity to identify more people who oppose him."

"Or strength in numbers might finally embolden more people to speak out," Emma suggested. "Dr. Hargrove mentioned others Walker has harmed. If we all joined together…"

"Perhaps," Mark allowed. "Meanwhile, we need to replace our horses. The ranch can't function without them."

"We could purchase new ones from Russ Miller at the livery," Emma suggested.

Mark shook his head. "Walker has likely threatened Miller not to sell to us. Walker will be watching, I'm certain. We'd need to travel to Pinecrest or beyond."

"Which requires horses in the first place," Emma noted with irony. "A circular problem."

Mark's lips quirked in a brief smile. "We could borrow Clara's wagon for the journey."

Emma considered this option. "What if," Emma began slowly, an idea forming, "what if we gave Walker an opportunity to incriminate himself?"

"What do you mean?"

Emma paced the room, her mind racing. "Walker probably believes his ambush succeeded in wounding or possibly killing one of us. What if we use that misconception? If he thought perhaps that I was seriously injured, perhaps dying, he might reveal something to the wrong person—someone he believes is sympathetic to his cause."

Mark's eyes narrowed as he followed her reasoning. "You're suggesting a deception."

"A strategic one," Emma clarified. "If Walker believed I was gravely wounded and unable to maintain my claim on the ranch, he might act prematurely, revealing his hand."

"It's risky," Mark warned. "If Walker discovers the ruse—"

"He'll be angry," Emma acknowledged. "But he's already trying to kill us. I don't see how provoking his temper makes our situation worse."

Mark considered her logic, his expression gradually shifting from concern to thoughtful calculation. "We'd need someone Walker trusts to carry the false information."

"Sophie," Emma suggested immediately. "Walker would have no reason to doubt news coming from within his own establishment."

"It could work," Mark conceded. "But we'd need to be prepared for his response. If he believes you're incapacitated, he might move against the ranch directly."

Emma squared her shoulders, wincing slightly as the movement pulled at her wound. "Then we'll be ready for him. It's time we took more of an initiative rather than merely reacting to his attacks."

The determination in her voice brought a look of admiration to Mark's face. "You are every bit as tenacious as your uncle was."

"I'll take that as high praise indeed," Emma replied with a smile.

They spent the few moments refining their plan. Mark would ride to town and discretely contact Sophie at the Silver Spur Saloon, providing her with the false information about Emma's condition. Meanwhile, Emma would prepare for a potential confrontation, ensuring defenses were in place should Walker or his men approach the ranch.

As Mark prepared to depart, Emma walked with him outside.

"Be careful in town," she cautioned. "Walker's men will be watching for you."

"I'll use the backstreets," Mark assured her, tightening the saddle cinch.

Emma nodded, her mind already calculating the next steps. "By this time tomorrow, we may have forced Walker's hand."

"For better or worse," Mark acknowledged, swinging into the saddle. His expression grew serious as he looked down at her. "Promise me you'll take no unnecessary risks while I'm gone. Walker is unpredictable when cornered."

"I promise to be prudent," Emma replied, reaching up to straighten his collar in a gesture that felt surprisingly natural. "But I won't cower in fear, either."

Mark's hand covered hers where it rested against his chest. "I wouldn't expect you to." His voice lowered. "Whatever comes, we face it together."

"Together," she affirmed, the word carrying weight far beyond its simple syllables.

With a final shared look of understanding, Mark rode away, his figure silhouetted against the afternoon sun. Emma watched until he disappeared from view, then turned back toward the house, her mind clear and her purpose firm.

Chapter 29

Emma was reading her bible later that day when the sound of approaching hoofbeats sent her heart racing. Too soon for Mark's return. She moved swiftly to the window, careful to remain hidden behind the curtain as she peered out.

Three riders approached the ranch house at a steady pace—not at the hurried gallop of an attack, but the deliberate advance of men with purpose. Emma recognized the center rider immediately: Jedediah Walker himself, flanked by Burke and another man she didn't recognize. Her stomach tightened. Walker rarely did his own dirty work.

"Lord, give me strength," she whispered, reaching for her rifle.

Emma positioned herself near the front window, where she had a clear view of the yard but remained concealed from the outside. She worked the lever action, chambering a round, and steadied her breathing. Her injured arm protested the movement, but adrenaline masked most of the pain.

The riders stopped several yards from the porch, spreading out slightly—a tactical formation that didn't escape Emma's notice. Walker dismounted first, adjusting his tailored vest with fastidious attention.

"Miss Abbott!" he called out, his voice carrying the practiced charm that had likely served him well in saloon negotiations. "I've come to pay my respects after hearing of your unfortunate accident!"

Emma remained silent, watching as Walker took several steps forward, his hands deliberately visible at his sides in a show of peaceful intentions.

"I understand you were injured yesterday," he continued, scanning the windows. "I wanted to personally express my concern and offer any assistance you might require."

Emma set the rifle within easy reach, but out of sight. She took a moment to adjust her appearance, pulling her hair loose from its pins to create a disheveled look, and used a handkerchief dampened with water to pale her complexion. She removed the neat bandage from her arm and replaced it with a hastily wrapped, blood-spotted one.

With a steadying breath, she moved back to the door, opening it partway and leaning heavily against the frame, as if requiring its support to remain upright.

"Mr. Walker," she acknowledged, her voice intentionally weak. "This is... unexpected."

Walker's eyes widened marginally at her appearance before his expression settled into practiced concern. "My dear Miss Abbott, you look terrible! I heard you'd been injured, but I had no idea your condition was so serious."

Emma allowed herself to sway slightly. "I appreciate your... concern. Though I find the timing curious, given recent events."

"Recent events?" Walker's brow furrowed in a performance of confusion. "I'm afraid I don't follow. I merely heard from one of my associates that gunshots were heard near your property yesterday, and that you might have been hurt."

"How considerate," Emma replied, permitting an edge of bitterness to enter her voice. "Though I suspect your concern has more to do with my land than my wellbeing."

"You're clearly feverish and confused, Miss Abbott. Gunshot wounds can become infected quite rapidly. Perhaps you should reconsider my previous offer—take the money and return to Boston, where proper medical care is available."

Emma gripped the door frame tighter, giving the impression of someone struggling to remain standing. "I'm not selling, Mr. Walker. Not today. Not ever."

Walker sighed, as if genuinely disappointed by her stubbornness. "Your uncle was equally obstinate, to his detriment." He stepped closer, lowering his voice. "Montana is a harsh territory, Miss Abbott. A woman alone, in your condition... it would be tragic if your situation deteriorated further without help nearby."

The threat was thinly veiled, but Emma refused to be intimidated. "I'm not alone, Mr. Walker." She straightened slightly, meeting his gaze directly. "And I'm stronger than I appear."

A flicker of annoyance crossed Walker's face. "McKay can't protect you forever. Men like him eventually revert to their true nature—or face the consequences of their past."

"Is that a prediction or a promise?" Emma challenged quietly.

Walker smiled, a cold expression that never reached his eyes. "Merely an observation based on experience. The West reveals people's true character, Miss Abbott. Some rise to the occasion; others... well, the frontier claims its share of dreams and dreamers alike."

He gestured to his men, who had remained mounted during the exchange. "I'll leave you to your recovery. My offer remains open—though the price may need adjustment given the... complications that have arisen."

As Walker turned to leave, Emma decided to bait the trap further. "Mr. Walker," she called, injecting a note of desperation in her voice as she staggered a bit for emphasis. "If my condition worsens... who might assist with legal matters? My affairs need organization, just in case..."

Walker paused, turning back with barely concealed interest. "Judge Henderson handles most legal concerns for people in the area. I'd be happy to speak with him on your behalf."

"That's very... kind," Emma replied, allowing herself to slump further against the door frame. "I may seek his counsel soon if things don't improve."

"A wise decision," Walker nodded, mounting his horse with practiced ease. "Good day, Miss Abbott. Do take care of yourself."

Emma waited until the three riders disappeared down the road before closing the door and exhaling deeply. The encounter had been unexpected but fortuitous—Walker clearly believed her injury was worse than it actually was, and he'd revealed more of his hand than he likely intended.

Her arm throbbed from the tension, and Emma unwrapped the hasty bandage, replacing it with a clean one.

Emma moved to her uncle's desk, pulling out blank paper to record the details of Walker's visit while they remained fresh in her mind. Every word, every implied threat might prove valuable when building their case. As she wrote, a plan began forming in her mind—one that might turn Walker's own schemes against him.

Chapter 30

Mark pressed himself against the alley wall as a pair of Walker's men passed by, their voices carrying in the quiet evening air.

"Boss seems mighty pleased about something," one said. "Haven't seen him smile like that in months."

"Abbott woman is worse off than we thought," the other replied with a chuckle. "Reckon she might not last a week?"

"Don't much matter. Walker's already talking to the judge about administering her property if she can't manage it."

Their laughter faded as they continued down the street, leaving Mark with a cold knot in his stomach. He'd planned to contact Sophie at the Silver Spur to initiate their deception about Emma's condition, but Walker was somehow already informed—and moving faster than anticipated.

Mark slipped through the backstreets toward Deputy Lewis's office, careful to avoid Main Street, where he'd be easily spotted. The law office was dark, but a light burned in a small corner room in the back, where Lewis sometimes slept while on duty. Mark rapped softly on the back door, three quick taps followed by two slower ones.

The door opened moments later, revealing Lewis with his gun drawn but pointed downward. Recognition dawned on his face, followed by concern.

"McKay. What's happened?"

"We need to talk," Mark replied tersely. "Privately."

Lewis ushered him inside, closing and locking the door behind them. The deputy's quarters were spartan—a narrow cot, a small table with a single chair, and a washstand. A pot of coffee simmered on a tiny stove in the corner.

"Walker's already making moves regarding Emma's property," Mark explained without preamble. "His men are saying he's in talks with Judge Henderson about administering it if she can't manage it herself."

Lewis frowned, setting his gun aside and pouring two cups of coffee. "That doesn't make sense. The judge wouldn't entertain such a notion unless Miss Abbott were incapacitated or worse."

"Which is exactly what Walker believes." Mark took the offered cup but remained standing. "We were planning to spread word that Emma's injury was more serious than it is in an attempt to bait Walker into revealing his hand. But he's somehow already convinced her condition is grave."

"Sophie," Lewis said thoughtfully. "She mentioned Walker was unusually interested when Dr. Hargrove came to town after visiting the ranch. Must have put the pieces together himself or, as I suspect, he has multiple men stationed everywhere watching and listening."

Mark nodded grimly. "And now he's accelerating his plans. How quickly could he persuade the judge to act?"

"Henderson's a corrupt old buzzard, but he maintains appearances," Lewis replied, rubbing his jaw thoughtfully. "He'd need some legal pretext—a claim that Miss Abbott is incapacitated and has no family to manage her affairs. Even then, there'd normally be notices posted, waiting periods..." He trailed off, his expression darkening. "Unless Henderson decides to bypass the usual procedures due to 'urgent circumstances.'"

"Which Walker would happily provide, no doubt," Mark said.

"I don't like this, McKay," Lewis said, setting his cup down with a decisive click. "Where is Emma?"

"At home... now I fear I shouldn't have left her alone."

Lewis regarded him for a moment. "You care for her. More than as just your employer."

It wasn't a question, and Mark saw no point in denying it. "Yes."

Lewis nodded slowly. "Then you should know Walker paid a call at the land office in Pinecrest yesterday. My counterpart there sent word this morning. He was asking about the process for contesting land claims based on verbal agreements prior to a death."

Mark's blood ran cold. "He's a scenario to suggest Thomas agreed to sell."

"Possibly... and likely has witnesses prepared to swear to it, too."

"I need to return to the ranch," Mark said, already moving toward the door. "Now."

Lewis grabbed his coat. "I'll come with you."

"What about the town?" Mark asked, knowing the deputy's sense of duty.

Lewis checked his revolver before sliding it into his holster. "Russ Miller owes me a favor. He can watch things for a few hours."

The two men moved quickly through the shadows toward the livery stable. As they approached, a figure detached itself from the darkness beside the door—Mark instinctively reached for his gun, but Lewis laid a restraining hand on his arm.

"Miller," Lewis greeted quietly. "We need your help."

Russ Miller, the burly livery owner, nodded in greeting. "Figured you might need different horses, considering." He glanced meaningfully at Mark. "Got two ready in the back stall. Best not use the main doors—Walker's men have been watching my place."

Mark eyed the man with cautious surprise. "Why help us?"

Miller's expression hardened. "Walker acquired my brother's mining claim last year after some convenient accidents. Hank never recovered from the loss—drinking himself stupid most nights now." He led them through a side entrance into the dimly lit stable. "These two are solid mounts, steady and sure-footed."

Two horses stood saddled in the back stall, one dark bay and one dappled gray. Mark ran a hand along the bay's flank, feeling the strong muscles beneath.

"What do we owe you?" Lewis asked, checking the gray's tack.

Miller shook his head. "Nothing. Just make sure Walker finally faces consequences for once." He hesitated, then added, "Word is, he visited the Abbott place earlier with his men. They returned looking mighty pleased with themselves."

Mark exchanged a grim look with Lewis. "All the more reason to hurry."

Miller handed each of them a rifle. "Take these as back up, too. Extra ammunition in the saddlebags."

"You've been planning this," Lewis observed.

A ghost of a smile touched Miller's weathered face. "I watch Walker closely. He's a mean buzzard. I assumed... just in case."

Mark mounted the bay, adjusting himself in the unfamiliar saddle. "We won't forget this, Miller."

"See that you don't," the livery owner replied. "And when this is over, I expect those horses back in the same condition they're leaving in."

Lewis chuckled as he swung into his saddle. "We'll do our best and watch over the town in my absence."

Minutes later, they were riding along the creek path, the moon providing just enough light to navigate by. Mark set a pace that balanced speed with caution—the terrain was treacherous in spots, and injuring the horses would only delay them further.

"Walker's moving faster than expected," Lewis commented as they reached flatter ground and increased their speed slightly. "If he's already convinced Emma is gravely injured, he might try to force her hand soon—pressure her to sign something while she's supposedly weakened."

Mark's jaw tightened at the thought. "Emma won't sign anything."

"But Walker doesn't know her like you do. He might think a woman alone, injured, would be easily intimidated into accepting his terms."

The mental image of Emma facing Walker's intimidation alone spurred Mark to urge his horse faster. "Let's cut across Tipper Ridge—it'll save twenty minutes."

Lewis raised an eyebrow. "That's rough country in the dark."

"Trust me," Mark replied.

With a nod, Lewis followed as Mark directed his mount off the main trail and up a narrow deer path that wound along the ridge. The terrain was challenging, requiring their full concentration, but Mark navigated with the confidence of someone who had traveled this route many times before.

As they crested the ridge, the valley opened before them, moonlight silvering the landscape. Mark's bay snorted, picking up a scent on the wind, and Mark immediately reined in, signaling Lewis to stop as well.

"What is it?" Lewis whispered, hand moving to his revolver.

Mark scanned the valley below, his eyes narrowed. "Smoke."

Following his gaze, Lewis spotted it too—a darker smudge against the night sky, rising from the direction of the Abbott ranch.

Without another word, they urged their horses forward, caution forgotten, as they galloped down the ridgeline toward the distant smoke.

Chapter 31

Emma extinguished the last of the flaming arrows with a soaked burlap sack, her lungs burning from smoke and exertion. Walker's men had struck just after sunset by launching fire arrows onto the roof of the toolshed from a distance.

When the first arrow struck the roof, setting the dry wood alight, Emma had grabbed her rifle and water buckets, fully aware she was exposing herself to potential danger. But she couldn't let the toolshed burn—not just for its value, but because the fire could easily spread to the barn nearby and surrounding dry grass.

As she worked to douse the flames, Emma had maintained a vigilant awareness of her surroundings, keeping her rifle slung across her back and positioning herself where she had clear sight lines to the property boundaries.

Now, with the immediate danger quelled, Emma stood in the yard, deliberately visible but within sprinting distance of the house if necessary. Her arm throbbed mercilessly from the exertion, blood seeping through the bandage where her wound had reopened during her efforts. She was genuinely exhausted.

"I know you're out there!" she screamed into the darkness. "If Mr. Walker wants my property, tell him to come face me himself instead of hiding behind cowardly tactics!"

Three riders emerged from the darkness—not skulking in from the tree line as she'd expected, but approaching directly up the main access road. Walker rode in front, flanked by Burke and Reynolds. Their confident approach suggested they believed her too weakened to pose any real threat.

"Miss Abbott," Walker called, his voice carrying a tone of reasonable concern that made Emma's skin crawl. "I see you've had some trouble. Fortunate, I decided to check on your condition this evening."

Emma didn't bother hiding her skepticism. "Fortunate indeed, considering the timing of this accident matches your arrival perfectly."

Walker tsked softly as he dismounted, keeping his movements slow and unthreatening. "Your injury seems to be affecting your judgment, my dear. Why would I damage property I will eventually own? Wildfires are common. A lightning strike, perhaps, or an ember from your chimney."

"Lightning from a clear sky? How convenient," Emma retorted, watching as Burke and Reynolds remained mounted, positioning themselves to flank her. She shifted slightly to keep all three men in her field of vision.

Walker advanced a few more steps, stopping when Emma's hand moved more obviously toward her rifle. "You're exhausted, Miss Abbott. Fighting a fire alone, while injured and feverish... you must see that this situation is untenable. A woman alone cannot manage a ranch of this size."

"I manage well enough," Emma replied, deliberately swaying slightly to reinforce his perception of her weakness.

Walker seized on the display, his expression softening with practiced concern. "You can barely stand. Please let me help you inside. We can discuss matters like civilized people."

Emma recognized the danger in accepting his offer, but also saw an opportunity. If she could get Walker to reveal his true intentions while she had control of the environment, it might provide the evidence they needed. She allowed her shoulders to slump in apparent defeat.

"Perhaps you're right," she conceded, her voice deliberately faint. "I should rest."

Walker smiled triumphantly, approaching with more confidence. "A wise decision. You've shown remarkable courage, but there comes a time when practicality must prevail."

Emma turned toward the house, maintaining awareness of the men's positions as she ascended the porch steps with deliberate slowness. Walker followed several paces behind, while Burke and Reynolds remained mounted, watching.

"Your men will stay outside," Emma stated, pausing at the door. It wasn't a question.

Walker nodded agreeably.

Emma entered the house first, leaving the door open for Walker to follow. She'd prepared the main room carefully earlier—a small fire burned in the hearth, adding to the impression of an invalid seeking comfort. A quilt lay across her rocking chair, and a pot of tea sat on a small table beside it, long since gone cold but preserving the appearance of an interrupted evening routine.

Most importantly, a pistol was concealed in the folds of the quilt.

Walker entered, removing his hat in a gesture of politeness that struck Emma as absurdly incongruous, given the circumstances. His eyes scanned the room with quick efficiency, noting exits and furnishings before returning to Emma.

"Please, sit," Emma invited, gesturing to a straight-backed chair positioned where the firelight would illuminate his face while leaving her partially shadowed in the rocking chair.

Walker seated himself, setting his hat aside. "I admire your composure, Miss Abbott, despite your circumstances. It's a quality I value."

"How flattering," Emma replied dryly, sinking into the rocking chair and arranging the blanket across her lap, her fingers finding the reassuring outline of the pistol beneath. "Though I know you are not here to compliment my character."

Walker smiled, the expression not reaching his eyes. "Direct as well. Another admirable trait. You're right, of course. I came because I'm genuinely concerned about your welfare—and because I believe we can resolve our... differences to mutual advantage."

"I'm listening," Emma said, leaning back as if conserving her strength.

Walker leaned forward slightly, his voice taking on a confidential tone. "Your situation has changed significantly. You're injured, feverish, isolated, and now facing a damaged toolshed that will require substantial repair. The hard truth, Miss Abbott, is that running a ranch requires the physical stamina that you currently lack."

"So I should simply sell to you and return to Boston?" Emma supplied, her tone carefully neutral.

"It would be the sensible course," Walker agreed smoothly. "I'm prepared to offer a generous sum—enough to establish you comfortably back East, or elsewhere."

Emma pretended to consider his words, watching him closely. "And if I decline?"

Something hardened in Walker's expression momentarily before he controlled it. "Then I fear your future here contains significant challenges. The territorial governor recently implemented provisions allowing for temporary administration of properties whose owners are incapacitated or unable to maintain them properly. As a concerned neighbor and established businessman, I would be the natural choice to assume temporary responsibility for your ranch."

There it was—the threat barely veiled within legal terminology. Emma felt a cold anger settle in her chest, but kept her expression neutral.

"That sounds remarkably convenient for you," she observed. "How long would such a temporary administration last?"

Walker smiled thinly. "That would depend on your recovery, of course. Judge Henderson would make the final determination based on periodic assessments of your capacity to manage the property."

"The same Judge Henderson who dismisses all complaints against you?" Emma asked innocently.

Walker's smile faltered slightly. "The judge is a fair man who understands the realities of frontier life. He recognizes that development requires certain... flexibilities in administration."

Emma allowed her gaze to drift toward the fire, as if considering her limited options. "And what of the gold on the north ridge? Would that factor into your temporary administration?"

"Yes,"

"How convenient for you," Emma remarked.

Walker's expression hardened. "You have spirit, Miss Abbott. I'll grant you that. But spirit alone won't save this ranch—or you. The realities of your situation remain unchanged. You're injured, alone, and facing circumstances beyond your capacity to manage."

He stood abruptly, moving to the window to glance outside before turning back to her. "I came here tonight prepared to be generous. My final offer is fifteen thousand dollars for the entire property—considerably above market value."

The sum was indeed substantial, reflecting Walker's desperation to acquire the gold deposit. Emma feigned consideration, her fingers remaining near the concealed pistol.

"And if I still decline?" she asked softly.

Walker's façade of civility slipped further. "Then I'll proceed with legal measures to assume control of a property whose owner is clearly incapable of managing it. Your injury, today's fire—these create a compelling case for intervention."

Emma allowed a small smile to cross her lips. "So either I sell willingly, or you'll take it anyway through legal manipulation. Not much of a choice, is it?"

"It's the only choice available to you," Walker replied bluntly. "Be practical, Miss Abbott. Even if you recovered fully, you lack the resources and connections to develop the gold deposit properly. The equipment, the workers, the processing facilities—all require capital and influence you simply don't possess."

"While you conveniently do," Emma noted.

Walker spread his hands in a gesture of pragmatic acceptance. "The West rewards those who understand its opportunities and limitations. Your uncle never grasped that—he was content to sit on valuable resources rather than developing them for progress."

"He valued the land for more than what could be extracted from it," Emma countered.

Walker's expression turned dismissive. "Sentimentality is a luxury few can afford on the frontier. Now, what is your decision? My offer expires when I leave this house."

Emma was preparing her response when a faint sound from outside caught her attention—hoofbeats approaching at speed. Walker heard it too, moving quickly back to the window.

"Expecting company, Miss Abbott?" he asked, his hand moving toward his jacket, where Emma suspected he carried a concealed weapon.

"Perhaps Deputy Lewis making his evening patrol," Emma suggested mildly, though hope surged within her. The approaching riders were moving too quickly for a casual visit.

Walker's jaw tightened as he peered into the darkness. "Burke! Reynolds!" he called. "Who's coming?"

Before his men could respond, two riders burst into the yard, pulling their mounts to a hard stop near the porch. Even in the dim light, Emma recognized Mark's distinctive silhouette immediately, with Deputy Lewis beside him. Relief flooded through her, though she maintained her composed expression.

"Unexpected developments," she observed to Walker, who had turned back to face her with barely concealed anger.

Emma tensed, ready to use the pistol if necessary. Before the situation could escalate further, heavy boots pounded across the porch, and the door burst open to reveal Mark, his expression a storm of concern and fury.

His eyes found Emma first, relief visibly washing over him when he saw her upright and alert. Then his gaze locked onto Walker, hardening instantly.

"Evening, Jed," Mark said, his voice deceptively casual, though his stance was anything but relaxed. "Bit late for a social call, isn't it?"

Walker's hand moved away from his concealed weapon as Deputy Lewis appeared in the doorway behind Mark, his badge visible on his vest.

"McKay," Walker acknowledged coldly. "Still involving yourself in matters that don't concern you, I see."

"Miss Abbott's welfare concerns me greatly," Mark replied, moving to stand beside Emma's chair, his position deliberately protective without blocking her agency.

Walker glanced between them, his expression calculating. "I see. Well, this explains much about her unusual attachment to this property. Thomas's loyal dog has found a new master—or should I say mistress?"

Emma rose from her chair with deliberate grace, letting the blanket fall away. "My answer remains unchanged, Mr. Walker. This land is not for sale—not at any price."

Walker's expression darkened. "You're making a grave mistake. Your situation—"

"Is not nearly as dire as you've been led to believe," Emma finished for him, "and Deputy Lewis can attest to my sound mind and complete capacity to manage my own affairs."

Lewis stepped forward, his thumbs hooked in his belt near his holster. "That I can, Miss Abbott. In fact, I'd be happy to provide a sworn statement to that effect for the territorial records—just to prevent any... misunderstandings about your competence."

Walker recognized the trap closing around him. His scheme to declare Emma incapacitated would fail if the local law enforcement officially documented her fitness. He forced a tight smile.

"I see you've outmaneuvered me for the moment, Miss Abbott. I underestimated your... resourcefulness."

"A common mistake when dealing with women," Emma replied with a pleasant smile that didn't reach her eyes.

Walker retrieved his hat, settling it on his head with deliberate calm. "This changes nothing in the long term. Gold brings its own complications—claim jumpers, development costs, transportation challenges. A refined lady from Boston will find such matters... overwhelming."

"Then it's fortunate I'm becoming less refined by the day," Emma countered.

Walker turned to leave but paused in the doorway, looking back at Mark. "She doesn't know everything about you, does she, McKay? When she does, we'll see if her faith in you remains so steadfast."

Mark stepped forward, tension radiating from his frame. "Your threats are getting tiresome, Jed. Or should I call you James Wallace, as you were known in Colorado?"

Walker's face blanched momentarily before his composure returned. "Be careful with accusations, McKay. Especially given your own... history."

"The difference is, his history is based on lies you created," Emma said, moving to stand beside Mark. "While yours is a documented fact."

Walker's eyes narrowed. "Documented? By whom?"

"Concerned citizens with long memories," Lewis supplied. "Amazing what people remember when given the chance to speak freely."

For the first time, genuine uncertainty crossed Walker's face. He glanced between the three of them, reassessing the situation.

"This isn't over," he said finally, his voice cold.

"No," Emma agreed. "But it soon will be."

After Walker departed, with Burke and Reynolds trailing behind him, Emma sank into the rocking chair, the evening's tension catching up with her. Mark was at her side instantly, kneeling to examine her blood-soaked bandage with gentle hands.

"The wound reopened," he observed, his voice tight with concern.

"Fighting the fire," Emma explained, wincing as he carefully peeled back the edge of the bandage. "Walker's men shot flaming arrows onto the barn roof. I couldn't let it burn."

"Of course you couldn't," Mark said, a hint of proud exasperation in his tone. "Deputy, there's clean bandaging in the kitchen cabinet."

As Lewis went to retrieve the medical supplies, Mark's eyes met Emma's, searching her face. "When we saw the smoke... I thought—" He broke off, unable to complete the sentence.

Emma reached up to touch his cheek, her heart swelling at the genuine fear and relief she saw in his expression. "I'm all right, truly. The fire was meant to flush me outside, make me seem more vulnerable than I am."

"It nearly worked," Mark said grimly.

"But it didn't," Emma replied. "And now we have more evidence of Walker's methods—and his plans. He admitted to seeking legal means to control the property based on claims of my incapacity."

Lewis returned with bandages and a bowl of clean water. "I heard most of your conversation through the window," he confirmed. "Walker was explicit enough about his intentions that it could be considered coercion, especially combined with the fire coincidentally occurring just before his arrival."

"Will it be enough?" Emma asked, wincing slightly as Mark began cleaning her reopened wound.

Lewis's expression was cautiously optimistic. "Combined with Professor Barclay's documentation of the gold deposit establishing motive, Clara's journal recording previous incidents, and Sophie's testimony about conversations she's overheard at the saloon... it's building into a compelling case. We need to avoid Judge Henderson, but the territorial marshal might take notice when he returns."

"In two weeks, correct?" Mark asked, applying fresh bandaging with gentle efficiency.

"Should be back within the week. I received a telegram earlier this afternoon letting me know," Lewis replied. "Walker is clearly accelerating his plans, so we need to stay vigilant and hope he makes a mistake."

Emma nodded thoughtfully, an idea forming as Mark finished bandaging her arm. "What if we accelerated our plans as well? The community meeting tomorrow evening at the church—we could use it to consolidate evidence and testimonies from everyone Walker has wronged."

"A public forum would make it harder for Henderson to dismiss the collective complaints," Lewis agreed, warming to the idea. "And if multiple respected citizens sign sworn statements and take a stand against him..."

"We'd still need to get those statements to the territorial marshal directly," Mark cautioned. "Walker has intercepted official communications before."

"Then we'll send a trusted messenger," Emma decided. "Someone Walker wouldn't suspect."

Chapter 32

Emma awoke to the sound of hammering coming from outside. Sunlight streamed through her bedroom window as she sat up quickly, wincing at the sharp pain in her injured arm. She pushed aside the quilt and walked to the window.

Mark worked steadily, replacing the scorched boards on the toolshed roof. His movements were precise and economical, each strike of the hammer deliberate. He was shirtless, and Emma watched the play of muscles across his back as he worked.

She turned away from the window, her cheeks warm.

Within minutes, Emma had dressed in a simple work skirt and blouse. She plaited her hair in a single braid. Her injured arm throbbed, but she ignored.

On the kitchen table sat a pot of coffee, still warm, and a plate with biscuits covered by a cloth. Beside it lay a note in Mark's bold handwriting: Eat something. You need your strength.

A smile touched Emma's lips as she poured herself coffee. Mark's concern warmed her heart. After Walker's departure last night,

Deputy Lewis had stayed for an hour, helping them formulate their plan for the community meeting. Mark had insisted she rest while they discussed the details, but Emma had remained firmly involved in the planning.

When Lewis finally departed, the lingering emotions between her and Mark had been palpable. Something had further shifted between them during the confrontation with Walker last night—a deeper understanding, a shared purpose that went beyond employer and employee.

Now, as she sipped her coffee and stared out the kitchen window, watching Mark work, she couldn't deny that she had fallen in love with him.

She finished her breakfast and headed outside, pulling on her work gloves as she crossed the yard.

"You should be resting," Mark called down from the roof when he spotted her.

"And you should know better than to expect that," Emma replied with a smile. "What can I do to help?"

Mark shook his head, but the corner of his mouth twitched upward. "Nothing up here. I'm nearly finished, anyway." He drove in one final nail and moved toward the ladder. "But we need to start preparing for tonight's meeting. Deputy Lewis will be here at noon with the documents."

As Mark descended the ladder, Emma noticed the dark circles under his eyes. "Did you sleep at all?"

"Enough," he answered, reaching the ground. He retrieved his shirt from where it hung on the ladder and slipped it on, buttoning it quickly. "I patrolled the property line every few hours. Walker's men were watching from the ridge, but they didn't approach."

"You can't keep this pace forever," Emma said softly. "You need rest too."

Mark's expression softened. "I'll rest when you're safe." He gathered his tools, deliberately breaking the moment of intimacy. "Professor Barclay sent word that he's completed his mineral survey. The documentation is all safely in the sheriff's office in the safe."

Emma followed him toward the house. "Have you heard from Clara? Is she coming?"

"She'll be here with Tommy this afternoon. She's bringing all her journals." Mark paused at the water pump to wash his hands and splash water on his face. "Russ Miller is spreading word among the ranchers. Samantha Turner is reaching out to the women in town."

Emma handed him a towel. "And Sophie? Will she be able to testify about what she's overheard at the saloon?"

Mark's expression darkened. "That's more complicated. Walker keeps his saloon girls under close watch. If he suspects Sophie is helping us..."

"Then we need to get her out," Emma said firmly.

Mark dried his face and hands, studying her with an intensity that made her heart quicken. "You've changed since you arrived in Blue Ridge."

"For better or worse?" she asked, trying to keep her tone light.

"You were brave from the start," Mark said. "But now you're a fighter, too."

His words warmed her more than they should have.

The sound of approaching horses drew their attention.

"Expecting anyone?" Mark asked.

Emma shook her head, squinting against the sun to see the approaching riders.

"It's Clara and Tommy. They're early," Mark said.

Indeed, Clara Jacobs rode toward them on her dappled mare, with young Tommy perched in front of her. As they drew closer, Emma could see Clara's face was tight with worry.

"What's wrong?" Emma called as they approached.

Clara reined her horse to a stop in the yard. "Walker's men have been asking about the meeting," she said without preamble. "They visited three families this morning, making threats, suggesting it would be 'unwise' to attend any gathering that might be 'detrimental to the town's interests.'"

Mark helped Tommy down from the horse, while Emma assisted Clara.

"Who did they threaten?" Mark asked.

"The Wilsons, the Grants, and us," Clara said, her voice steady despite the fear in her eyes. "Two men came just after breakfast. They said it would be a shame if our roof caught fire while we slept."

Tommy clutched Mark's hand, looking up with solemn eyes. "I wasn't scared," he insisted. "But Ma said we should come here where it's safer."

Emma knelt despite her protesting arm and met Tommy's gaze. "Your ma is very wise. And very brave, just like you."

Clara touched her son's shoulder. "Tommy, why don't you check on those new kittens in the barn that Miss Emma told you about last time?"

The boy's face lit up. "Can I?"

"Stay within shouting distance," Mark instructed, ruffling the boy's hair.

As Tommy raced toward the barn, Clara's composed facade crumbled slightly. "I wasn't sure where else to go."

"You did exactly right coming here," Emma assured her. "We'll protect each other." She glanced at Mark. "This changes our plans for the meeting. If Walker is intimidating people…"

"We need to move up the timetable," Mark finished. "If Walker knows about the meeting, he might already be planning to disrupt it."

Clara nodded grimly. "That's what I thought, too. But what can we do? Some folks will be too scared to come now."

Before either Mark or Emma could respond, another set of riders appeared on the horizon.

"Popular morning," Mark muttered, positioning himself slightly in front of the women as he squinted at the approaching figures. After a moment, his posture relaxed. "It's Lewis. And Patrick McGinty with him."

The deputy and the storekeeper rode into the yard moments later, both men looking grim.

"We have trouble," Lewis announced as he dismounted. "Walker's intimidating folks all over town. Patrick here came to warn me after Walker's men visited his mercantile."

McGinty nodded, his usually cheerful face serious. "They made it clear my store might suffer unfortunate accidents if I supported any 'slander' against Walker." His Irish brogue thickened with anger. "As if his reputation deserves any respect!"

"They threatened a few families this morning as well," Emma explained. "Clara and Tommy just arrived, seeking refuge."

"Walker's moving fast. He must have informants who told him about the meeting," Deputy Sam said.

"We're losing our advantage of surprise," Mark said.

"What are we going to do?" Clara asked. "If people are too frightened to attend the meeting…"

Emma straightened her shoulders, her mind racing through possibilities. "We bring the meeting to them."

Four pairs of eyes turned to her questioningly.

"If people are afraid to gather in one place, then we divide and conquer," Emma explained, her idea taking shape as she spoke. "We split into pairs, visit as many families as we can personally, and collect their testimonies and signatures privately."

Mark nodded slowly. "It could work. People might speak more freely in their own homes without fear of Walker's men watching who attends a public gathering."

"We'd need to move quickly," Lewis added. "Cover as many households as possible before Walker realizes what we're doing."

"And we'd need to gather together after we finish and safely hide the testimonies outside of town until the territorial marshal arrives," Clara pointed out as she turned to Deputy Sam. "I wouldn't put it past Walker and his men to destroy the sheriff's office if they even think you were harboring mounting evidence against them."

McGinty snapped his fingers. "The old missionary church! Father Simmons left years ago, but the building still stands empty beyond the creek outside of town."

"Perfect," Emma said. "We'll need paper, ink, and reliable messengers to coordinate between teams."

"I've plenty of both at the store," McGinty offered. "And my nephew Seamus has quick feet and knows how to keep secrets."

Lewis nodded decisively. "Then it's settled. We'll divide the town and outlying farms among us. Collect as many testimonies as possible today, meet at the missionary church at sundown, and consolidate our evidence."

"What about Sophie?" Emma asked. "We still need her testimony about Walker's conversations in the saloon."

A shadow crossed Mark's face. "I'll handle that. I'll slip into the back entrance of the saloon. Sophie usually takes breaks in the kitchen."

Emma felt a spike of worry. "That's too dangerous. If Walker catches you…"

"It's our best option," Mark countered gently.

"Fine, but you don't go alone. Take Deputy Lewis with you."

Lewis nodded. "Agreed. I'll position myself near the saloon in case of trouble."

"Then I'll pair with Clara," Emma said. "We can visit the families on the east side of town."

"And I'll take the west side," McGinty offered.

"What about Tommy?" Clara asked, glancing toward the barn, where her son was visible playing with the barn kittens.

"He can stay here with Samantha Turner," Emma suggested. "She's coming this afternoon to help prepare for the meeting. She'll look after him."

"Then we have a plan," Lewis said firmly. "McGinty, ride back to your store and gather supplies. I'll meet you there in an hour, and we'll distribute the supplies to everyone."

As the men mounted up, Mark pulled Emma aside. "Are you sure about this? Your arm is still healing, and if Walker's men spot you…"

"I'll be careful," Emma promised. "And I'll have Clara with me. We'll avoid any direct confrontation if possible." She squeezed his arm. "Just promise me the same. Don't take unnecessary risks at the saloon."

Something flickered in Mark's eyes—a tenderness that made Emma's breath catch. "I'll come back to you," he said softly. "That's a promise I intend to keep."

The intensity of his gaze held her for a long moment before he turned away to confer with Lewis. Emma pressed a hand to her racing heart, trying to compose herself.

Clara approached, a knowing smile on her face. "That man cares deeply for you."

Emma flushed. "And I care for him. We've been through a lot together."

Emma watched as Mark and Lewis rode out, heading toward town. McGinty followed shortly after, promising to send his nephew with supplies as soon as possible.

"We should prepare," Emma said, turning to Clara. "We'll need to decide which families to visit first."

Clara touched Emma's good arm. "First, you need to change that bandage. You're still bleeding."

Emma glanced down at her arm, surprised to see fresh blood seeping through the white cloth. In all the excitement, she'd barely noticed the pain.

"I suppose you're right," she conceded.

As they walked toward the house, Emma cast one last look at Mark's retreating figure. A prayer rose unbidden in her mind: Lord, keep him safe. Bring him back to me.

Chapter 33

The Silver Spur Saloon stood quiet in the afternoon heat, most of its patrons either sleeping off the previous night's excesses or working until the evening's entertainment began. Mark surveyed the building from the shadows of the alley across the street, noting the positions of the two men lounging on the front porch.

"Walker doubled his security," Lewis observed quietly from beside him. "Those aren't his usual doormen."

"No," Mark agreed. "And both are carrying guns and know how to use them."

"How do you want to play this?" Lewis asked.

Mark studied the building's layout once more. "The door to the saloon in the back alley. The kitchen staff use it during the day. Sophie should be preparing for the evening rush now, mostly alone."

"And if she's not?"

"Then we retreat and find another way," Mark said firmly.

Lewis nodded. "I'll create a distraction at the front. Nothing obvious—just enough to keep the men's attention away from the back.

I'll move around to cover the rear exit if I can. If all else fails, meet me at the Livery as soon as possible."

Mark agreed with the plan, and they separated, with Lewis heading toward the main street while Mark circled through backyards and service lanes to approach the saloon from behind.

The back alley was deserted except for a mangy dog picking through discarded food scraps. Mark approached the door cautiously, listening for voices inside. Hearing none, he knocked softly—three taps, a pause, then two more.

The door opened a crack, and Sophie's wary eyes peered out. They widened in recognition.

"Mark! What are you—" She glanced nervously over her shoulder before whispering, "You shouldn't be here."

"I need to talk to you," Mark replied quietly. "It's important."

Sophie hesitated, then opened the door just wide enough for him to slip inside. The kitchen was warm and smelled of baking bread and stewing meat. A large pot simmered on the stove, but otherwise, the space was empty.

"Everyone's out front or upstairs resting," Sophie explained, wiping her hands on her apron. "But Walker could return any minute. He's been in and out all day, angry about something."

"That something is a meeting we have planned for tonight," Mark explained quickly. "He found out about it and started threatening folks. We need your help now more than ever. You've heard things working here—conversations, plans. Your testimony could be crucial."

Sophie wrapped her arms around herself, suddenly looking very young and scared. "If I speak against him, he'll know it was me. No one else would have heard those private conversations."

"We can protect you," Mark promised. "Once the territorial marshal has the evidence—"

"The marshal won't be here for days," Sophie interrupted. "What happens to me in the meantime?"

"What if we got you away from here? Somewhere safe until the marshal arrives?"

Hope flickered briefly in Sophie's eyes before dimming. "Where? Blue Ridge is Walker's town. And I can't just disappear—he'd send men to find me."

Before Mark could respond, a floorboard creaked overhead. Sophie froze, her eyes darting to the ceiling.

"You need to go," she whispered urgently.

Mark hesitated, unwilling to leave without securing her help.

"Please," Sophie begged. "I'll think about what you've said, but you need to leave now."

The sound of footsteps on the stairs decided the matter. Mark squeezed Sophie's hand in silent promise and slipped back out the door just as voices became audible from the saloon's interior.

He pressed himself against the wall beside the door, listening.

"Sophie! Where's that stew?" a gruff male voice called.

"Coming, Mr. Burke," Sophie replied, her voice admirably steady. "Just checking the bread."

"Walker wants extra food prepared tonight. He's invited Judge Henderson and some business associates for a private meeting."

Mark's jaw tightened. Walker was gathering his allies.

The conversation continued inside, but Mark had heard enough. He needed to warn the others about this development. He moved silently down the alley.

As he rounded the corner of the building, a figure stepped directly into his path.

"Well now, if it isn't the loyal ranch hand," Jedediah Walker said, his voice smooth as silk and twice as dangerous. He held a small derringer casually in his right hand, the barrel pointed squarely at Mark's chest. "A bit far from the ranch, aren't you?"

Mark kept his expression neutral, his mind racing through escape options. Walker stood alone, but that didn't mean reinforcements weren't nearby.

"Just picking up supplies," Mark replied evenly.

Walker's smile didn't reach his eyes. "In the back alley behind my establishment? How convenient." He gestured with the derringer. "I think we should continue this conversation somewhere more private. My office, perhaps?"

"I'm expected back at the ranch," Mark said, making no move toward the saloon. "Miss Abbott will send people looking if I'm delayed."

"Miss Abbott is busy with her own... activities today," Walker replied.

Mark weighed his options. Refusing would likely result in Walker calling for his men, while agreeing might provide an opportunity to gather intelligence about Walker's plans.

"After you," Mark said finally, gesturing for Walker to lead.

Walker chuckled. "Oh no, I insist. You first." He motioned with the derringer toward a side door of the saloon.

Mark had no choice but to comply, acutely aware of Walker following closely behind, the small but deadly pistol trained on his back. The side door led to a narrow hallway used by the saloon's private customers who preferred discretion.

"Up the stairs, then first door on the right," Walker directed.

Mark climbed the stairs, his mind cataloging every detail of the building's layout for potential escape routes. The upstairs hallway was dimly lit, with four doors leading to private rooms and one larger door at the far end that Mark assumed was Walker's personal quarters.

The first door on the right opened into a lavishly appointed office with a large desk, leather chairs, and bookshelves filled with ledgers and bound folios. Walker gestured Mark inside, then closed and locked the door behind them.

"Please, sit," Walker invited, indicating one of the chairs opposite the desk.

Mark remained standing. "I prefer to stand."

Walker shrugged, lowering himself into the chair behind the desk, though he kept the derringer visible. "Suit yourself. Though this may take some time."

"What do you want, Walker?"

"Direct, as always," Walker observed, leaning back in his chair. "I've always appreciated that about you, McKay. No pretense, no games. Just straightforward action." He set the derringer on the desk, within easy reach, but no longer pointing directly at Mark. "It's why I found it so useful to frame you in Colorado."

The casual admission of guilt surprised Mark, though he kept his expression impassive. "Is that supposed to anger me?"

"No, it's meant to remind you that I'm always several steps ahead," Walker replied. "Just as I am now. Your little evidence-gathering expedition today? Already compromised. Half the people you're counting on won't talk, and the other half will lie to protect their interests."

Mark said nothing, letting Walker continue.

"You see, loyalty is a commodity in places like Blue Ridge," Walker explained. "Some buy it with money, others with fear. I prefer a combination—the carrot and the stick, so to speak." He opened a drawer and removed a sheet of paper. "For instance, this statement from Eli

Granger, testifying that he saw you tampering with Miss Abbott's barn the night it caught fire."

Mark's jaw tightened. "Granger would never sign that."

"Not willingly, perhaps," Walker conceded. "But when faced with losing his blacksmith shop or signing a simple piece of paper... well, men make practical choices."

"What's your point?" Mark demanded, fighting to maintain his composure.

Walker leaned forward. "My point, McKay, is that you're fighting a losing battle. And I have something you don't—respectability, business connections, and a clean record."

Mark remained silent, unwilling to reveal how deeply Walker's words cut.

"But it doesn't have to be this way," Walker continued, his tone shifting to something almost conciliatory. "I'm prepared to offer you a way out—a chance to leave this territory with a clean slate and enough money to start fresh elsewhere."

"In exchange for what?"

"Something very simple," Walker smiled thinly. "Convince Emma Abbott to sell me her ranch."

Mark couldn't contain a short, disbelieving laugh. "You can't be serious."

"Entirely serious," Walker insisted. "She trusts you. Values your opinion. Ask her to go away with you, start a life together somewhere else. Make up whatever you want. Just convince her to sell to me."

"And if I refuse?"

Walker's smile vanished. "Then I'll ensure the territorial marshal receives sworn statements about your activities in Colorado—amended, of course, to include violent crimes beyond the original accusations. Your bounty will increase tenfold, and you'll spend the rest of your life looking over your shoulder or end up in jail or hanged."

Mark's mind raced.

"How do I know you'd keep your end of the bargain?" Mark asked, feigning consideration of the offer.

Walker's expression brightened, sensing victory. "I'd provide written confirmation that all charges against you were fabricated—to be held by a neutral third party until the sale is complete. Help me acquire the Abbott ranch, and you walk away a free man with five thousand dollars in your pocket. Oppose me, and you'll surely die."

Mark took a moment to appear contemplative. "I'll need time to consider this."

"Of course," Walker agreed magnanimously. "You have until tomorrow morning. Eight o'clock, at Miss Abbott's ranch. I'll arrive to discuss the sale, and you'll have convinced her it's the sensible option." His eyes hardened. "Don't disappoint me, McKay. You've seen what happens to those who do."

Mark nodded curtly, turning toward the door. "We're finished here then."

"For now," Walker agreed, unlocking the door. His voice dropped to a menacing whisper. "If you warn the deputy about our little chat, I'll know. I have eyes everywhere in this town."

Mark left without responding, his face betraying nothing. He descended the stairs and exited through the side door, expecting at any moment to feel a bullet in his back. But Walker let him go, confident in the trap he'd laid.

Once outside, Mark stuck to the back alleys, circling away from the saloon. Deputy Lewis waited anxiously in the shadow of the livery stable.

"What happened?" Lewis demanded when Mark appeared.

"Walker intercepted me," Mark explained tersely. "Made me an offer to betray Emma in exchange for clearing my name."

Deputy Sam nodded his head, "The bounty on your head... we can talk about that later. Did he mention the evidence gathering?"

"He knows," Mark confirmed grimly. "Claims he's already intimidated half the town into silence."

"This is not good."

"We proceed as planned. But we need to be more careful. Walker is meeting with Judge Henderson tonight, likely planning countermeasures."

"What about Sophie?" Lewis asked.

Mark shook his head. "She's scared, and with good reason. I wasn't able to secure her testimony."

Lewis sighed. "We should head back to the ranch and warn Emma about Walker's knowledge of our plans."

As they retrieved their horses from behind Miller's livery, Mark wrestled with whether to tell Lewis more about Walker's ultimatum.

"There's something else," Mark said finally as they mounted up. "Walker's coming to the ranch tomorrow morning, expecting me to have convinced Emma to sell."

"And will you?"

"No," he said firmly. "But we can use his visit to our advantage. If we can get Walker to reveal his plans, his threats, while witnesses are present..."

Lewis nodded slowly. "It could strengthen our case. But it's risky, especially for Emma."

"Which is why we'll be prepared," Mark insisted. "We'll have trusted men hidden on the property, ready to intervene if Walker tries anything."

The deputy studied him for a long moment before nodding. "All right. But we tell Emma everything. This affects her most directly, and she deserves to make her own decisions."

"Agreed," Mark said, nudging his horse forward. "Let's go. We have a lot to prepare before sundown."

Chapter 34

Emma reviewed the signed testimonies as she sat at the table in her home, a sense of cautious hope building within her. She and Clara had gathered sworn statements documenting Walker's intimidation, fraud, and other misdeeds, while Samantha, who sat nearby, had watched over Tommy.

"This is all more awful than I expected. Walker is a terrible, vindictive devil of a man," Clara said, organizing the papers into neat piles. "And now he is threatening people. I fear this is going to get worse. He's dangerous."

"Some threats have the opposite effect," Emma observed. "They remind people what they're fighting against."

Tommy sat, contentedly drawing pictures, at the far end of the table while the women worked.

"Do you think testimonies will be enough?" Samantha asked.

"We can't be certain, but these testimonies alone reveal a pattern. Each testimony together paints a picture of systematic corruption, intimidation, and violence. The others being gathered can only add to this horrible tapestry of evil."

Clara nodded in agreement. "And Professor Barclay's mineral survey provides a clear, documented motive for Walker's interest in the ranch property."

The sound of approaching horses drew their attention. Emma moved to the window, relieved to see Mark and Deputy Lewis riding into the yard.

"They're back," she announced, noting the grim expressions on both men's faces. "Something's happened."

She hurried outside to meet them, Clara and Samantha following close behind.

"Walker knows about our plan," Mark said without preamble as he dismounted. "He intercepted me near the saloon."

Emma's heart lurched. "Are you hurt?"

"I'm fine," Mark assured her, though the tension in his jaw suggested otherwise. "But Walker's gathering his allies tonight—Judge Henderson and others."

Lewis dismounted more slowly, his expression troubled. "We need to pray Walker does not catch on to our plan to meet at the missionary church."

"We should leave soon. Sunset is less than two hours away," Emma said.

"There's more," Mark said, glancing at Lewis before continuing. "Walker's coming here tomorrow morning. He expects me to have convinced you to sell the ranch by then."

Emma's eyes widened. "What?"

Mark explained his encounter with Walker, including the offer to clear his name in exchange for betraying her. His voice remained steady, but Emma could see the anger tightly controlled beneath his calm exterior.

"He's desperate," Emma concluded when Mark finished.

"Or he's confident in his position and is simply offering you a last chance to sell before he takes more drastic measures," Clara suggested worriedly.

"Either way, we need to be prepared for his visit tomorrow," Lewis said. "If Walker comes here expecting compliance and finds resistance instead..."

"He'll show his true nature," Emma finished.

Mark shook his head. "It's too dangerous. If Walker feels cornered, there's no telling what he might do."

"I'm not afraid of Jedediah Walker," Emma stated firmly.

"You should be," Mark replied, his voice tight with concern. "I've seen what he's capable of when his interests are threatened."

Emma stepped closer to him, lowering her voice. "And I've seen what I'm capable of when my home is threatened. I won't hide or run, Mark."

Something flickered in his eyes—pride, admiration, and something deeper that made Emma's heart race.

"No one's suggesting you run," Lewis interjected pragmatically. "But we can take precautions. I'll position trusted men around the property early tomorrow—out of sight, but close enough to intervene if needed."

"And I'll stay the night here," Samantha offered.

"And Tommy and I will return here after the meeting tonight as well," Clara added. "Safety in numbers."

Emma nodded gratefully. "Thank you. All of you." She turned back to Mark, who still looked troubled. "We'll face him together. That's how we've handled everything else."

After a moment, Mark nodded reluctantly. "But we take every precaution."

"Agreed," Emma said. "Now, we should prepare for the meeting tonight."

As the group moved inside to complete their preparations, Mark gently caught Emma's arm, holding her back.

"There's something else Walker said," he told her quietly when the others were out of earshot. "He claimed he will get a sworn statement from Eli Granger, saying I sabotaged your barn before the fire."

Emma's brow furrowed. "That's absurd. Eli would never—"

"Not willingly," Mark agreed. "But Walker implied he will threaten Eli's livelihood to secure his cooperation."

"Then we'll speak to Eli at the meeting tonight and warn him," Emma decided.

Mark's expression remained troubled. "Walker's desperate and dangerous. I don't want you anywhere near him tomorrow morning."

Emma placed her hand over his where it still rested on her arm. "I know you're concerned, but this is my fight, too. My ranch, my future."

The intensity in Mark's eyes made her breath catch. "Your safety matters more than any ranch."

***

As sunset approached, Emma changed into a fresh blouse in her bedroom and prayed, asking God to watch over them all.

Mark waited alone in the main room, standing by the window with a distant expression.

"The others are loading the wagons," he explained without turning as she entered the room. "Lewis thinks it's safer if we all travel together."

Emma approached slowly, concerned by the tension evident in his posture. "What's troubling you?"

Mark turned to face her, his expression conflicted. "If something goes wrong tomorrow morning..."

"It won't," Emma assured him.

"But if it does," he persisted. "If Walker brings more men than we anticipate, if the situation turns violent..."

"Then we'll handle it as we've handled everything else," Emma said firmly. "With courage and faith."

Mark shook his head, his eyes never leaving hers. He stepped closer, close enough that she could feel the warmth radiating from him. "You know that I would never accept Walker's offer to clear my name by conning you into selling this property, right? I would never do that. Not at any price."

"I know that," Emma said.

"No, you don't understand," Mark insisted. "It's not just loyalty or honor that keeps me fighting alongside you. It's—"

Mark hesitated, his intense blue eyes searching hers, vulnerability evident in his expression, unlike anything Emma had seen from him before.

"It's that I've come to care for you deeply, Emma," he finally said, his voice low and earnest. "More than I thought possible."

Emma's breath caught in her throat. The world seemed too narrow to just this moment, this room, this man standing before her with his heart in his eyes.

"When I came to Montana, I was running from the past," Mark continued. "I never expected to find a future worth fighting for. But then you arrived, determined and fearless, and everything changed." His hand reached up tentatively to brush a stray strand of hair from her face. "Whatever happens, my loyalty isn't just to this land or your uncle's memory. It's to you."

Emma's heart pounded in her chest. She had suspected his feelings mirrored her own, but hearing the words spoken aloud made them real in a way that both thrilled and terrified her.

"The wagons are ready! We need to leave now if we want to make the meeting before dark!" Deputy Lewis called from outside.

Mark's hand fell away, though his eyes remained locked with hers.

"We should go," Emma said reluctantly, though she made no move toward the door.

"Emma," Mark said, her name almost a plea on his lips.

Before she could reconsider, Emma closed the small distance between them and placed her hand on his chest, feeling his heart beating rapidly beneath her palm.

"I care for you too," she whispered. "I have fallen in love with you. And when this is over—when Walker no longer threatens everything—we'll have time to discover what that means for both of us."

The smile that transformed Mark's face took her breath away. It was unguarded, genuine, illuminating features usually kept carefully controlled. Without hesitation, he covered her hand with his own, squeezing it gently.

"I love you," he said simply.

Chapter 35

Emma sat wedged between Mark and Deputy Lewis on the narrow bench seat of the wagon, acutely aware of Mark's steady presence beside her.

The sun hung low on the horizon, painting the mountains in shades of amber and purple. Any other evening, Emma might have paused to appreciate the beauty, but tonight her thoughts remained fixed on the meeting ahead—and on Walker's impending visit tomorrow.

"We should arrive just before the others," Lewis said, breaking the contemplative silence.

"You think Walker's men are watching us?" Mark asked, his eyes scanning the tree line as they traveled.

"Possibly," Lewis replied. "I haven't seen any yet, but that doesn't mean they aren't out there."

Emma clutched the oilskin packet containing the testimonies closer to her chest. "We need to be vigilant."

As they rounded the bend that led to the missionary church, Emma spotted several horses and wagons already gathered in the small clearing. The church windows glowed with lamplight, warm squares of yellow against the darkening landscape.

"More people than I expected," Mark observed, tension evident in his voice.

Lewis nodded grimly. "Word spreads fast when people sense change coming."

The deputy slowed the wagon as they approached, allowing Mark to scan the surroundings before they came to a complete stop. Emma noted the subtle nod between the men before Mark jumped down and extended his hand to help her from the wagon.

His fingers closed around hers with a firm gentleness that sent warmth spreading through her despite the evening chill. Their eyes met briefly, the connection between them deeper now that words had finally been spoken.

"Stay close," he murmured as her feet touched the ground.

Professor Barclay hurried from the church steps to meet them, his normally composed academic demeanor replaced by barely contained excitement.

"You've arrived just in time," he said breathlessly. "We've received unexpected support!"

"What kind of support?" Lewis asked, reaching to help Clara down from the wagon behind theirs.

Before Barclay could answer, the church door swung open to reveal Reverend Thompson and a man Emma didn't recognize—tall, broad-shouldered, with the unmistakable bearing of authority. His well-worn duster couldn't disguise the practiced way he surveyed the newcomers, nor the slight bulge of a holstered pistol beneath his coat.

Mark stiffened beside her. "Marshal Collins."

"He's back early?" Lewis said, surprise evident in his voice.

"Apparently, the circuit judge sent urgent word," Barclay explained, walking with them toward the church. "Something about suspicious land transactions requiring immediate attention."

Emma caught the meaningful glance that passed between Mark and Lewis. The pieces were falling into place faster than they'd anticipated.

"The Lord works in mysterious ways," Clara murmured beside her.

As they entered the church, Emma was struck by the number of people gathered. Nearly thirty townspeople filled the simple wooden pews, their expressions ranging from determined to fearful. McGinty stood near the altar in animated conversation with Dr. Hargrove and Lydia Williams. Josiah Smith occupied a corner bench, looking distinctly uncomfortable but nodding respectfully as they entered.

The conversations hushed as Marshal Collins stepped forward. His weathered face remained impassive, though his eyes lingered on Mark with unmistakable recognition.

"Deputy Lewis," he acknowledged, before turning to Emma. "And you must be Miss Abbott."

"Marshal," Emma greeted him with a respectful nod. "I'm pleased you could join us. We hadn't expected your return until next week."

"Nor had I expected to cut my circuit short," Collins replied.

Something in his tone suggested he knew more than he was revealing. Emma exchanged a glance with Mark, whose posture remained alert, ready for trouble.

"We've gathered testimonies documenting Jedediah Walker's activities," Emma explained, holding out the oilskin packet. "Intimidation, property destruction, fraudulent claims—"

"And a falsified murder charge in Colorado," Mark added quietly.

The marshal's eyes narrowed slightly. "That's a serious accusation, Mr. McKay."

Mark held his gaze steadily. "One I'm prepared to substantiate."

A moment of tense silence stretched between them before Reverend Thompson cleared his throat. "Perhaps we should begin the meeting? Many folks here have traveled some distance despite the risks."

Collins nodded. "Of course. Let's hear what your community has to say."

The marshal gestured toward the front of the church, and the group moved forward. Emma noticed Mark hanging back slightly, his wariness evident. She slowed her pace to walk beside him.

"Are you all right?" she whispered.

"I don't trust coincidences," Mark replied softly. "The marshal returning early, just as we're gathering evidence against Walker..."

"You think he's aligned with Walker?"

"I think we need to be cautious." His hand brushed hers briefly. "Until we understand his intentions."

They took seats in the front pew as Professor Barclay and Deputy Lewis organized the presentation of testimonies. Emma watched as McGinty stood to speak first, describing Walker's control of freight prices and how it affected the merchants of Blue Ridge.

One by one, the townspeople came forward. A rancher described cattle mysteriously disappearing after he refused to sell land adjacent to Walker's holdings. Lydia Williams detailed threats made against her late husband's newspaper when he attempted to investigate Walker's business dealings. Dr. Hargrove explained how medical supplies had been "delayed" after she treated a homesteader Walker wanted removed.

The pattern grew clearer with each testimony—a systematic campaign of intimidation and control stretching back years, touching every aspect of life in Blue Ridge.

When Clara stood to read from her journal, documenting dates and details of incidents she'd recorded, Emma felt the mood in the church shift. These weren't just isolated grievances, but evidence of corruption that had infected the entire community.

Throughout the presentations, Marshal Collins listened without comment, his expression inscrutable. Occasionally, he made notes in a small leather-bound book, but he asked no questions, offered no reactions.

Finally, Professor Barclay presented his mineral survey of the Abbott property, explaining the geological formations that indicated significant gold deposits.

"This provides a clear motive for Mr. Walker's persistent interest in the property," Barclay concluded. "And explains his increasingly aggressive tactics since Miss Abbott's arrival."

As the professor returned to his seat, Marshal Collins closed his notebook and surveyed the assembled townspeople.

"You've presented compelling accounts," Collins said finally. "But accusations alone aren't sufficient for legal action."

A ripple of disappointment moved through the gathering. Emma felt Mark tense beside her.

"However," the marshal continued, as he reached into his coat and withdrew a folded document. "I received this telegraph from the Colorado territorial authorities. It seems new evidence has emerged in an old murder case—evidence that exonerates the primary suspect and implicates someone else entirely."

Emma's heart raced. Mark sat perfectly still beside her, his breathing measured and controlled.

"The suspect who fled arrest was known in Colorado as Mark McKay," Collins continued, his eyes finding Mark in the crowd. "A man incorrectly charged with murdering Harrison Pierce, who worked in Silver Creek, Colorado, at the assayer's office and was also a mining inspector investigating fraud in several operations near Denver."

A murmur rippled through the church. Many eyes turned toward Mark, who met the marshal's gaze unflinchingly.

"New testimony places James Wallace, now known as Jedediah Walker, at the scene of the crime," Collins said. "And establishes his motive for eliminating Inspector Pierce, who had uncovered evidence of Walker's widespread criminal activities."

The marshal's words hung in the air for a moment before the church erupted in whispers. Emma reached for Mark's hand, finding it clenched in a tight fist on the pew between them. She covered it with her own, feeling it gradually relax beneath her touch.

"I don't understand," Deputy Lewis said, rising from his seat. "How did this information surface after all this time?"

Collins's expression remained neutral. "It seems Mr. Wallace—or Walker—made enemies in Colorado, just as he has here. One of his former associates recently found religion on his deathbed and made a full confession to authorities, including details of how Walker arranged Pierce's murder and framed McKay."

The marshal turned his attention fully to Mark. "The Colorado authorities have formally withdrawn all charges against you, Mr. McKay."

Emma felt the shudder that passed through Mark at these words, complete freedom he had not dared hope for, delivered unexpectedly in a small church in Montana Territory.

"What about Walker?" someone called from the back of the church. "Will he be arrested?"

Collins held up a hand for quiet. "I have a warrant for Jedediah Walker's arrest on charges of murder, fraud, and corruption in

Colorado Territory. However, I'd like to add territorial charges based on his activities here, which would prevent him from ever returning should he somehow evade the Colorado justice system."

The marshal turned to Deputy Lewis. "That's where your collected testimonies become valuable, deputy. They establish a pattern of behavior consistent with his crimes in Colorado and provide grounds for additional charges here in Montana Territory."

Hope surged through the gathering, reflected in straightened postures and animated whispers. Emma squeezed Mark's hand, feeling him return the pressure with equal intensity.

"What's the plan, Marshal?" Lewis asked.

"Walker doesn't know I've returned," Collins replied. "Nor does he know about the Colorado warrant. That gives us an advantage." He scanned the church. "I understand he plans to visit the Abbott ranch tomorrow morning?"

Emma nodded. "He expects me to agree to sell the property."

"Then we'll be waiting for him," Collins said decisively. "We'll position men around the property tonight. When Walker arrives in the morning, we'll serve the warrant and take him into custody."

"He won't come alone," Mark warned. "He'll have men with him."

"Neither will we," the marshal assured him. "I've already deputized four reliable men from Pinecrest who accompanied me back to Blue Ridge. With Deputy Lewis and yourself, Mr. McKay, we should have sufficient manpower to handle Walker and his associates."

Collins addressed the broader gathering. "I'll need three volunteers to ride to surrounding ranches tonight to warn them of possible resistance from Walker's remaining men after the arrest."

Hands shot up immediately. The marshal selected three riders, giving them instructions before turning back to Mark and Emma.

"Miss Abbott, I'd recommend you and Mrs. Jacobs remain in town tonight for safety. Walker may have men watching your ranch already."

"No." Emma's response was immediate and firm. "If Walker has men watching the ranch and sees it empty, he'll suspect something's wrong. He needs to believe tomorrow morning will proceed as he expects."

Mark nodded in agreement. "Emma's right. Walker's suspicious by nature. Any deviation from normal patterns will alert him."

Marshal Collins considered this, then nodded reluctantly. "Very well. Deputy Lewis, you go with them. Stay hidden in Miss Abbott's home tonight and then exit before dawn in the morning before Walker arrives."

The meeting concluded with arrangements for the morning's operation. As people began to disperse, many approached Mark to offer congratulations on his exoneration. Emma watched his stunned reactions to each handshake and back slap, the reality of his freedom still sinking in.

While Mark was occupied, Marshal Collins approached Emma privately. "Miss Abbott, there's something else you should know."

She turned to him, noting the gravity in his expression. "What is it, Marshal?"

"The deathbed confession in Colorado mentioned more than just Inspector Pierce's murder," he said quietly. "The man also implicated himself and Walker in the death of your uncle."

Emma's blood ran cold. "My uncle? But his death was attributed to natural causes."

"According to the confession, Walker and this man visited your uncle shortly before his death, threatening him over the gold discovery. Allegedly, poison was slipped into your uncle's beverage." Collins watched her carefully. "I can't prove it, of course. But I thought you should know."

Emma struggled to maintain her composure as this new information settled in her mind.

"Thank you for telling me, Marshal," she managed finally. "All the more reason to see justice served tomorrow."

Collins nodded grimly. "Indeed, Miss Abbott. Indeed."

Chapter 36

The return journey to the ranch proceeded in tense silence. Emma sat between Mark and Deputy Lewis again, but this time with Clara beside her on the crowded bench. Two of Marshal Collin's deputies followed behind in her wagon, maintaining a discreet distance.

Night had fallen completely, the wagon's lantern casting just enough light to illuminate the rutted road. Stars pricked the vast Montana sky, countless pinpoints of light in the darkness.

"Are you all right?" Clara asked, noticing Emma's distant expression.

Emma nodded, though her mind still reeled from the marshal's revelation about her uncle. "Just thinking about tomorrow."

"It will all be over soon," Clara reassured her. "One way or another."

From Emma's other side, Mark shifted and reached for her hand in silent support. The small contact steadied her, reminding her of their earlier conversation and the promise of what might come after Walker was gone.

As they approached the ranch, Lewis extinguished the lantern. They proceeded the final quarter-mile in darkness, alert for any sign of Walker's men watching the property.

"No obvious lookouts," Lewis murmured as the house came into view, a dark silhouette against the starlit sky. "But that doesn't mean they're not there."

He stopped the wagon a hundred yards from the house. Lewis and Mark helped the women down.

"We need to approach normally," Mark instructed quietly. "As if returning from a regular church meeting. Once inside, keep lantern light to a minimum and stay away from windows."

Emma nodded, taking Clara's arm as they walked the remaining distance to the house. Every shadow seemed to hold potential danger, every rustle in the surrounding bushes a possible observer.

They reached the porch without incident. Mark insisted on entering first, checking each room before allowing the others inside. When he finally signaled the all-clear, Emma felt the tension drain from her shoulders.

Lewis moved to the kitchen. "I'll make a pot of coffee. It's going to be a long night."

Clara followed him, offering to prepare a light meal for everyone. Left alone in the main room of the home with Mark, Emma finally had a moment to absorb everything that had happened at the meeting.

"You're free," she said, watching his profile in the dim light filtering through the windows. "The charges are withdrawn."

Mark turned to her, his expression a complex mixture of disbelief and relief. "I'm glad it's all formally documented, but I've sensed for some time that I was no longer a wanted man," he admitted. "I assumed things were developing behind the scenes—after all, if I were still truly wanted, someone would have come for me by now. I also sensed Deputy Lewis knew of my bounty and didn't act on it... for what reasons, I may never know." He paused, his shoulders relaxing slightly. "Still, I couldn't bring myself to trust the justice system completely."

"What will you do now?" Emma asked, suddenly afraid of his answer. Would he stay? Or would he choose to start fresh somewhere else, somewhere without the shadows of his past?

Mark stepped closer, his eyes never leaving hers. "That depends largely on you, Emma Abbott."

Her breath caught. "On me?"

"Earlier today, I told you I care for you," he said, his voice low and intense. "That hasn't changed. But now, instead of offering you a man with a price on his head and a false murder charge hanging over him, I can offer you someone with a future. A real future."

Emma's heart pounded as she absorbed his words. "I didn't care about the charges, Mark. I cared about you—who you are, not what someone falsely accused you of being."

A ghost of a smile touched his lips. "That's one of the many reasons I love you."

The word hung in the air between them, simple yet profound. Love. Not caring, not affection, but love—clear and unambiguous.

Lewis appeared in the doorway. "One of the marshal's deputies just checked in. All outbuildings are safe, no one hiding within, the horses in the barn are fine. A rider was spotted on the ridge to the north. Probably one of Walker's men keeping watch."

Mark stepped back slightly, though his eyes remained on Emma. "Good to know. We'll need to plan our positions for the morning carefully."

Lewis nodded. "Clara's made sandwiches. We should eat while we can, then get some rest in shifts. I'll remain in the kitchen throughout the night. The marshal deputy and I will converse through the window or the back door in the kitchen."

"I'll take first watch from the front of the house then," Mark offered.

With a final meaningful glance at Emma, he followed Lewis toward the kitchen. Emma remained rooted in place, his declaration echoing in her mind.

Love.

Her uncle's journals had described love as the most transformative force in human experience. Standing there in the dimly lit room, feeling the certainty blooming in her own heart, Emma finally understood what he meant.

Chapter 37

The night passed slowly, each hour marked by changing watches and whispered reports. Emma managed a few hours of restless sleep. Mark refused to rest, moving between watch positions.

Before dawn, Marshal Collins came. They gathered in the kitchen, keeping their voices low as they finalized positions for Walker's arrival.

"Walker typically travels with at least two men," Lewis explained, indicating points on a rough map Mark had drawn of the property. "Burke and Reynolds, most likely."

Mark nodded in agreement. "They'll approach from the main road, expecting no resistance more than likely."

"My men are positioned here, here, and here," Collins said, marking locations that provided coverage of all approaches to the house. "Lewis, you'll take the north side near the corral. McKay, you'll remain inside with the Emma as planned. Clara, Tommy, and Samantha stay in the loft hidden and make no sounds."

Emma sat at the table, Clara beside her with a comforting hand on her arm. "What if Walker suspects something? What if he doesn't come?"

"He'll come," Mark said with certainty. "His greed won't let him miss this opportunity."

Collins checked his pocket watch. "First light in 30 minutes. Everyone to positions. No one moves until I give the signal."

The men dispersed silently, each heading to their assigned location. Emma and Clara remained at the table, while Mark positioned himself near the front window, where he could observe the approach road without being seen.

The house was quiet, the predawn stillness broken only by the soft ticking of the mantel clock. Emma found herself counting heartbeats, each one bringing them closer to confrontation.

Clara opened the Bible, reading silently by the faint light of dawn beginning to filter through the windows. After a moment, she found a passage and turned the book toward Emma.

"Be strong and courageous," Emma read softly. "Do not be afraid; do not be discouraged, for the Lord your God will be with you wherever you go."

"Joshua 1:9," Clara said with a gentle smile. "My husband read it to me on our wedding day, and again before every challenge we faced together."

Emma squeezed her friend's hand gratefully.

From the front room, Mark's voice came in a harsh whisper. "Riders coming."

Emma and Clara exchanged glances before moving carefully to join him. Kneeling below the window level, Emma peered over the sill at the approaching riders.

Three men on horseback moved at a leisurely pace toward the house. Walker rode in front, dressed more formally than usual in a black coat and vest. Burke and Reynolds flanked him, their hands resting casually near their holstered pistols.

"Just as expected," Mark murmured. "Walker's dressed for business. He's expecting to leave here with a signed deed."

Emma swallowed hard, her mouth suddenly dry. Despite all their preparations, the sight of Walker approaching sent a chill through her.

"I'll be right beside you," Mark promised, sensing her anxiety. "Just follow the marshal's plan."

The riders drew closer, their features becoming more distinct in the early morning light. Walker's expression showed confidence bordering on smugness. He clearly anticipated no trouble.

"Burke's peeling off toward the barn," Mark noted. "Reynolds is staying with Walker."

Emma watched as Walker and Reynolds dismounted, tying their horses to the hitching post before approaching the porch.

"Places," Mark whispered, helping Emma to her feet.

Clara retreated to the loft while Mark moved to stand beside the door, out of sight from the entrance. Emma took her position in the center of the room, facing the door with her shoulders squared and chin lifted in defiance.

Three sharp knocks echoed through the house.

"Miss Abbott," Walker called, his voice pleasant, but carrying an undercurrent of authority. "Jedediah Walker, here to see you, as arranged."

Taking a deep breath, Emma moved to open the door. Walker stood on the threshold, hat in hand, his smile not reaching his eyes.

"Good morning, Miss Abbott," he greeted her smoothly.

"Please come in, Mr. Walker," Emma replied with forced civility, stepping aside to allow him entry.

Walker entered confidently, Reynolds following a step behind. Both men stopped abruptly when they spotted Mark standing by the wall.

"McKay," Walker acknowledged, his smile faltering slightly. "I see you're still... advising Miss Abbott."

"I am," Mark answered evenly.

Walker's eyes narrowed as he assessed the situation. "I had hoped our discussion yesterday might have clarified certain realities for you both."

"It certainly clarified things for me," Mark agreed, his tone deceptively casual. "Though perhaps not in the way you intended."

A flash of uncertainty crossed Walker's face before his confident mask returned. He turned his attention back to Emma. "Miss Abbott, I've brought the paperwork for the sale. Fifteen thousand dollars. A very fair price for a property."

Emma met his gaze steadily. "I'm afraid I won't be selling the ranch—not today, not ever."

Walker's expression hardened. "I strongly advise you to reconsider. Montana Territory can be very dangerous for a woman alone. As you've experienced firsthand."

The threat hung in the air between them. Behind Walker, Reynolds shifted his weight, his hand drifting closer to his holstered pistol.

"Are you threatening Miss Abbott?" Mark asked, his voice dangerously quiet.

Walker smiled thinly. "Merely stating facts about frontier life."

"I believe I'll manage just fine... Mr. Wallace," Emma replied calmly.

The color drained from Walker's face.

"I don't know what you're talking about," Walker said stiffly.

"I think you do," came Marshal Collin's voice from the doorway. He stood with his badge displayed prominently, Deputy Lewis beside him. "James Wallace, I have a warrant for your arrest on charges of murder and fraud in Colorado Territory."

Walker's hand moved toward his jacket, but Mark was faster. In one fluid motion, he drew his pistol and aimed it squarely at Walker's chest.

"I wouldn't," Mark advised quietly.

Walker froze, his eyes darting between the marshal and Mark, calculating odds that were rapidly deteriorating. Outside, shouts indicated that Burke had encountered Collins's deputies near the barn.

"This is absurd," Walker blustered. "I've never even been to Colorado!"

"Strange," Collins remarked, entering the room with his own weapon drawn. "Because Harrison Pierce's murder was witnessed by your associate Mitchell Reed, who recently provided a detailed confession before his death."

Walker's face contorted with rage. "Reed was a drunk and a liar!"

"He was dying and seeking redemption," Collins corrected. "And his testimony is corroborated by documents recovered from his possession—documents that outline your mining fraud operation in considerable detail."

Lewis moved forward to disarm Reynolds, who surrendered without resistance. Outside, the sounds of struggle had ceased, suggesting Burke had been similarly subdued.

"You have nothing," Walker snarled, desperation edging into his voice. "No proof that would stand in court."

"We have Reed's sworn testimony," Collins countered. "We have financial records. And now, thanks to the good people of Blue Ridge, we have evidence of your continued pattern of intimidation and fraud here in Montana Territory."

Walker's gaze snapped to Emma, hatred burning in his eyes. "You," he hissed. "Just like your uncle—too stubborn to recognize a good offer when it's presented."

"My uncle," Emma said softly, her voice steady despite the anger rising within her. "Whom you threaten up to his death?"

"Thomas Abbott was a fool who undervalued what he had. Like niece, like uncle, it seems."

Collins nodded to Lewis. "Take him into custody, Deputy."

As Lewis moved to handcuff him, Walker made his final desperate play. With surprising speed for a man his age, he reached into his coat and withdrew a small derringer pistol concealed in an inner pocket.

Several things happened simultaneously: Reynolds shouted a warning; Mark lunged toward Emma, pushing her to the floor; Lewis drew his weapon; and Clara, peered over the loft's edge at exactly the wrong moment and gasped.

Walker swung his pistol toward the sound, aiming at Clara. Without hesitation, Mark fired.

The shot echoed deafeningly in the confined space. Walker staggered backward, the derringer falling from his grasp, unfired. He looked down in disbelief at the spreading crimson stain on his expensive vest before crumpling to the floor.

Marshal Collins rushed forward to examine Walker. After a moment, he looked up and shook his head.

"He's gone," he pronounced.

A heavy silence fell over the room, broken only by Clara's quiet prayers from where she knelt in the loft. Emma remained on the floor where Mark had pushed her, his protective arm still around her shoulders.

"A clean shot," Collins said. "Necessary force in defense of others. I'll note that in my report."

Lewis escorted a subdued Reynolds outside to join Burke in custody. Collins followed, instructing two deputies to handle Walker's body.

Emma trembled violently. The confrontation, Walker's threats, the sudden violence—it overwhelmed her carefully maintained composure.

Mark helped her to sit on the rocking chair, his own hands not entirely steady. "Are you hurt?" he asked urgently, examining her for injuries.

"No," Emma managed. "Just... shaken."

Clara brought a glass of water, which Emma accepted gratefully.

"I'm sorry you had to witness that," he said, his voice rough with emotion. "I never wanted—"

"You saved Clara's life," Emma interrupted. "Maybe mine too. There's nothing to apologize for."

Mark's thumbs traced gentle circles on the backs of her hands. "It's over now," he said. "Really over."

The reality of those words settled over them both. Walker was gone. The threat he represented to her land, to Mark's freedom, to their future—all of it had ended in that single chaotic moment.

"What happens now?" Emma asked.

Mark's eyes met hers, steady and sure. "Now we begin again. Without shadows, without threats. Just us and whatever we choose to build together."

"Together," Emma repeated, the word carrying all her hopes, all her newfound certainty. "I'd like that very much."

Mark smiled—a real smile that transformed his entire face. "So would I."

From outside came the sounds of activity as the marshals prepared to transport Walker's body and the prisoners to town.

"Before all this," Mark said hesitantly, "I told you something important. Something I've never said to anyone before."

Emma nodded, her heart quickening. "You said you love me."

"I do," he confirmed, his voice gaining confidence. "I love you, Emma Abbott. Your courage, your determination, your compassion for others. I love who I am when I'm with you—not a fugitive, not a ranch hand, but a man worthy of standing beside you."

Emma raised her hand to his face, tracing the strong line of his jaw with gentle fingers. "And I love you, Mark McKay. I think I have from the first day I met you."

Mark turned his head slightly to press a kiss to her palm. "Even when I was gruff and suspicious?"

"Especially then," Emma admitted with a small laugh. "Because even at your most guarded, you still chose to help me, to teach me, to protect me."

Mark rose from his kneeling position on the floor. He gently pulled Emma to a standing position and drew her gently into his arms. Emma went willingly, resting her head against his chest, feeling the steady beat of his heart beneath her cheek.

"Your uncle would be proud of you," Mark murmured into her hair. "You've protected his land, brought justice to the man who threatened him, and built a place for yourself in this community."

Emma smiled against his shirt. "I think he'd be proud of us both."

"He gave me a chance when no one else would," Mark said quietly. "And now, because of you, I have a future I never thought possible."

Emma lifted her head to look into his eyes. "What does that future include, Mark McKay?"

His gaze was tender as he brushed a strand of hair from her face. "Whatever you want it to include, Emma Abbott. I'm not a wealthy man, but I know this land. I can help you build the ranch into everything you want it to be. Or if you prefer to return to Boston eventually—"

"No," Emma interrupted firmly. "My future is here. With you."

The joy that spread across Mark's face made her heart swell. Slowly, giving her every opportunity to pull away, he lowered his head until his lips hovered just above hers.

"May I?" he whispered.

In answer, Emma closed the remaining distance between them, pressing her lips to his in a kiss that held all the promise of their newly secured future.

The kiss deepened, tender yet insistent, a sealed covenant between them. When they finally parted, Emma knew with absolute certainty that she had found her true home—not in the ranch house around them or the land stretching to the horizon, but in the arms of the man who had risked everything to stand beside her.

Outside, boots sounded on the porch steps. Reluctantly, they moved apart as Marshal Collins entered.

"The prisoners are secured," he reported. "We'll be heading to town shortly. Miss Abbott, I'll need a formal statement from you when you're feeling up to it."

"Of course, Marshal Collins. I'll come to town this afternoon."

Collins nodded, his gaze moving between Emma and Mark with a knowing assessment. "Mr. McKay, I've sent a telegraph to Colorado confirming your exoneration. The official documentation should arrive within the week."

"Thank you, Marshal," Mark said. "For everything."

After Collins departed, Emma and Mark stepped onto the porch to watch the procession of lawmen, prisoners, and Walker's body begin the journey toward Blue Ridge. The morning sun bathed the ranch in golden light, the mountains rising majestically in the distance.

Clara, Samantha, and Tommy joined them.

"It's over" Clara said.

Emma nodded. "It's over."

Clara smiled knowingly at the sight of Emma and Mark standing close together, their shoulders touching. "No, my dear," she corrected gently. "I believe it's just beginning."

As if to confirm her words, Mark's hand found Emma's, their fingers intertwining naturally. Emma smiled up at him, seeing in his eyes the same certainty that filled her heart.

The future stretched before them—uncertain in its details but secure in its foundation. Together, they would build something lasting on this Montana land, a legacy worthy of Thomas Abbott's dreams and their own newfound love.

The Lord's plan, Emma reflected, had been greater and more wonderful than anything she could have imagined when she first stepped off that stagecoach in Blue Ridge. Through trial and danger, she had found not just a home, but a partner with whom to share it.

"What shall we do first?" Emma asked, surveying the ranch that was now without threat or shadow.

Mark smiled, lifting their joined hands to press a kiss to her fingers. "Marry me, Emma Abbott."

Epilogue

Emma smoothed the front of her dress for the tenth time as the wagon rattled down the path toward Blue Ridge. Mark, beside her on the bench seat, reached over and captured her restless hand in his.

"You're certain about this?" he asked, his voice steady but his eyes searching hers. "We could wait, have a proper ceremony with more preparation."

Emma squeezed his hand in return. "I've never been more certain of anything in my life." She smiled as the morning's events replayed in her mind. Not two hours after Walker's body had been taken away, she and Mark had stood in her kitchen, planning their next steps.

"I don't want to wait," she'd told him decisively. "Not after everything we've faced. Life is too precious, too uncertain."

Mark had looked at her with such tender intensity that her breath caught. "Today, then," he'd agreed. "If Reverend Thompson is willing."

Now, as Blue Ridge came into view, Emma felt a curious blend of nervousness and complete certainty. The town looked different somehow—brighter, more welcoming without Walker's shadow hanging over it.

Small clusters of townspeople gathered on the boardwalks, watching their approach with undisguised interest. News of Walker's death had clearly outpaced their wagon.

McGinty stood outside his store, waving enthusiastically as they passed. "Abbott! McKay!" he called.

Mark reined in the horses. "It's over. Thank you for all your help."

The storekeeper's face split into a broad grin. "This calls for a celebration!"

"We may have other plans," Emma said, exchanging a meaningful glance with Mark that didn't escape McGinty's notice.

His eyebrows shot up. "Is that so?" The shopkeeper's gaze dropped to their clasped hands, and his smile widened further. "Well, I'll be..." He touched the brim of his hat. "Congratulations in advance, then."

They continued toward the church, aware of curious eyes following their progress. Emma sat straighter, chin lifted, unembarrassed by the attention. Let them look. Let them see what choosing one's own path could lead to.

The church stood quiet and unassuming at the end of the main street. Its whitewashed exterior gleamed in the midday sun, the simple cross above the door a beacon of the faith that had sustained them through their recent trials.

Mark helped Emma down from the wagon, his touch lingering a moment longer than necessary. "Ready?" he asked softly.

Emma nodded, and together they climbed the steps to the church door. Mark knocked firmly.

Moments later, Reverend Thompson appeared, his expression shifting from polite inquiry to warm recognition. "Miss Abbott, Mr. McKay. I've just heard about this morning's events. Please, come in."

He ushered them into the cool dimness of the church.

"Reverend," Emma began, suddenly finding words difficult. "We've come to ask—"

"We'd like you to marry us," Mark finished for her, his voice steady. "Today, if possible."

The Reverend's bushy eyebrows rose, but his smile was genuine. "I see." He gestured to the front pew. "Please, sit. This is a significant decision, especially coming so soon after this morning's traumatic events."

They sat side by side, shoulders touching, while Reverend Thompson pulled a chair to face them.

"You've both experienced profound changes recently," the Reverend said gently. "The end of a threat, the clearing of Mr. McKay's name. These are reasons to celebrate, certainly. But marriage is a lifetime commitment before God."

"It's not impulsive, Reverend," Emma assured him. "Perhaps in timing, but not in conviction."

Mark nodded. "I've cared for Emma since she first arrived in Blue Ridge. I simply didn't have the right to act on those feelings until now."

"I'm ready to build a life with Mark," Emma said.

Reverend Thompson studied them both, his kind eyes moving from one face to the other. "You're both certain? Marriage on the frontier is no easy undertaking, even without the unusual circumstances that have brought you together."

"The circumstances may be unusual," Mark acknowledged, "but our feelings aren't. If anything, facing danger together has only confirmed what we already knew."

The Reverend smiled. "Very well. I'd normally suggest a period of formal engagement, but frontier life often requires practical adjustments to traditional practices." He leaned back in his chair. "I can perform the ceremony this afternoon. But first, I'd like to speak with each of you separately—a brief pastoral counseling that I require of all couples, no matter how hasty or elaborate the wedding."

Emma and Mark exchanged glances, then nodded in agreement.

"Excellent. Mr. McKay, perhaps you could step outside while I speak with Miss Abbott? There's a bench in the small garden behind the church."

Mark squeezed Emma's hand before rising. "I'll be right outside."

When they were alone, Reverend Thompson looked at Emma. "You've had quite a journey since arriving in Blue Ridge, Miss Abbott."

"I have," Emma agreed. "Nothing like I expected when I left Boston."

"Life rarely follows our expectations," the Reverend observed. "The Lord often has other plans, greater than we can imagine. Jeremiah 29:11 reminds us, 'For I know the plans I have for you, plans to prosper you and not to harm you, plans to give you hope and a future.'"

Emma smiled. "My uncle Thomas was fond of that verse. He quoted it in one of his final letters to me."

"A wise man, your uncle." The Reverend's expression grew more serious. "Now, tell me honestly, Emma. This decision to marry Mark—is it influenced by gratitude for his protection? By the heightened emotions of danger and its resolution?"

Emma considered the question carefully. "I won't deny those experiences have deepened my feelings," she admitted. "But they didn't create them. I began to care for Mark slowly... when he taught me to ride western-style, when he patiently explained ranching techniques, when I saw his gentle care for the land and animals."

"And his past? The accusations, though now disproven?"

"Never mattered," Emma said firmly. "I judged Mark by his actions, not by others' words about him. Just as I hope to be judged myself."

Reverend Thompson nodded approvingly. "And your faith? Will it be a cornerstone of your marriage?"

"It will," Emma affirmed. "Both Mark and I have experienced God's provision in unexpected ways."

The Reverend patted her hand. "I believe you, my dear. Let me speak with Mr. McKay now."

Emma switched places with Mark, taking her turn on the garden bench. The small enclosed space behind the church offered a peaceful respite, with late summer wildflowers blooming along the simple picket fence. She traced the worn wooden slats of the bench, wondering what other brides had sat here before her, hearts full of hope for the future.

Inside, Mark sat across from Reverend Thompson, his posture straight but not tense. "I assume you have many questions for me, Reverend."

"I do, Mr. McKay. Marriage is not a commitment I take lightly, nor should you." The Reverend leaned forward. "Emma Abbott is an educated, well-bred young woman who has chosen a difficult path for her life. What can you offer her that would make such sacrifices worthwhile?"

Mark didn't answer immediately, giving the question the consideration it deserved. "Materially? Nothing. I have some savings, skills with livestock and land management, and now that my name is cleared, the freedom to conduct business openly."

"And beyond that?"

"Loyalty. Protection. Partnership." Mark met the Reverend's gaze directly. "I can offer Emma my complete commitment to her happiness and wellbeing. I can promise to respect her independence while standing beside her through whatever challenges we face. And I can give her my word that I'll never stop trying to be worthy of the trust she's placed in me."

Reverend Thompson nodded slowly. "And your faith, Mr. McKay?"

"My faith is... practical," Mark admitted. "I believe in a God who sees worth in each person, who offers second chances. I've experienced that grace through Thomas Abbott and now through Emma. I may not be eloquent in matters of theology, but I'm committed to living honorably before God and man."

"Well said." The Reverend stood. "I believe you and Emma are entering this marriage with clear eyes and sincere hearts. I'd be honored to perform the ceremony today."

Mark's relief was visible. "Thank you, Reverend."

"I suggest three o'clock this afternoon. That will give you time to make necessary preparations, and me time to ready the church." He smiled. "Though simple, a wedding should still be treated as the sacred occasion it is."

"Of course," Mark agreed. "We'll return at three."

When he stepped into the garden, Emma rose immediately, searching his face. "Well?"

Mark's slow smile told her everything. "Three o'clock today. We're getting married, Emma."

She threw her arms around his neck, propriety forgotten in the private garden. Mark's arms encircled her waist, lifting her slightly as he embraced her.

"I want to tell Clara," Emma said when they separated. "And we'll need witnesses."

Mark nodded.

They thanked Reverend Thompson once again and departed, only to find the town's grapevine had indeed been busy. Mildred Harper intercepted them before they'd gone ten paces from the church.

"Is it true?" she demanded, eyes bright with excitement. "Are you two getting married today?"

Emma blinked in surprise. "How did you—"

"Honey, a blind man could see what was between you two," Mildred chuckled. "And McGinty isn't exactly known for his discretion."

Mark laughed. "Yes, it's true. Three o'clock today, if you'd like to attend."

Mildred clasped her hands together. "Oh, I wouldn't miss it! This is wonderful news! We must celebrate properly. Emma, dear, do you have a dress? Flowers? Oh, there's so much to do!"

Mildred linked arms with her and was guiding her toward the Blue Ridge Inn. "Mark, you go see about a proper suit at the mercantile. McGinty keeps a few for occasions just like this. Emma will come with me."

Mark opened his mouth to protest, but caught Emma's amused glance. With a resigned shrug, he headed toward the mercantile while Mildred swept Emma away.

The next few hours passed in a whirlwind of activity. Word spread through Blue Ridge like wildfire, and what had begun as a simple, private ceremony quickly transformed into a community celebration.

Lydia arrived at the Inn with her best dress in hand, ready to alter it to fit Emma for the occasion. Clara brought wildflowers gathered by Tommy, who proudly announced he would serve as ring bearer. Dr. Emily contributed a blue handkerchief tucked discreetly into Emma's sleeve.

"Something borrowed, something blue," she explained with a smile. "Old world traditions have their place, even in Montana Territory."

The women worked together, turning the plainest room in Mildred's inn into an impromptu bridal chamber. Their chatter filled the space with warmth and friendship, a feminine camaraderie Emma had never truly experienced in Boston's competitive social circles.

"I never expected this," Emma admitted as Clara pinned fresh wildflowers into her hair. "When I came to Montana, I thought I was leaving everything behind. Instead, I've found a new family."

"That's frontier life," Clara replied. "We hold each other up because we must. And celebrations are all the sweeter when shared in good company."

At quarter to three, Emma stood before a small mirror, hardly recognizing her reflection. Her borrowed deep blue traveling dress had been skillfully modified with lace trim from Lydia's collection. The wildflowers in her hair formed a simple crown, more beautiful than any formal arrangement. Her cheeks were flushed with anticipation, her eyes bright.

"You look lovely," Mildred declared, adjusting a final fold in the dress. "A proper frontier bride."

Emma smiled at her reflection. Not a Boston debutante, not a society wife, but a woman who had chosen her own path. "Thank you. All of you. I never expected such kindness."

"Nonsense," Dr. Emily said briskly, though her eyes were warm. "You've earned your place in this community, Emma. Today we celebrate not just your marriage, but the defeat of a man who threatened us all."

A knock at the door interrupted them. Deputy Lewis stood there, looking uncharacteristically nervous in his best uniform.

"Miss Abbott," he said, removing his hat. "I, uh, heard about the wedding. Congratulations." He cleared his throat. "I was wondering—that is, I understand your father isn't present, and the tradition normally calls for..."

Emma understood immediately. "Deputy Lewis, would you do me the honor of walking me down the aisle?"

Relief washed over his face. "I'd be privileged, ma'am."

The group made its way to the church, which had undergone its own transformation. Evergreen boughs and wildflowers adorned the simple altar. Lanterns were lit despite the afternoon sun, casting a warm light throughout the space. Most surprising of all was the number of people already seated in the pews—shopkeepers, ranchers, townswomen—all dressed in their Sunday best.

"It appears you're having a proper wedding after all," Deputy Lewis murmured as they paused at the church door.

Emma took a deep breath. "So it seems."

Professor Barclay, seated at the small organ, began to play. The assembled guests rose, turning to watch her progress.

As Emma walked down the aisle, she focused on Mark, standing tall beside Reverend Thompson at the altar. He wore a black suit that complemented his lean frame surprisingly well. His dark hair was neatly combed, his face freshly shaven. But it was his expression as he watched her approach that took Emma's breath away—wonder, love, and complete happiness.

Deputy Lewis placed her hand on Marks when they reached the altar. "Take care of her," he said.

"With my life," Mark promised.

Reverend Thompson opened his Bible, surveying the gathered congregation with evident pleasure. "Dearly beloved, we are gathered here in the sight of God and these witnesses to join this man and this woman in holy matrimony."

The ceremony was simple yet profound, the ancient words taking on new meaning in the context of all they had survived together. When the time came to exchange vows, Mark's steady voice filled the church.

"I, Mark McKay, take thee, Emma Abbott, to be my wedded wife, to have and to hold from this day forward, for better, for worse, for richer, for poorer, in sickness and in health, to love and to cherish, till death do us part, according to God's holy ordinance; and thereto I pledge thee my faith."

Emma's voice trembled slightly as she repeated the vows, but her eyes remained fixed on Mark's, drawing strength from his certainty.

Tommy brought forward the rings—Mark's a simple gold band purchased hastily from McGinty's limited selection, Emma's a delicate silver ring from Mildred, the very ring she had worn during her short marriage after arriving in Blue Ridge. They exchanged them with hands that had weathered hardship yet remained gentle with each other.

"By the authority vested in me by God and the Montana Territory," Reverend Thompson concluded, "I now pronounce you husband and wife. What God has joined together, let no man put asunder." He smiled warmly. "You may kiss your bride, Mr. McKay."

Mark's kiss was tender yet unmistakably possessive, a sealing of promises made. The church erupted in applause and cheers, the celebration of a community that had found its freedom from fear.

As they turned to face their friends, Emma caught sight of familiar faces throughout the church—McGinty beaming proudly, Clara wiping away tears. Even Mildred's face was wet from tears. These people had become her family in ways she could never have imagined.

"Mrs. McKay," Mark whispered as they walked back down the aisle together.

Emma squeezed his hand. "Mr. McKay."

Leave A Review

If you enjoyed this book, please consider leaving an honest review
on Amazon

Visit Our Website:

www.vivianbelle.com

Visit Our Amazon Author Page HERE

Find Us On Social Media:

Facebook

Facebook Author Page

Instagram

www.ingramcontent.com/pod-product-compliance
Lightning Source LLC
Chambersburg PA
CBHW011848300726
48970CB00009B/2695